HOMELESS LOVE

A Novel By:

C.F. HAWTHORNE

P.O. Box 33046
Riverside, California 92519
(800) 431-1579
www.cfhawthorne.com

ISBN 0-9752568-0-7
First printing, May 2004

10 9 8 7 6 5 4 3 2

Printed in the United States of America

DEDICATION

This novel is dedicated to the world.

Love is not yours too keep, but too share.

Love is a gift, as it is given so can it
be taken away.

SFMH
C.F. Hawthorne

ACKNOWLEDGEMENTS

First, I give all glory and honor to Jesus Christ,
my Lord and Savior.
I thank thee O Lord for blessing me with a second novel.
I thank thee O Lord for the friends that thee
have placed in my life.
I thank thee O Lord for the knowledge
that I have acquired along the way.
I thank thee O Lord for loving my friends and me.

Dwayne, Bradley, Avari, and Cher, my cat…thanks so much for being in my life. I'm truly enjoying the journey that we've been blessed to travel.

To our dog Sunny, you're gone but not forgotten. We miss you Sunny boy. SFMH

To my cousins, Rozelia Felton, Renee and John Harris, Cynthia Richardson, and Cynthia Lee Harris, Maranda Benton, Murray and Raynette Gill. Too all that I may have missed thanks for giving me such a wonderful extended family.

To the Focus Group Angels, - Jacqueline Hamilton, Jacquelin Thomas, Deborah Holmes, Carmellia Chavers, Tina Carter and Miriam Pace. I cannot thank you guys enough for coming into my life. Please stay right where you are, because it fits, and I will forever be grateful for your friendship.

Much love goes out to the crazy women at the Family Law Court. Thanks once again for your encouraging words.

A Special Family Law Thanks:

Maranda Benton, Raynette Gill, Laura Coflet, Gia Davis, Teresa Shaffer, Genetta Banks, Diana Howard, Linda Tolber, Carolyn Jones, Brenda Halliburton, Geri Gilmore, Rosalind Green and Anita Diez thanks for your excitement.

Look over your shoulder ladies, here comes the COPS. It must be against the law to have friends like you. Thanks for being in my life.

Special thanks goes out to Elaine Wells, you sold more of my first novel "For Every Black Eye" than I did in one week. You go girl. Thanks for your faith in me.

Thanks to my readers and encouraging warriors. I pray that all of my novels, I'm blessed to write, gives you as much pleasure as the first one. I'm truly not a writer without readers and I thank you.

To all the book clubs that allowed me to come into their lives, I thank you. To all the bookstores that have allowed me to fulfill my dream as a writer and sign in your stores, I thank you from the bottom of my heart. Even the ones that didn't pay me.

I would also like to thank Steven Switzer who gets a kick out of introducing me to my Local 777 Union family. Always vote Union. They save jobs.

To Rhoda Smith, my editor - thanks for the last word!

To Kathy Sloan thanks for the late night discussions on whether it is breasts or breastisis.

I saved the best for last, my grandmother. Grandma Dorothy you are my shero, and I thank you for the woman that I am, if it had not been for you, no telling what I would have become. I thank you Grandma Dorothy for never leaving me, and the butt thrashing. Ouch!!!!!!

To anyone that I did not mention it's not because I didn't want to, but I simply didn't want Chapter 1 to open like this. Therefore, I had to stop somewhere.

I love you guys,
Thanks for being
In my life.

Chapter One

ꙮ

"**O**h, hell no!" I shouted as I approached my office and saw this creepy, Rastafarian looking, homeless man sleeping on my front stoop.

He jumped to his feet and began shouting how sorry he was that I caught him snoozing. Snoozing as if my Legal Process Service Business was the freakin' Holiday Inn.

"I must have overslept," he said as he gathered his things under his arm. "I'm really sorry."

Who the hell did he take me for... a counselor at a homeless shelter? Lord help the day, like I gave a shit about his apologies. I walked passed him.

"I have no room for I'm sorry. I've had enough to last me a lifetime," I told him as I approached my doorway.

I heard a quick intake of breath, as if I was bothering him. "I understand," he hissed.

I turned around to face him. "No, you don't, so get the hell away from here."

His voice drifted into a hushed whisper, "I'm sorry. I meant no harm."

I really didn't give a shit if he meant me any harm or not, I wanted him gone. "This is private property, not Fairmont Park," I said as I tried to get that damn key into the lock. "Find another place to snooze." I could feel him staring at me, but when I turned to face him, he was glaring down the street, then he turned back to face me.

"Think of me as a watchdog—if I'm here, then you'll always be protected," he slurred, with a little smile.

My heart was thumping as I pushed open the door. "I don't need a watchdog. I have an alarm system, protection 24/7 and you're invading my privacy, so please leave and find yourself another place to sleep!" I shouted with a little more force in my voice.

"Can't you just help a brother out?" he asked as he slung his duffel bag over his shoulder.

"Hell no!" I shouted without thinking. "I'm sick and tired of helping folks out. Can you help a sister out and stay your drunken ass off my property? I don't have any obligation to you. Now leave and don't ever come back, or I'll call the police. Then you'll have a place to sleep for a couple of months—the county jail!" I slammed the door so hard the plate glass rattled. I leaned against the frame as drops of moisture clung to my forehead. Taking a quick glance through the window, I watched him walk away slowly. I saw a smile on his bushy, foul face when he glanced back over his shoulder. I suppressed the urge to run out there and kick the shit out of him. How in the hell could I help him out when my life was spinning out of control?
Immediately I threw myself into my work like always.

About an hour and a half later Alex rushed her simple tail into the office with some stupid excuse about why she was late.

"I'm sorry but his alarm clock didn't go off like it was supposed to." She shrieked, avoiding my eyes.

I held up my hands in an effort to stop the bullshit from invading my space. "Alex, it's damn near 8 o'clock. We agreed to meet at 6 a.m. so we could go over these files. I don't know why in the hell I let you talk me into coming into the office this early on a Saturday morning anyway. I have other things to do."

"I know, but I couldn't get up this morning. I went to this bad ass club in Orange County last night and time just got away from me," she swayed her hips from side to side. "Maybe when I move in with you, we won't have this little problem."

I wasn't in the mood for her lame excuses. I'd just had my second panic attack when the realization of what that crazy hobo could've done to me. I swallowed so hard a knot formed in my throat. I slammed my fist down on my desk. "What the hell does moving in with me have to do with you getting to work on time? I'm totally confused Alex."

She gasped and, put her hands on her hips and said. "You know how much I hate my little cramped ass apartment, that's why I'm never there. So when we move in together I'll be your carpool buddy and I'll get to work when you get to work." She smiled and clapped her hands together as if the problem was really solved.

"I get to work at 6 in the morning, and you don't have to be here until 8."

Alex laughed out loud, "You got a problem then, ain't no way I'm gonna punch in at six in the morning."

"I don't have a problem, you have the problem!" I shouted, slamming my fist down on my desk again. Alex knew she had me by the balls, she knew there was no way in hell I was going to fire her. That would prove The Judge right. He was always saying that you can't work with family, and I was determined to prove him wrong.

"Nina, I'm sorry," she said softly, blinking her big bright eyes at me.

"You are always sorry, Alex, you don't understand I'm under a lot of pressure. Someone is trying to sabotage my company, The Judge is getting on my last nerve, and Mother is very ill. So you need to get your shit together."

"I know that you're under a lot of pressure, that's no reason to take it out on me. I said I was sorry. What more do you want from me? You're not this pissed when I come in late on a regular work day," she said as if she were in denial of the fact that getting to work on time was her responsibility.

"I'm not paying you overtime Alex."

"Dock me an hour, hell I don't care, better yet, I'll give you the files and leave you and your bad attitude here alone."

"Get out of my office girl," I said as calmly as I could.

She left in a huff, slamming the door behind her. I sat at my desk, only a few seconds from a nervous breakdown. As I listened to her slamming drawers and cussing like a sailor, I just couldn't believe what I was hearing. Was she really trying to make this my fault? My family really had a way of making me feel guilty.

I tried to remain calm as I floated above my crumbling world. She was right. Whatever happened to the levelheaded woman I used to be? What happened to the young and powerful Judge Harold T. Moore's daughter?

Suddenly Alex's voice sliced through the clatter in my head. "Nina I'm talking to you," she said as she walked around the desk, stared at me for a few seconds, and then knelt down beside me. I squinted because she sounded as if she were speaking underwater. She wiped tears from my eyes that I didn't know were there. "What's wrong, Nina? This isn't like you. Is it Mother?" I heard her say.

I shook my head as my pitiful life spun around me.

"Then what is it? You didn't talk to our crazy ass sister did you? Because I had a conversation with her last night that sent me into another world, that girl needs help."

I shook my head slowly again. "No, I didn't speak to Rachel." I replied, trying hard to regain my composure, but I could feel that I was losing control.

Alex stood; my eyes followed her. "Did you speak to The Judge this morning?" She asked.

I couldn't answer because that familiar pain of loneliness began to form in my throat.

"Why do you let him control your life like that, Nina? That man is as crazy as Rachel!"

"No," I whispered and blinked away those tiny little bastard tears.

"Then, what's wrong?" She asked wiping my cheeks again.

I lowered my head. "I guess what Aunt Louise says is true: some women can go crazy from loneliness."

"Nina, that woman is deaf and crazy herself. The entire Moore family is crazy. So don't invest too much of your time in that old crazy ass woman. She says shit like that because she's lonely her damn self."

I took a deep breath and gazed up at her. "That's what I'm talking about, lil sis. I don't want to grow old and lonely. I should have men falling at my feet. I'm young, successful, and wealthy. Instead I'm running homeless Rastafarian, wannabes off my damn doorstep."

"Homeless what?" She gasped softly.

I pointed toward the front door. "One was sleeping on my porch this morning when I came in."

Alex's eyes were wide with astonishment when I gazed back at her, she fell to her knees. "Oh, my God, are you okay? Did he hurt you?"

"He didn't do anything to me, Alex, he was probably too drunk," I replied softly, waving off the panic that was about to escalate into hysteria. "He wasn't hurting anything, just down on his luck." I shrugged.

The veins in her forehead popped out like a demon; she squinted her eyes, sucked in all the air around us and stood to her feet. "Wasn't hurting anything?" She shrieked.

"Exactly, he asked if he could sleep on my front porch."

She began pacing back and forth, peeping out of the window, closing the blinds. "What balls, asking you if he could freeload." She said, as she continued to pace.

"Well, I told him no, so calm down."

"I hope that you called the police."

"No, I didn't, what could they do?"

She stopped and stared at me. "I bet The Judge knows what to do!"

"Alex, I'm not calling The Judge. If it happens, again I'll call the cops, but not our father. That man already has too much of my life in his hands."

Suddenly, her eyes lit up with anger. "Why wait for a repeat performance?" She screamed. "Call the cops now, so they can be on the lookout for him."

I sort of laughed, I couldn't believe she still had so much fear of homeless people. I couldn't give a shit about them. I just didn't want any of them sleeping on my doorstep. I have a reputation to live up to.

"What if he kills you?" She shouted.

"Calm down, he didn't hurt me," I shrugged. "He just needed a place to sleep."

"Nina, you're too trusting. I swear to God if I was here, I would have put my foot up his drunk ass and kicked him in the face."

Oh brother! This child has some serious problems. "Listen, Alex, you need to calm down; you and The Judge get so worked up over these homeless folks, just leave them alone."

"I know damn well you ain't siding with those homeless freaks, girl. The Judge would have your ass. You need to be more careful, it's probably the same guy you saw lurking around the neighborhood."

"I'm not siding with them. And as far as The Judge goes, he's the one always quoting bible scripture, yet he won't feed the homeless. What's up with that?"

"I don't know. Hell! That's The Judge."

I wiped my eyes and blindly stared at the papers that were on my desk. "Like Mother said, we need to pray for the weak."

"You pray, Nina Marie. I'm calling the fucking cops."

I looked at her, "I can't believe you're thinking that way. Mother taught us to take care of our own."

"Is he our own?" She asked, folding her arms across her chest. She morphed into our father right before my eyes.

"What?"

"Is he black?"

I sighed. "Yes, but what does that have to do with anything?"

She threw up her hands. "That's even worse, no wonder you can't find a good black man." She pointed toward the window. "They're all homeless."

"That's ridiculous!" I said as I watched Alex's demeanor mimic The Judge's. "How in the world did you come to that conclusion? You don't give a damn about homeless people, and you damn sure don't care if they're black or not."

She rolled her eyes and the right side of her lip curled up just a little. "I see those weak ass men walking around town like there's nothing to do in this world but wait." She said, pacing back and forth in front of me.

"You don't see those men Alex, so stop lying. If a man doesn't have on a three-piece suit and drive a luxury car, you don't give them the time of day!"

She stopped pacing. "And something's wrong with that?"

"Not every man has what you need financially, but they can provide what you need emotionally."

"Hell, Nina, I'll see a psychiatrist for my emotional instability." She flung her long blond braids over her shoulders. "If I'm gonna spend time with a man, its gotta be worth my while, and I don't know what you're talking about, you've had your share of white collar workers. So miss me with the bullshit."

"Alex, that's just what the're full of. Bullshit. I think it's time that I start to look for love in more than just material possessions. Maybe the guy that works at the Shell gas station just might have what I need."

"Are you crazy? The Judge would have your head for even thinking of something like that."

I hugged myself and looked away. "You would never understand the pain that loneliness can bring."

She walked up to me and kissed me on the forehead. "Being alone isn't that bad."

I pushed her away. "How would you know? When was the last time you spent a Friday night alone. When was the last time you spent any night alone?" I shouted.

"You don't have to be alone. I find guys for you all the time. You speak to them one time, then you never call back, and you never take their calls. So maybe you're alone by choice."

"Alex the guys you hang out with scarcely have a vocabulary."

"So?"

"So I need someone I can at least communicate with."

I saw a smile cross her face, she knew I was right. Then her eyes lit up. "What about that doctor I hooked you up with a few months ago."

I threw up my hands. "I barely told the man my name before he slid his tongue down my throat. I need more than that Alex and one day I'll find him."

"But."

"But, until then, I'll keep praying and waiting."

"I'll pray for the right man to come along, but I ain't waiting for him." She smiled. "He's gonna hafta catch up with me in a club or somewhere other than home."

"Whatever, Miss Thang." I snapped my fingers. "But it's late and I'm paying you by the hour. So let's get to work so I can get back to my empty bed.

℘

Alex and I were going over every employee file and we were still no closer to finding out who was trying to sabotage my company.

"What about complaining Stanley?" Alex asked handing me his employee record.

"I don't think Stanley would do this. He just got his little girl back from Child Protective Services. He knows the importance of court files. Not him." I handed the file back to her, shaking my head.

"Okay, what about Karen."

"No way." I said nodding again. "What would she gain from shredding documents and making sure that we found them? No, put her back, she's clean."

"Nina."

"Divorcee and two small boys, Alex. She's clean."

'Too trusting.' She said under her breath as she threw the file to the floor. "Then what about Ms. Redhead, from Houston?"

I took the file from her hand. "I don't know Alex. What would Sabrina have to gain if I lost my business?" I asked as I studied her file.

"Hell, I don't know. What would the culprit gain period, if you lost this company?"

I thought about the question before I answered it. "I'll have the shame and embarrassment of failure."

"Right." Alex nodded.

"I would have to admit to The Judge that he was right and I was wrong."

"Wrong about what?" She frowned.

"Wrong for leaving his law firm."

"He knows we can't work for him."

I glanced at the stack of files that I spent all of Friday night correcting. "No, Alex, he doesn't know that we can't work for him."

Her right brow rose. "He better ask somebody."

"He doesn't have to ask anybody anything. He's The Judge remember." I said dropping the file on the floor. "Now, back to Sabrina, she's the nicest person you'd ever want to meet. She steps in and puts out fires, she deals with those irate customers quite well, and whenever your butt is late, I pointed to her, she steps in and helps. I can't begin to image it's Sabrina."

"I know the girl is all over the place. Willing to jump in

and save the day, which earned her the first crack at the Orange County office manager position, but if you ask me. I still think she's hiding something."

"Like what?" I asked.

She clapped her hands together. "I don't know, but have you looked into her pale face, and what's up with those big, thick ass red lips." Alex shook her head. "There's something about her I don't like."

"There's something about everybody that you don't like." I smirked and picked up another file. "Sabrina has been my back office senior lead person, for over a year."

"And when did all the trouble start?"

"Two months ago."

"Oh." She replied and looked back at the file she was reading.

"And for the sake of you gossiping around the office, I offered Sabrina the OC position because her son is very ill."

Alex looked up from the file she was reading. "What's wrong with him?"

"He has a crippling childhood disease, she needs this job, that's why Sabrina couldn't possibly be the culprit, if I lose the business she loses the medical coverage."

"So maybe that's what she's hiding. The fact that her son is all jacked up."

I stared in dismay at Alex, before I replied. "Yes dear." I said softly. "That could be it."

"Then we don't have anyone else." Alex said holding up her empty hands. "I don't have an answer for you. You may need to consider hiring a PI for this one."

"I can't take on a PI, I just paid thirty-five thousand back in sanctions fees. I don't have that kind of money. Not with the San Diego office opening up so soon."

Alex sucked her teeth. "When will Orange County open?"

I sat the next employee file aside. "The contractors are shooting for December." I passed a hand through my hair, and picked up another file, breathed heavily and opened it. "If this keeps up Alex, I many not have a business by December." I batted away tears. "The Judge will never let me live this down, if I lost the company."

"You got that right." Alex said. "You know he thinks that men should be the head of everything."

I nodded in agreement, as Alex twisted in her seat.

"And you know me." She continued. "The only thing a man should be ahead of in my life, is at the head of my bed." She laughed and clapped her hands again. "Otherwise they're worthless."

"Good Lord, Alex." I said rolling my eyes.

"Speaking of worthless men." She smirked. "Why doesn't The Judge ever say anything about Rachel's worthless husband missing Sunday dinners. I don't know why Marc and Rachel can get away with so much while the rest of us are put under a microscope." She said.

"Well, you know he and Rachel have always been tight." I added. "When we were younger I accepted their relationship because of Rachel's mom being killed, but now I feel as if I'm still fighting for his approval."

"Because you are, Nina." She said softly.

"This is true." I agreed and continued to search for the person who was trying to bring me down.

Franklin

"Frank, man I can't believe she threw you out on your ass," Bones' laughter echoed through the bus station where we met everyday for breakfast.

"I can't believe it either," I said sliding into the seat across from him. I took out my breakfast and poured it into my coffee.

"I'm not about to give up the best sleeping place in the city, I'll tell you that much," I winked.

Homeless Love

"Man, it's her place, you don't pay rent over there."

"You don't pay rent at this bus station, but you're here everyday; Lilly in the bakery shop gives you free coffee and sticky buns everyday, and you don't pay for that. Nina should think of me as her watchdog, I keep other dirty folks away from her front stoop," I said with a smile as I brushed off my sleeves.

"If she catches you again she's gonna call the cops. You gotta take them high society folks at their word. They don't understand that we're homeless by circumstances and not by choice."

"Whatever Bones."

"Just make sure that you stay out of sight. You heard about that judge down in San Diego, didn't you?"

I shook my head. "Keeping up with current events isn't my thing." I smiled as my old friend sucked air between the spaces where his teeth used to be.

"Anyway," he continued. "This mean ass judge tried to kick all the homeless folks out of San Diego."

I inhaled the aroma of the coffee and whiskey. "Did they leave?"

Bones scratched his hairy face. "And go where?" he huffed.

"I don't know," I shook my head.

"No, they didn't leave man; they do just what you do, stay out of sight."

I glanced into my cup. "I'll stay out of her sight and out of her mind, but I will not be out of a good place to sleep."

"What you gonna do?" He asked.

I looked up at him. "I'm going to lay low, set my alarm clock and be out of there before she can let her top down on that green BMW." I winked. "Besides, if she would have stayed her little tail in bed where she was supposed to be, she would never have known I was there."

"She got a little butt?" Bones grinned.

"Well, no she don't, it's sort of big--she ain't no small girl."

"Oh, so she has some meat on her bones?" He winked again.

"Hey, don't be thinking about Nina like that." I complained.

"I thought you said you don't have time for no woman?"

"I don't."

"So why your feathers all ruffled?" He smiled.

"A guy can fantasize, can't he? We're never going to hook up. What do I have to offer her? Hell, she has everything." I gazed into my half empty cup of whiskey. "I have nothing to offer her. I can't even chase away the sadness that I see on her pretty little face, and it drives me insane. It just makes my heart hurt."

A few minutes of silence passed between us before Bones spoke, "I don't understand how a person can be so sad and have so much. I thought money could buy you at least a smile."

I nodded. "She's one unhappy lady," I answered, as I sipped from the paper cup.

"Maybe her man got her upset?"

I almost choked on the whiskey. "She doesn't have a man!" I spat.

"How you know? Hell, you don't live with her."

I shook my head. "She's always alone. Besides this is a different kind of sadness, a painful sadness."

"How can you say that Frank, you act like you know this woman?"

"I've seen it before, trust me; I know the look, I've watched her almost every night." I looked away when my pulse begin to beat rapidly, my mind wandered back to Nina's beautiful round face. I sat up straight, smiled, and cleared my thoughts.

"She so beautiful Bones, her hair is past her shoulders, and when she smiles, she lights up the room. If she were my lady," I pointed at him, "she wouldn't be sitting behind a desk until three in the morning. Hell, I'd be holding her in my arms until the sun came up."

"Yeah, right man, before you do that you gotta let go of that bottle."

The smile fell from my face. "You should change your name from Bones to Dream Killer."

"Hey man, I'm sorry," he held up both hands. "But the truth is the truth."

"Why you gotta bring up some shit like that. I know what I have to do."

He pointed to my cup. "I just want you to see how that bottle is keeping you from your dreams."

"And what's keeping you from your dreams?" I asked defensively.

"Man, I told you when we first met, I have a tumor in my head and I have seizures, so I can't work for very long."

"Well, that's what you tell me, how do I know it's the truth?"

When he squinted, folds of skin flipped down over his eyes. His weather-beaten dark face grew stern as he turned his baseball cap to one side. "It's the truth, do I need to bring you my medical records?"

"Naw, man, I'm just messing with you; let's just forget it, and you're right—if I leave this mess alone," I said gulping down the rest of the whiskey, "maybe I can have a dream."

He raised his bushy eyebrows. "How you know so much about Nina anyway?"

I lowered my head. "I got my ways, I guess you can say my days in the real world taught me a great deal about folks."

"Yeah, right," he laughed.

"I was trained well," I winked.

"Who you kidding? The streets taught you how to dig through trash cans and read folks mail."

"That too," I smiled. "If people only knew the information a homeless person, or anybody for that matter, can get from a trash can, they'd burn everything that had their name on it, including the newspaper."

"So is that how you know so much about Nina, by digging through her trash?"

I laughed. "You got it."

Chapter Two

Nina

The digital clock on my desk flashed 10:15 a.m., forcing me to realize that I still had a full day ahead of me. I had tried for almost a week to get to work early enough to catch that homeless Rastafarian, but I guess he got the message, because I never saw him again. Thank God for small miracles.

"Nina," Alex said tapping lightly on the office door.

"Yes," I replied softly.

"This is a reminder call you have a meeting today in San Diego at two o'clock."

"It's today?" I frowned. So much was going on in my life, I couldn't remember if I was coming or going.

She raised her eyebrows as she stood in my doorway with her arms folded across her chest. "Yes, it's Friday, and the meeting is at two o'clock today," she repeated in a very slow drawl. "I put the message on your desk, and The Judge wants you to drop by and see Mother while you're out there."

Passing a hand through my hair I took a deep breath. "How in the hell did he know I was going to be in San Diego today?"

"I don't know, Nina." She threw her hands in the air. "How does he find out anything?"

I couldn't believe this little heifer was standing there as if she didn't report everything to The Judge. Just like when we were kids.

Homeless Love

"I just can't understand how in the hell this man always seem to know what's going on in Riverside and he lives almost two hours away."

"Well, get ready, because he knows about your little homeless incident also."

"What?" I growled. She shrugged her shoulders as if to say: wasn't me, I held up my hand. "Never mind, Alex, I'm in no mood to defend myself to him, my reputation is at stake, my clients are dropping off like flies, their paperwork isn't being delivered to the courthouse as promised, and I'm looking like a schmuck; and by the way, did you talk to the cell phone company, regarding my bill?"

"No, I haven't." She said softly.

"Get the hell out of my office."

"What the hell is wrong with you?" She frowned and rolled her eyes.

"What's wrong with me? If I can't find out what's going on, I'm gonna lose my mind right along with my business," I stood and walked over to the plate glass window. I hugged myself trying to keep my emotions intact, which obviously wasn't working.

Alex walked up behind me. "We're working on it Nina, but I still say you should tell Harold, I know he can help us."

I shook my head. "He'll only tell The Judge, then I'll never get anything done," I screamed. "I feel like every demon in hell is riding me. I don't need my brother in on it, too."

She put her arms around my shaking shoulders. "It's okay Nina, things are going to get better. We're gonna get to the bottom of who's trying to screw up this company. Then I'm gonna kick the shit out of the culprit."

"Yeah, okay, Alex; I need to get ready for San Diego. I'll talk to you later," I said, turning her around and pushing her toward the door.

"Damn, Nina, you don't have to be so rude."

"I'm sorry, I just need to be alone to get ready for The

Judge and all his bullshit about the bloodline and marrying well and babies. So good-bye."

I sat there, angry with myself for not being able to control these damn tears that insisted on flowing at the drop of a dime. I also became irate that I was letting something as simple as loneliness control me to the point of not paying attention to my company. If only I could take men off my menu for a while, I think life would be much easier for me, but somehow I continued to allow The Judge's insensitive words to send me flying into the wrong man's arms every time.

I'm tired of the Michael's of the world: 'my woman should take care of me.' I'm tired of the Mark's of the world: 'I have to visit my daughter this weekend.' I had no idea that a 35-year-old man could have a 26-year-old daughter. And I'm truly tired of the Rick's of the world: leaving people at the altar. What the hell is wrong with him? Alex buzzed my office intercom several times before I answered. I pushed the button down so hard I thought I broke it. "What?"

She cleared her throat. "Are you still upset? I have good news."

I took a deep breath and exhaled, "No, I'm not upset, what's the good news?"

"You don't have to go to San Diego."

I slumped back in my chair. "Why not, did I lose the account?" I was losing everything else.

"No, you didn't lose the account, a few of the attorneys had to reschedule, so I rescheduled the entire meeting."

I breathed a sigh of relief. "You always amaze me, sis." I really did love Alex; she was the only one in the Moore family that was half sane, although I worry about her catching a disease or worse a bullet in the head from screwing around with some angry wife's husband. I still have yet to find out how she catches so many good men, and I get stuck with the leftover nuts. Maybe I'll start praying to God to send me a man to love. Any man will do!

"Nina, did you hear what I said?"

I blinked twice. "I'm sorry, I must have zoned out. What

did you say?"

"I said, you know I got your back."

"And I got yours, lil sis."

⅋

Several hours later, long after everyone had gone home to their families and lives beyond this office, I was still there not willing to face another Friday night home alone. I took the bottle of cognac from the bottom drawer, poured some into a glass and made a toast. "Here's to another lonely weekend." I threw back the double shot of Hennessey. After pouring another one I strolled over to the picture window that I loved so much. I leaned against the cool windowpane, and traced a lonely raindrop cascading down the glass. Not realizing I was crying, I closed my eyes to shut out the excruciating pain of loneliness, and I began to pray for myself for the first time in my life. I prayed to God to send me someone to love, and someone my family could love as well, especially The Judge.

The phone rang before I had a chance to go into details. I glanced up at the clock and smiled, knowing exactly who would call me at the office this late.

Picking up the phone, I sat down, swung around and put my feet on top of my crystal clear desk.

"Yeah I know, you found a big, handsome, black man to share your bed, and I should have been with you because you found one for me, too." I laughed as I repeated Alex's lines before she had a chance to spring them on me.

"Nina?" A cold, deep, hard voice echoed in my ear sending chills up my spine, stopping my heart from beating.

My stocking feet hit the floor, and my throat instantly became dry. "Judge?" I said softly.

"Who else were you expecting to be calling you at 3 o'clock in the morning at your office."

C.F. Hawthorne

I sat up straight and looked around the room. "No one," I answered as I began straightening up my cluttered desk.

"Oh, come now, Nina." he said with a slow drawl. "You must have been expecting someone, or you would not have answered the phone in such an unprofessional manner."

I cleared my throat as The Judge babbled on. I let my shoulders drop and picked up a folder from my pile. This was the beginning of a long conversation with The Judge. He had been boozing and when he was drinking, he gets into this self-righteous mood. Then, he'll pick a victim to call to let them know why he was better than they were. I didn't practice law the way he did. I didn't have the client base that he had at my age. I didn't do anything the way he did. He was married with four kids at my age. So he was always going to be better than I was. I blocked out the sound of his babbling until his tone hardened.

"Nina?"

I held my breath fearing he'd read my mind. "Yes sir."

"Why didn't you call your mother today?"

"I get so busy around here and before I know it, time has slipped by."

"I see, but you have enough time to wait for a phone call from one of your lowlife friends, to tell you about a big, unclothed, black man, but you don't have enough time to call your sick mother?"

"I speak to Mother just about everyday."

"You didn't call today." he slurred.

I clutched the phone tightly in my hand. "It doesn't matter if I didn't call today. I'll call her in the morning."

"Everyday! Nina Marie Moore, you will call your Mother everyday. You only talk to her when Alexandra calls."

"That's because she's on the phone with Mother all the time. She's on the phone more than she's working."

"Fire her then!" he shouted.

I rolled my eyes. "She's family," I managed to say between

his babbling, "remember the bloodline."

"If she's not doing the job, let her go."

"All our lives you've preached about the importance of family and the bloodline." I took a calming breath. I couldn't say I hated him, but he got on my last damn nerve and even more now, that this damn biological clock was ticking like mad.

"When family is keeping you down, sometimes you have to cut your losses."

Well whatever! I thought as I passed the time correcting more mistakes.

"I fired you!"

"Excuse me!" That caught my attention; now for once I could finally win an argument. "You didn't fire me, I left."

He was quiet for all of a minute, not even enough time for me to gloat. "You have your side and I have the truth, so fire her and move on with your perfect little life."

What the fuck is wrong with this man? "I will not fire her," I said through clenched teeth. "She's - -."

"What?" He interrupted.

I tried to clear the unevenness out of my voice, knowing there was no point in arguing with The Judge. He always changed the rules in the middle of the game so he could win, even in court.

"You don't have to fire her, I'll call and demand that she quit."

"Yes, Judge." I answered, not allowing his threats to intimidate me. Alex was the only one that stood up to him. Mother said it's because Alex is a free sprit and you can't control a free spirit. I say it's because she's just like him. Insane.

He continued to speak as if I were listening. "And once she's no longer working for you. I'd like to hear what excuses you'll come up with why you can't call your sick mother."

I was quiet as he rambled on, I knew anything that I would say would only lead to a longer conversation.

"Nina, are you listening to me?" He shouted.

"Yes, Judge, I am." *I don't give a shit but I'm listening.* "But,

I really need to finish up here so I can go home."

"No, what you need to do is stop staying in that damn office until three or four in the morning."

"Judge?"

"What?"

"I really have to go."

There was a pause, and once he began to speak his tone became even. "Why don't you spend one of your lonely nights with that D.A. I was trying to set you up with?"

"Who, Chuck?" I frowned.

"Yes, he's a brilliant man and he adores you."

I shook my head. The Judge was giving me a migraine.

"Nina Marie Moore, Charles is a very wealthy man and we need to surround ourselves with money and power. So why not give him a couple hours of your dateless life? It's for the good of the family."

"I'm not going on a date with Chuck."

"And why not?" he shouted.

"He's an old wrinkled white man!" I said, keeping my voice in check.

"And?"

"And, I don't want to date old wrinkled white men."

"Well, it's better than sitting home; oh, excuse me, it's better than sitting at that damn office all night without a date, waiting for your scandalous friends to call."

My blood boiled. One of these days, Judge. Honor your Mother and Father is going to go right out the window.

"You're working your life away. You can go to dinner with Chuck and see what happens. Who knows?" He cackled. "I just might get a rich and powerful grandson out of the deal," he said, coughing into the phone.

"So this is all about you and the family?" I said once the coughing stopped. "And not me?"

"It would be good for everyone, including you."

"I can't, Judge."

He was silent for a few seconds. "What I don't understand is, why you can't give Chuck a chance. He's a good man, Nina Marie."

"But, he's not the man I want."

"You should be willing to take any man. You're always sitting in that damn office every night until the crack of dawn. I don't see why you bought that big house in the hills. You're hardly there. Why don't you just turn one of those offices into a bedroom, then you never have to leave that building."

Now that he managed to make me feel like dirt, I whispered. "Is that why you called me tonight, to talk about my pathetic life? Well, I'm happy with my life just the way it is. Now if you don't mind I have a lot of work to do!"

I held my breath as I waited for The Judge to speak. My stomach knotted, and my head began to pound. I hated it when he made me feel like a child or a criminal in his courtroom. I hated that I could not stand up to him, hang up in his face, or throw him off a cliff in Big Bear. I hated the fact that the almighty Harold T. Moore, Sr. was my father, the man who controlled most of San Diego through the judicial system.

The Judge cleared his throat. "Apparently, you have no respect for the person who raised you and put you through college so that you could become the successful business woman you are today. Therefore, I'm finished with this one-sided conversation."

"See, there you go."

"Well, the Bible does say to honor your mother and your father, and you're not doing that my child."

I gripped the phone so tightly my hand ached. I wanted to hang up, but that meant I would have to call him in the morning to apologize. I damn sure didn't want to sit through another lecture of I told you so, not to mention how disappointed my poor, ill Mother would be. I just had to wait out another storm with this foolish man.

"Call your mother in the morning," The Judge demanded then slammed the phone down before I had a chance to reply.

I listened to the buzzing tone in my ear, gripping the receiver until my knuckles throbbed. I slammed the phone down and kicked the trash can that was next to my desk.

"Oh, shit!" I hopped around the room. "Hell, I'm going home," I said as I slipped my shoes on and grabbed my raincoat and umbrella. My purse and brief case were near the door. I picked them up along with the usual weekend work; set the alarm, and slammed the door behind me, forgetting to check for my keys.

'Just calm down, you can't keep letting him upset you,' Relief swept over me when I touched the keys which were wedged between my wallet and the lining of my purse. I brought the keys into view and began my nightly ritual of button clicking. I clicked a button and the doors unlocked, another click and the engine started; By the time I finished clicking buttons the rain had gone.

Only in California can the rain cease and the moon shine so brightly, all in a matter of seconds.

I walked down three steps and around the corner toward my car. I clicked another button and the top of my sea green convertible went down. Throwing my things into the back seat, I snapped the top securely into place and slid behind the wheel of the car. I fumbled with the radio station until I found something to complement the solitude that had built up around me. Good music instantly takes me away from the insanity I call my life. I reapplied the sweet chocolate lipstick and sprayed on a few squirts of Ozan, a perfume I bought while vacationing in London. I buckled my seat belt, revved the engine, and peeled out of the driveway trying to run away from this lonely night. I made a left on 7th Street and another on Market. I slowed down as I gawked at so many homeless people in downtown Riverside.

By the time I made it to the 91 freeway, the open road and the wet morning air made my burden seem even heavier. I decided to keep driving.

I always kept a packed overnight bag in the trunk of my

car. I never knew when the notion would hit me to keep going, and I could end up anywhere, usually the Newport Beach Marriott, or the cabin in Big Bear.

I searched for my cell phone and remembered the damn thing was turned off again. This time someone had cloned my number and I refused to pay the $2,500 cell phone bill. Not to mention the other two cell phones were mysteriously turned off with large phone bills. I must be up to $9,000 in cell phone bills. I shook off the thought of my money slowly slipping away.

I turned up the radio and made a mental note to call Alex, once I got to the hotel. She would lose her mind if she couldn't find me, even though she'll be entwined in a new lover's arms tonight. I drove the 91 freeway to the 55 south at about 75 miles per hour until I turned into the parking lot of the Newport Beach Marriott.

Once in the room, I felt cold and lonely. I threw my briefcase on the sofa and went into the bedroom. I called Alex's apartment, then my place. After several rings, a sleepy voice picked up the phone.

"Hmm, hello." she whispered softly.

"Alex?"

Another soft whisper. "Yes."

"What are you doing?" I asked as if I didn't know.

"Nothing," she mumbled softly.

"I'm in Newport Beach." I said, as I tried not to feel jealous of my sister and her lover.

"Why you out there?" She asked softly.

I sniffed. "Just wanted a change, that's all."

"Ohhh, Nina hold on," she groaned.

I could hear muffled sounds and short moans. "Are you using a condom, girl?"

"Nina, hold on a minute! Damn."

"Alexandra?" I screamed into the phone.

"Nina, stop tripping; yes, I'm using a condom, you never let me run out of the damn things. Now I'll call you in the morning.

What's your room number?"

I brushed away the tears that were choking my voice as I heard Alex's lover begging her to return to him. "1107," I managed to say.

"Okay, big sis got it," she said hurriedly.

"I love you, Alex," I sang into the phone, "and please, use a condom." I could tell by the sucking of her teeth she was irritated with me, but I didn't care. I couldn't afford to lose her to some stupid disease.

Ignoring me, she said, "You should have come out with me, I found one just for you and he was fine as hell." She chuckled softly.

I took a deep breath and held it in until I was strong enough to speak. "Maybe next time, little sis."

"I'll keep an eye out for you." she said as her voice faded. I placed the receiver in its cradle and practically took the mini bar to bed with me.

Franklin

I jerked out of my sleep, from behind the dumpster, when her car sped out of the driveway. I tried desperately to clear my clouded vision and focus on my father's wristwatch, but I was too drunk to see a damn thing. I gathered my things, wiped the corners of my mouth and headed for home, the doorway at the front of the building. With a Black Velvet whiskey bottle still clutched in my fist.

After taking a few more swigs, I screwed the lid on tight and stuck it into my duffel bag where I retrieved three freshly washed blankets that smelled like Downey and began to prepare for a deep coma-like sleep.

I took the tiny alarm clock out of the duffel bag and set it for 5 a.m., making sure I was long gone before Nina arrived or she would evict me from my home, on her front stoop. Imagining it was Nina's beautiful full mouth, I moistened my lips and tenderly licked the reed as the untouchable image of Nina's astonishing face haunted my memory.

Of all the abandoned buildings, I've sought shelter in, this building where I could see Nina by moonlight, had proven to be the best place in town. She helped me to get through more than one painful night.

I shook my head and frantically searched the duffel bag for the bottle, reality was creeping back into my life and whiskey was the only way to fight it off. I was waging a war against my past, against the demons demanding my history, becoming my reality. Black Velvet took care of that reality bullshit. I cradled the fifth of whiskey in my arms as if it were a newborn child. My savior, my salvation I thought, as hot unforgiving tears fell on the label and slid down the side of the bottle.

Getting off the streets and stopping the boozing, wasn't reality because my memories always came back with a vengeance. I took another swig of whiskey and closed my eyes as the numbness descended on my heart. I tried to plunge further into the resting place of my mind as it too became dead like my spirit.

I wanted to forget about JoLee and what I'd done to her. I would pray like Bones told me to, but what was the point in that? God had shown me just how much he cared when he took my family away from me.

Chapter Three

Nina

I rose to the sound of 'We will, we will rock you,' being drummed out on my hotel door. I fell out of bed to the floor with a loud thud. When I managed to get my feet loose from the tangled sheets, I stumbled to the door and leaned against it, completely out of breath. My head was hurting like a two-dollar whore.

When the face appeared at the tiny peephole, I swung it open. "What the hell are you doing here?"

"I thought you might need some company," Alex grinned pushing me aside as she dropped the Coach bag on the floor.

I slammed the door, brushed past her and headed for the bed, pulling the sheet over my head.

"What's wrong with you?"

"Nothing's wrong with me. Why did you come here so early in the damn morning?" I asked softly. "Are you on drugs or something?"

"No, my addiction ain't synthetic, it's man made."

"Synthetic means 'man made,' crazy," I huffed from under the sheets. "Just say your addiction is men."

"Well, you know what I mean."

"No, I don't know what you mean, now keep quiet so I can go back to sleep."

"Don't you want to hear about last night?"

"No, and it wasn't last night it was this morning."

When she dropped down on the bed next to me, it felt like a million needles were sticking me in my head. "Okay fine, and by the way, The Judge called for you this morning."

"Again?" I shouted flinging the covers from my face and grabbing my head all at once.

She bounced her feet on the carpet. "Yep."

I sat up in bed. "I spoke to him right before I left the office. Did you tell him where I was?"

Alex rose to her feet. "No, I didn't tell him anything. What's in there?" She asked, pointing to the other side of the suite, like a curious child, and then she went to investigate.

"It's just another room." I followed Alex with my eyes as much as my throbbing head would allow. "What did you tell him?"

"I told him you went to the market." She replied and opened the drapes to let the brightest sun I ever did see into the room.

I protected my eyes with my hand like a vampire. "Please close it, Alex, I spent the night with Jack Daniels."

"It's a beautiful Saturday morning, Nina."

"Whatever, girl; why did you say the market?"

"Listen, big sis." Alex said, flinging her waist length braids to her back. "A blind man can find you. When you're not at the office, you're at home, if you are not home you're at the market." She slapped her hips, then slid her hands around her back and tried to slip them into her pockets, but those tight ass pants of hers prevented that transaction. "It's that simple." She added with a wink.

I stood and walked over to the drapes to close them. "Baby girl, I do have a life outside the office, and those pants are too tight."

She looked down at her jeans. "What are you trying to say, my pants are too tight?" She winked again and licked her brown lips.

"Hell yes, that's exactly what I'm saying, did you bring

something else to wear?"

"Yes." She smiled.

"Then, go and put it on."

Alex disappeared into the other room to get the overnight bag. I laid back and covered my head, waiting for last night's party with the mini bar to subside.

Moments later she emerged half naked and smiling. "Ju like?" She asked in a playful Spanish accent.

I dragged the sheet from my face and became instantly awake. "Where in the hell are you going with that on?" I blinked. She strolled across the room and stood before the full-length mirror in a two-piece yellow bathing suit that showed vividly against her midnight skin. "I thought we could go to Balboa Beach." She said as she jiggled her big ass in the mirror.

"You can't wear a thong on a public beach, girl."

"This is not a thong." She smiled and jiggled more ass. "It's a regular bikini, it's just a little small."

"A little small? Alex, I hear the damn thing screaming it's so tight. It's that hot out there, that you have to wear something like that?"

She licked her finger and touched her backside. "I wouldn't know, big sis. I'm always hot. Sizzling hot." She smiled. "Now, go and put on your bathing suit, so we can catch a few men."

"Alex, I wouldn't be caught dead in a bathing suit and especially not in public." Like a Mother hen, I pointed toward the bathroom. "Now, go back into that room and find something else to cover your body."

"Oh, Nina, come on it's a beautiful day and I don't want to be pinned down with clothes."

"Girl, you must be crazy if you think I'm going to be seen with you in public looking like you're auditioning for a porn flick or something. Now go!" I shouted.

Alex disappeared into the bathroom and slammed the door behind her. I sat on the edge of the king size bed and reached for the remote control.

"We better call Mother." She yelled. "If The Judge finds out we didn't call her today, he'll have a shit fit."

I stretched across the bed and reached for the phone, praying that my mother would answer. I breathed a sigh of relief when I heard the tiny sweet voice whisper.

"Hello."

"Hi, Mama, I love you."

"Danny Glover don't live here."

"Excuse me."

"I said, Danny Glover don't live here."

"Aunt Louise, it's me! Nina!" I shouted so my 85 year old deaf aunt could at least hear my name.

"Oh! Hi Tana baby, where you at sugar? Mark and the boys was at church on Sunday, but I didn't see you."

"Lizzie, Lizzie." I shouted over and over again. Hoping that she would put my mother on the phone. I don't know why Aunt Louise even answers the phone, she can't hear worth a damn.

"Hello."

Oh! Thank God, I was relieved that my mother took the phone. "Hi Mama, I love you."

"I love you too, but you know The Judge don't like for you to call me Mama, he says that's too country."

"I like calling you Mama."

"Are you trying to upset him?"

"No, ma'am." I lied, that's exactly what I was trying to do, just in case he was listening in on the other end. "How are you today?"

"Well, I'm doing better child. Who is this, Nina?"

"Yes ma'am, it's Nina."

"Oh, how wonderful of you to call. Rachel called early this morning and so did Harold. The Judge said Alex hasn't called, but you know how wild that child is, she's probably on her way down here to surprise me."

"Alex isn't going to San Diego today."

"No?"

"No, ma'am. She's spending the day with me. We're going to the beach, would you like to come?"

"Oh, no baby, Aunt Louise is visiting with me so your father could go fishing. But thanks for asking. You girls have a great time in all that sand."

"Yes ma'am." I was glad that she declined. I couldn't handle Aunt Louise in public.

"Rachel saw you eating lunch by yourself the other day, she said you looked so sad. Are you alright, baby?"

Shit! I knew the joy wasn't going to last too long. "Yes, I'm fine, but what was Rachel doing in Riverside? I thought she never left San Diego." I ignored the mocking voice of Rachel that was playing around in my head.

"I think she had to meet someone. She would've said something to you, but she saw that you were deep in thought."

Silence slipped in again and then she spoke. "Nina, you really should call Rachel, she's not doing well."

"Mother." I took a deep breath. I don't know why she had jumped on this bandwagon of mending fences.

"She asked about you this morning."

"Why is she asking about me?" I shouted, forgetting how much arguing upsets her. "Sorry, Mother." I sang when her silence penetrated my ears. "What did she want to know?"

"Oh, you know the usual. How are you? What are you doing? Things like that."

I was so irritated with my mother for being weak. "What else Mother?" I asked while trying to keep my composure. "Mother?"

"Nina, I know that you girls love each other, but I can't for the life of me figure out why the two of you can't get along."

"Tell me what else she asked, then I'll tell you why we can't get along."

Mother fell silent once again; she cleared her throat and let out a deep sigh.

"What did she ask?"

There was another deep throaty sigh, and then she spoke softly. "She asked if you were still on the prowl for a husband."

I held the phone firmly, sat up straight and said, "I'm not on the prowl for a husband."

"But, Alex said that you attend a great deal of those singles functions."

I'm going to kill Alex, I thought as my Mother repeated my entire life to me. "Mother, that doesn't mean that I'm looking for a husband."

"Nina, don't judge your sister's words so harshly, she's only concerned about you."

"You have no idea about Rachel, she's scandalous, hateful, and very manipulative. You should open your eyes to your family."

"I know dear."

"And, so what if I were looking for a man? The whole world is searching for someone. I didn't invent the singles club, so there must be a need for it."

"I know dear, but if you weren't so picky maybe you could find a good man and make me and The Judge very happy grandparents."

"I'm not picky. I just want him black, working and good looking. Is that too much to ask for?"

"No, child, but that nice young man The Judge has for you--he's good looking and working, why can't you just go out with him? Two out of three isn't bad."

"Mother. Chuck is older than Jesus." They really needed to get off my back about that old white man. I had no desire to be a trophy wife.

"Your father is older then I am. Older men take care of their wives."

"I don't need a man to take care of me, I can do that. I need him to love me, and I don't think Chuck can do that!"

"Oh, Baby, one time won't hurt. Just to make The Judge happy so I don't have to hear about it all the time."

"That's not what I want, and I'm already trying to make The Judge happy I . . .."

"Nina." She sighed. "He's so disappointed in you for leaving the practice to open those process service things. Do you realize how embarrassing that was for him?"

"They're not things, they're companies, and I'm sorry that he's disappointed in me, but he already has too much control over my life." I took a deep breath to calm myself. I had to abandon the conversation before my words hurt the wrong person. "Listen, Mother, I have to go; I'll call you again once we return from the beach."

"Today?" She said, I could almost hear her smiling through the phone. Which meant I better tell Alex to remind me to make the call.

"Yes ma'am, today. And Mother, when Rachel's gossiping about me, please tell her to mind her own business."

"Nina."

"Never mind." There was no way in hell she would ever say anything mean. "I'll tell her myself when I see her at Sunday dinner. You take care and I love you, tell The Judge I love him too, and Aunt Louise. . . . if she can hear you," I mumbled under my breath.

"Okay, baby, I'll do that."

I hung up the phone and screamed. Alex rushed out of the bathroom with a face towel, dripping wet.

"What's wrong, what happened? Is Mother alright?"

"Yes, she's fine."

"Why did you scream?" She frowned.

"Because that bitch Rachel has been gossiping to Mother, I'm sick of her."

She dropped her shoulders. "You're just now getting sick of it?" she asked, with a significant lifting of her brow. "How long have you been knowing Rachel, 35 years?" She shrugged her shoulders and dismissed my brief temper tantrum.

I walked into the bathroom behind her. "Get your butt out of here so I can use it. I'm paying for this room."

"You better stop pushing me around or I'll call Rachel and tell her that you were in Newport Beach with a strange man that you picked up in a bar."

I swatted Alex on her big ass. "Heifer."

Franklin

After I realized Nina wasn't coming in that morning, I caught my breath and calmly made it to the bus station bathroom. I hurried and brushed away the stale taste of the whiskey from my mouth and finished my daily bath in the sink. The fresh smell of coffee filled my nostrils. I secured the off white cap on top of my dredlocks and headed for the coffee shop where Bones was waiting with the java. "You want some?" I offered hoping he'd say no as I filled the paper cup with whiskey.

"Not this early in the morning. You need to give your liver a break." He added, shaking his head.

I smiled and toasted Bones. "I will man, but not today."

"I'll keep praying for you."

I inhaled the aroma of the warm whiskey and sighed. "Pray for yourself."

"I do. Where you sleep last night? I couldn't find you," He said changing the subject fast.

With the first sip of the warm whiskey, my heart rate slowed and I eased back into my body.

"At my usual spot. You know when it gets dark you have to disappear or the cops will add more drama to your life."

Bones nodded. "And I know how you wanna stay invisible to the cops."

"I don't need any trouble." I winked, as the warmth from the whisky grew cold in my mouth. "Man, I can remember a time when I drank my alcohol from fine crystal glasses. On the rocks, shaken, but not stirred." I tapped my mouth and shook my head. "I bet that's how Nina drinks her wine all the time." I added.

"Probably, but you better stay your black ass away from her place."

I waved him off and refilled my coffee cup with more whiskey. "Where you been sleeping?" I nodded.

"Here and there, you know me, I'm gonna find a place to crash. I got connections." Bones laughed and a hard chest-busting cough followed. He hit his upper body with his fist.

I raised an eyebrow and backed away. "Damn!"

"Smoker's cough." Bones smirked. "But you ain't gotta worry about this."

"Why not?" I frowned, as I protected my whiskey with my hand.

"Cause you don't smoke, fool."

I relaxed and leaned back into Bones' conversation. "You go to a doctor for that?"

His eyes fluttered. "I ain't got a doctor."

"What about the free clinic? I get checked there all the time." Bones coughed again and I frowned again.

"Man, all I get from the free clinic is a handful of free condoms." He winked.

"What you need condoms for?" I asked, with the frowns of confusion pasted on my face.

A sly grin spread across his grubby old face as he swayed in his seat. "Cause when the mood hits me, I don't want to hear wait, we ain't got no protection, and I sure as hell don't want to hear 'I'm pregnant.'" He snapped his fingers.

"Man, who gonna let you touch them." I laughed.

Homeless Love

"Riverside got homeless women, and they need loving too."

"Bones, you one crazy dude."

He shrugged his shoulders. "Don't let this old face fool you." He grinned and scratched his two-day-old whiskers, which made his weathered skin appear to be tougher than leather.

I smiled and sipped more whiskey.

He cocked his tattered New York baseball cap to one side. "Everybody needs loving, Frank, even a man like you."

"You got to be crazy getting involved with a woman and you don't have nothing to offer her."

Bones patted his chest. "I got me, Frank, and that has to be enough, and she can have all the love that I have to give."

"Well, I just want to stay healthy and not get laid." I added.

"You've been on the streets too long, baby, I still want both." He added.

I glanced down at my watch. "I'm happy for you, man, but I got a bus to catch."

"Where you going?"

"I have a gig to play today, on the other side of town."

g

It was very late when I started to get the shakes; I finished playing at the Side Walk Café and caught the next bus back to downtown Riverside. I headed right to my favorite spot, J and J Liquor Store, where I bought a fifth of whiskey for lunch and dinner. The café owners always fed me after a gig, so I didn't see the need to buy more food.

I located a sweet little spot under a tree in Fairmont Park, where I settled my tired body down until it was time to go to Nina's.

"Hey, Frank, why don't you play something for us man." Big Ted shouted, another homeless man who lost both his legs in Vietnam.

I reached for my sax, moistened my lips, and closed my

eyes as I played a soft imitation of Brown Sugar, one of Nina's favorite songs. I played until self-pity, shame, and disappointment overwhelmed me, disturbing the voices inside my head.

I hurried and seized the brown liquor and forced down the blazing wetness as I tried to drown my sorrows. I squeezed my eyes tighter, trying to force out the demons that were lurking in the shadows of my sobriety.

I took another swallow of the fiery liquor as the sounds of my wife's cries the night our only child died raced through my head. The child that we spent countless nights praying for, the child that God gave us and saw fit to take away, because it was His will. I rested my head on the tree trunk and waited for the whiskey to take effect.

When I closed my eyes I saw her beautiful, red painted nails clawing at my heart like a mad woman; her screams felt like daggers in my head. The hatred she had for me weakened my soul and damned me to a life of eternal hell on earth. I gasped for breath as the scorching air began to swallow me whole.

I took another swig and another and another, until I could think no more; until I could no longer remember that night, that day, that moment in my pitiful life. I glanced down at my father's watch and tried to make out the time, when I saw a shadow. I struggled to my feet, stumbling with each step. "Hey what time is it?" I slurred, and swayed in front of the silhouette.

I didn't realize I was standing so close until a fist slammed into my chest. The blow sent me crashing to earth. Too intoxicated to fight back I stayed on the ground and humbled myself to the embarrassing kick to my pride. I crawled back into the shadows of the trees where I became invisible to the world once again. I didn't feel like a man, nor did I feel like a human being, and the stranger's words continued to hammer my soul like a boxer. 'It makes me sick to think that you're human repeated over and over, until I slipped into the warmth of the darkness. Hoping that it would be forever.

"Frank, man, come on let's go." I heard Bones shout, snatching me from my solitude. I picked up my gear and blindly followed my friend. When we found another sweet spot on Third Street, in an abandoned building across from a taco shop that was always crowded. I breathed a long sigh of relief.

As I began slipping back and forth, in and out of my lonely world, with my empty dreams, in empty spaces of my mind, I let it all go. "I know a man ain't supposed to cry, Bones, but for once I wish someone would change the damn rules, consider our sorrows. Just once."

"Frank, don't go there," Bones insisted.

But there is where I needed to be. I tried to focus on the blurred vision in front of me. I put my hands on his head and cried on his shoulders. "I didn't mean it, Bones, really I didn't. Shit happens you know. I know I was wrong, and I'll pay for the wreckage of my past, but I didn't mean to kill them."

"Trust in God, Frank, He'll bring you through it."

"Why in the hell you always say that bullshit to me? I can't trust in a God that allowed a person like me to keep living, while an innocent child dies. I can't, Bones. I'm through."

Bones gave me a polite pat on my shoulders as the sweet darkness of drunkenness surrounded me, calming me, allowing me to travel into total intoxication without fear.

I don't know how long I was passed out, but it wasn't long enough, because it was still bright outside. Bones' shouts cut through my head like a knife.

"Frank, we gotta bail, man. The cops doing a sweep in this building." I could hear him scream as he tried to lift me from the rat-infested floor, but I wanted to cling to the whiskey, just a little while longer. It allowed me to enjoy my family the way it used to be.

"We gotta go, Frank."

"Leave me alone, I don't give a shit, let them find me." I cried and tried to capture the sweet smell of my wife and baby girl.

But pain in the ass Bones, managed to get me to a sitting position.

"Frank, man, you don't want to go back to prison, so get up, let's get the hell out of here."

"Prison is where I should be." Anguish began to spread through my body like a virus.

"That's in the past, man, and you suffered enough. You can't keep punishing yourself. Now get your black ass up and move."

As I struggled to stand, warm tears ran down my face. "It ain't in the past. It's right here; I killed them, and I haven't suffered enough, just leave me, man, just leave me, and let me die."

"You know what, we already been through this shit."

"Then leave me alone with my pain."

"I've taken care of you for this long, you must be crazy if you think I'm gonna leave you now. You're like a brother to me," he whispered. "Like a brother."

"I don't want a damn brother--I just want to be left alone," I shouted and swung at Bones; I missed. "Why can't you leave me alone?"

"That's your problem. You're alone and you shouldn't be. Let's get out of here before the cops come or you'll end up back where you really don't want be, in prison, sober for life!"

As he began to struggle with my 190-pounds, the duffel bag and the saxophone, all of which were weighing him down, sobriety started to catch up with me--something I tried to stay away from. I always kept a buzz going. I pushed against Bones, but my effort was wasted against his sober stance.

"I don't know, man, I just . . . just can't stop drinking once I start thinking."

"You can stop drinking if you let go of the past. Going on binge after binge isn't solving your problem," he said as we wobbled out of the building.

"I'm trying, man."

"No, you're not, how many times do I have to tell you, you have to let the past go or it will destroy you. You've wrapped yourself in a blanket of guilt."

I closed my eyes and felt utterly miserable. Grief and despair tore at my heart. He simply didn't understand how much I needed to drink. "I can never let go of the past, it's the reason I'm here. Why I deserve to be here." My legs slipped from under me and we went crashing to the ground. "Get off my back and leave me the hell alone." I rocked, hitting the ground with my fist. "Get off my fucking back!"

Bones waited for a few minutes then offered his hand. "Let's try this again." He grinned that damn wicked, toothless grin.

"No!" I slapped his hand away, staggered to my feet and headed for the rosebush.

Unzipping my pants, I sighed as waves of relief made me shiver. My eyes remained closed throughout the duration of my piss. After what felt like a lifetime, I lifted my lids only to find myself pissing down my damn pants leg.

"Oh! Hell man, now you see what you made me do." I stumbled back and fell into the rosebush.

"I'm standing over here, you pissed down your leg, not me." Bones laughed. "Besides it happens to the best of us," he said through a series of coughs.

"Well, it only happens to me when I'm with you," I shouted as I began to really sober up from the ass whipping the rosebush was putting on me. "Just leave me alone," I shouted when the thorns released me. I gathered my things and started to walk away.

"Frank," Bones called as he walked briskly behind me.

"What?" I snapped.

"It's still early, we have time to make it to the shelter."

I pulled the white cap tightly on my head. "The what?"

"The shelter. If we're one of the first 50 men, then we'll get a cot and something to eat."

"I told you I don't like shelters, it's just an open space with a bunch of men jammed together, coughing and hacking all over each other. That's probably where you got that cough from." I shook my head. "No, thank you, that's not for me." I tried to walk faster, but the pain began to explode in my head like Beethoven's Fifth Symphony. "I'll be locked down for the rest of the night; I can't handle it; no thank you."

"But you can get a shower, a hot meal, rest for the night, and start out fresh in the morning."

"I don't have time for all that. I need to make more money."

"I don't think you have a choice in this matter," he shouted.

"Like hell I don't!" I replied and headed in the direction I thought to be downtown Riverside.

When Bones stepped in front of me, the pressure in me increased with frightening intensity. "You can't play on the street corner," he said as if I were a child.

I pushed him out of my way and continued my pace. "And why the hell not?"

"You got piss running down your leg." He smiled and pointed to the large wet spot on my pants. "If you go into any eatery looking like that, they'll never let you play there again. So come with me, get a shower, get something to eat, and get a good night's sleep."

"Bones, man, I can't be locked up all night. What if the demons come and I need a drink."

"It's just for one night, Frank. You need the rest." He grabbed me by the arm and led me to the Salvation Army.

Chapter Four

Nina

Around 5:45 Monday morning, I was slipping the key into the lock of my office building. My arms were loaded down with large folders, which needed to be retyped and rerouted to the right jurisdiction. I had no idea what happened Friday, but between The Judge, my boring love life and this company, I was losing my mind.

Alex became a horny bimbo while we were in Newport Beach, and left me to entertain some strange Geri curl dripping, gold crocked teeth, greasy, Barry White wannabe-- who obviously thought I was just like my sister - fast.

I dropped the folders on my desk, inhaled the aroma of coffee and shook the image of Alex's prison rejects from my mind. I headed to the back to put away the sticky buns I bought from the bus station bakery.

If these were the kind of men she found for me at the clubs she went to, I wanted to be alone. When I returned to my office, I noticed the front door was still open.

Without thinking, I rushed to close and lock it. Then I glanced around the room and even tiptoed to the tiny closet behind my desk, listening for any unusual sounds. There was no need for me to identify it, I just needed to hear it, and I was getting the hell out of there.

Shrugging off the anxiety that crept into my soul, I headed for the kitchen. When I returned to my office, I sat behind my desk and sipped the hot orange mocha coffee--compliments of Lilly, the young lady at the bus station bakery.

Smiling at the old Victorian home that I transformed into an office building, I was glad that I decided to leave the fireplace in its original state; it gave the reception area a cozy, friendly atmosphere on cold mornings when my clients walked in for their appointments.

I placed my cup on my desk and shook my head at how disappointed The Judge was in this place. I knew he hated it because I loved it. I walked toward the plate glass window, which had a magnificent view of other old Victorian office buildings, that used to be homes.

The well-manicured lawns, large hedges, and the beautiful trees gave a feeling of just that, being home. I lowered my head and began to turn away when a silhouette of a man caught my eye. Then suddenly he was gone.

I could feel a panic attack seeping through my blood as I remembered the homeless Rastafarian and the glossy evil look that was in his eyes. I shook off the unnecessary fear and went back to my desk, as I leaned back in my chair; I took a deep breath as the calming sound of Pamela Williams 'Eight Days of Ecstasy' CD took a load off my mind. That sister cold blow a saxophone in such a way it eased all my stress away. Her music made Friday's little fiasco seem harmless.

I was just about to slip into the workload, which was waiting for me when I heard something hit my window several times. I rose to take a peek, but I didn't see anything, so I closed the blinds and tried again to slip into the aftermath of Friday's chaos.

Around 7:45, I heard something at the front door. I jumped to my feet, the sound of Richard's voice settled my nerves.

"Nina, I need to talk to you, honey," he said as he tapped lightly on the office door.

I frowned and rolled my eyes. Knowing Richard, if he

was saying anything past good morning this early, it wasn't good news. He's simply not a morning person. "Come in," I said bracing myself. The last time he had something to say, I ended up buying a new car, because the other one was stolen. Thank goodness, I had the Jeep until I got around to buying the Beemer.

When he entered my office, I could see flames in his eyes that matched the scarlet suit he was wearing. "Where's the fire Richard?" I asked trying to make light of his expression.

He dropped a stack of files on my desk, took out a dusky rose silk handkerchief from his lapel, wiped his forehead and fell down into the chair in front of my desk. He passed a hand over his slicked hair and twisted his ponytail. "Child, the fire is in Mr. Sanchez' behind, this man is pissed off."

I noticed he had added a new thumb ring to his many collections of rings he had on each finger. "Was this from Friday?"

Richard rolled his eyes and smacked his lips. "You got it, boss lady."

I tried to suppress a smile. Richard was so dramatic when there was a crisis. He was known as a hand-flailing, eye-rolling, lip-smacking, foot-stomping drama queen. Lord, help the day; I was glad he sat down, otherwise he would have been swaying his hips all over my office, and I couldn't take him seriously when he started walking like a woman. I shook my head and looked into my cup. "Okay, darling, tell me the problem."

He snatched a folder from the pile that he brought in. "Nina, we sat on his divorce papers for almost three weeks," he said shaking the file in my face.

"Okay." I mumbled wondering what the problem was.

Richard stabbed the piles of folders with his manicured index finger. "Honey, he wants his wife served today."

"We don't have a problem. Just file the document first thing this morning and serve her." I replied sipping the cold coffee.

"He wants us to serve her free of charge."

"Why do you look so worried? We can handle this. It's not a problem, it's part of the process." I added with a smile.

"Not if the heifer moved to Costa Rica," he said with his arms folded, swinging his legs.

I sat up straight and stared at him.

"Okay." He sang, sticking his lips out.

"Are you serious?"

"Honey, I'm very serious, so is Mr. Sanchez," he said snapping his fingers.

"Do a proof of service by mail."

"Nope, can't do that."

"And why not?"

"We don't have an address for the old goat."

"Okay. Still not a problem." I leaned back in my chair. "Let's do a notice of publication in the news paper."

"Nope," he said, shaking his head with his eyes closed.

"Why not, Richard?"

Richard shook his head. "I spent most of my weekend talking to Mr. Sanchez. He wants her personally served as promised, papers in hand, no questions asked kinda service." He said folding his handkerchief and neatly placing it back into his lapel.

"I don't think we can help him; we'll have to bite the bullet on this one; refer him to someone else."

"We can't." He huffed. "He's threatening to go to newspaper and anyone else who'll listen to him. Your company's reputation is at stake and you know The Judge will have a picnic knowing that this corporation is struggling. He wants you to come back and work for him or at least let a man run this empire you've built." Richard sang.

I immediately sat up. "Okay, okay you made your point. Get my brother on the phone!" I shouted and grabbed the remote control, pausing the music. "Tell him we need him to locate Mrs. Sanchez' address in Costa Rica."

"Lord, child, how in the world is that boy supposed to do that?"

"Friends, family, hell--I don't know, he's the private investigator. I'm going to meet with Mr. Sanchez and see if I can smooth this over."

"Short of offering him your BMW what can you do?"

"I don't know, but I'll think of something. Get the staff ready for the meeting. I'll be in there in a few minutes." Richard stood in front of me without moving. "Go, Richard, go."

"There's more," he said raising his eyebrows.

I trembled a little at his expression and eased back into my chair. "What?" I moaned as my stomach did flips.

He sighed heavily and looked down at the stack of files, which appeared to be about ten feet tall at this point. "I took these divorce files home over the weekend."

I listened as his voice filled with anguish.

"They've been dismissed."

"What!"

"Nina, these people are still married," he said handing me a stack of dismissed court cases.

"No." I shook my head.

"Well, according to these documents, you requested the divorce cases to be dismissed."

"What divorce cases?" I frowned shaking my head in total dismay.

"The ones that you represented pro bono."

"Excuse me." Sabrina said, sticking her head in the office.

I looked in her direction. "What are you doing here so early?"

"I had a few things to do, before the day gets to busy. You need to sign these forms, they have to go out today."

I closed my eyes for a brief second; the feeling of my world crashing down hovered over me like a long forgotten sin.

"Give them to me." I said waving her in. "I'm so over-whelmed by the torment of the past few months, Richard, I don't think I can handle anymore of this shit."

"You'll be okay Nina."

After I signed the last document, I looked up at Sabrina. "Didn't you find those original medical insurance documents half shredded?"

She nodded. "In the back office." She added as she left the room.

"My cell phone constantly gets turned off and the bill is so outrageous it's ridiculous."

"Honey, hold on to your seat because there's more." He huffed again, shoving more files in my face.

I inspected the files briefly and was confused. "What is this?"

His free hand moved recklessly to his neck. "These files were delivered to the wrong court in Orange County last week." His eyes narrowed and his back became rigidly straight. "And they've been dismissed as well."

My head pounded and my face grew hot with anger. "What's happening?"

"Nina, I don't know, but the Riverside Family Law files were delivered to Orange County Criminal and then forwarded to Corona Family Law. The Corona Family Law files ended up in Blythe. The list goes on and on. Everything is all screwed up, honey!" he said waving his hands in the air.

The room became very still, my throat went dry and my palms began to sweat. I tried to remain calm, but shit was happening so fast I wanted to reach out and hurt someone.

"A few other things has happened with documents that we can't explain; if this continues you'll have to take drastic measures to ensure the integrity of this company," he said softly as if someone were listening.

"And that means what?" I asked leaning into him.

"I know how much you hate it." He said, twisting his

lips to one side. "But you'll have to start kicking ass and taking names."

I lowered my head.

"Nina, listen, it's going to be an even bigger problem when those clients start complaining to the Bar Association and the Better Business Bureau. You can't have any bad publicity, girl, you're about to open the San Diego office."

My face automatically fell into my hands. "Richard, please."

"Please my red alligator shoes, what if they decide to sue you?"

"For what?" I snapped, looking at him.

"You're the attorney, Nina, have you forgotten about breach of contract. You did promise these folks fast, reliable service, 100% worry free. Didn't you?"

"Oh, hell, Richard, I can't take any more of this shit I have to get out of here," I shouted as I picked up my keys and headed for the front door.

"The Judge is on the line," Sabrina said as I passed by her.

I glanced at the clock. "It's 9:30, where's Alex?"

"I don't know." She shrugged her shoulders.

"Tell him I'm not in."

"Yes, ma'am."

"Will you be long?" She asked.

My nerves tensed immediately. "Excuse me?" I squinted.

"We have a staff meeting at ten. If you're going to be long I can reschedule it for tomorrow."

I felt as if a hand had closed around my throat. "Yes, you do that, Sabrina."

As I pushed opened the door with my keys in my hand, Alex and I came face to face."

"Nina . . . I."

"Not now, Alex," I said, brushing past her. "Not now."

I walked through the back door of the Street Kar Café, after an unsuccessful, useless meeting with Mr. Sanchez. I could hear sensual soft music flowing from a saxophone. After placing my order, I went to take a peek at the musician, but a mass of people had gathered around. The whisper of the melody incarcerated my heart and eased the horrifying day off my shoulders.

"Five forty." The white haired girl said, sporting two nose rings connecting to a chain that was dangling from her earlobe.

"Who's that?" I asked as I pressed the $20 bill into the palm of the girl's hand.

"Oh, just some guy who plays here every once in awhile."

I raised an eyebrow. "Oh, really?"

"Yeah." The girl answered as she offered me the change.

"Give it to the musician." I motioned with my head.

"I will, but don't call him that. Is your order for here or to go?" She asked all in one breath.

"To go, and don't call him what?" I asked surprisingly.

"A musician! He hates to be called a musician."

"Why?"

"I don't know!"

"Then, what is he?"

Casually she answered. "I don't know!"

"Ok. The man has a right to his opinion."

I turned to lean against the wall, but the whispering of my name from the saxophone forced me into a nearby chair. My body slipped into a magnificent breathtaking trance. I closed my eyes as his music engulfed me, relaxing every tense muscle in my body. I wanted so much to allow the melody to take me away, to take control of everything and to ease the tension from my soul. I would have, if the crazy looking kid hadn't interrupted my stupor with her silly cough. Lord only knows how long that child was standing there gawking at me.

I snatched my lunch from her hands, rolled my eyes and

almost ran out the back door of the café, my embarrassment in tow.

For the rest of the day, my nerves were on edge. The music had awakened something inside of me that I thought I had put to rest many years ago.

ᵹ

When I turned into my driveway and pushed the button to my four-car garage, a wave of sadness rushed over me along with a slap of reality.

I was being honored as the Woman of the Year, and I was sitting on top of the world, yet I felt as if my life was still incomplete.

I grabbed my purse from the back seat, and made a mental note to make the deposit in the morning. I headed inside the house. The sweet sultry sounds of jazz greeted me at the door, which was relaxing because I loathed walking into a quiet house. I pushed a few buttons to set the alarm and start the fireplace; I grabbed the half empty bottle of wine from the fridge and gulped it down, not bothering to get a glass.

The phone rang, chasing off the pity party that was looming over my head. I tried to disguise my annoyance when I answered. "What?"

"Whatcha doing, girl?"

I grabbed another bottle of wine out of the refrigerator. "Nothing, Richard."

"I'm surprised that you're home and not at the office?"

"I was just about to settle down next to this cozy fire and listen to my Áveri JáNea CD." I glanced around my enormous living room. "You know, Richard," I said, feeling the buzz of the wine taking effect. "I'm glad that Alex spends time in this house with me; otherwise most of the rooms would never get used."

"I know what you mean, honey child. Does anyone use your game room?"

Homeless Love

"Alex does. She spends most of her time entertaining her many male friends. Especially during football season. That's the only time that 51-inch Trinitron gets turned on."

"I don't know why you bought such a big TV anyway, you should have bought a JVC sound system like the one I have."

"The young man at the store said he hadn't had a sale in a long time, so I thought I'd help him out. I never thought about a sound system, he was selling TV's so I bought a TV."

"You're always helping folks out, you need to help yourself out, honey babe."

I cradled the phone on my shoulders as I opened the wine. "I'm okay," I huffed.

"Why don't you buy a saxophone?"

"For what?"

"Well, you love jazz so much."

"I don't know how to play." I hissed.

"You can always take lessons."

Ignoring his comment, I consumed the glass of wine before he spoke again.

"You should think about it."

"Nah, I'm fine, besides I get more enjoyment listening to others play."

"Honey, you got the blues." He stated with much attitude. "And you should do something to release the tension."

"Is that why you called me?"

"Actually yes. I was calling to check on you. You seemed so down at the office today. I know things are looking bleak, but. . ."

"Well, I'm fine and I have to go before you get too deep into my business."

"Okay, girl, go and take a long soak in that Jacuzzi bathtub that's big enough for ten folks."

"I will, Richard."

"And remember sister-to-sister, I'm here for you."

"You're not a sister, Richard."

"Well, I'm one tonight, girlfriend," He shouted as he hung up the phone.

"Lord, help the day!" I said as I started on that foreboding journey up those lonely, long ass 13 stairs.

ଞ

The hot water consoled my tense skin. My hair was pulled up in a bun with a few ringlets hanging in my eyes. Raspberry candles lined the bathroom floor against the wall. I tipped my head back and allowed the powerful massage jets to be my unsatisfying lover tonight.

About an hour later, I emerged from the cold water, reached for the pink terrycloth, floral robe, and descended downstairs to finish reading over the contract for the San Diego office.

I settled on the lambskin rug in front of the fireplace, as Wayman Tisdale picked the bass so smoothly, I began to drift into space.

I held my breath as my fingers began to ease the tension from my body as the rhythm and I became one.

The hairs on my arms immediately stood up, my lips trembled as I tried to remain calm, but my back arched involuntarily, and my toes dug deeper into the lambskin. I rocked back and forth trying to deny myself the pleasure my fingers sought. The touch from my hand was almost unbearable. I was at the point of no return when David Childs' the radio announcer's sultry voice sang to me.

'The temperature is 62 degrees in Southern California, we will be expecting some rain, not much, but enough to get you wet.'

I sighed and bit my lower lip until it throbbed like my pulse. My misery was so acute it felt like physical pain. I strolled back up those 13 lonely stairs, which I counted every time I took that long pathetic journey to my empty bedroom. I decided to return to the place that gave me the most comfort: My office.

Chapter Five

Franklin

J sat in the shadow of Nina's doorway softly playing *Ain't No Sunshine When She's Gone*. My heart ached to touch her, to hold her in my arms, but my past never let me get close to her, not even in my dreams.

I tried convincing myself I wasn't afraid to face my past if it meant I could have Nina, but I knew in my hour of darkness my prayer would not be answered. I've prayed for Him to take the cries of my daughter out of my head. He doesn't give a damn about my sorrows. When I close my eyes, I can still see my baby girl, crying and spitting up blood. He doesn't care.

With shaking hands, I untwisted the cap and swiftly sucked down the brown liquid as fast as I could, it burned like hot lava in my throat.

"This is my God." I screamed to the heavens as whiskey trickled down each side of my mouth.

I sucked more of the holy water until it was empty, the warmth of my God began to bless me by taking JoLee's gut piercing, heart wrenching, screams from my mind, allowing me to slip out of this painful ass world.

But no sooner than I began to agree with the alcoholic deity, I was snatched back by another ear-piercing scream, which was followed by a few blows to my side. I struggled to my feet, immobile for a moment, but trying to balance myself.

"Didn't I tell you to stay the hell off my property? "I'm

calling the police."

"Wait!" I yelled as my right hand reached for the silhouette. But it moved away and my right foot slipped off the first step. The concrete walkway was the only reason I didn't fall right to hell.

"Honey, I'm sorry." I cried, as blood dripped from my wound and cascaded into my cloudy eyes. I staggered to my feet and stumbled toward the silhouette of my gorgeous wife, I inhaled her perfume, allowing it to carry me away, but her screams sent me deeper into the pit of hell.

Nina

I drove down Market Street fast and as frightened as any woman would be after being attacked. The further I drove, the more homeless people I saw. Hysteria drove me mad, until nothing was familiar. I hit the brakes and brought the Jeep to a complete halt in the middle of the street. I caught my breath and reached into the backseat for my purse.

"Shit!" I hit the steering wheel realizing I dropped everything in my haste to get away. I drove until I found a pay phone, made a call to the Riverside Sheriff Department and waited. A few minutes' later, two sheriff cars pulled into the gas station parking lot.

When I got out of the Jeep to greet them, I knew I wasn't going to get anywhere, when I spotted Officer "fat ass" Perez. One of The Judges' arch enemies. He managed to pop his fat stomach out of the black and white car.

"Well Ms. Moore, another homeless man attack." He said sarcastically laughing.

"Yes." I said, staring right into his chubby face. "I left him on the sidewalk."

"On the sidewalk. Ms. Moore."

"Yes, what the hell was I going to with him?"

"I really don't know Ms. Moore. Show me where this homeless man is." He said as he turned to stuff his potbelly back into his car.

℘

By the time the sheriff and I arrived back at the office, the homeless Rastafarian was gone. The officers' flashlights beamed like beacons as they probed outside of the building, checking the dumpster, rosebushes, and parked cars. Still no sign of anyone having been there.

Nerves dried my throat like a wasteland. "Well." I mumbled.

"Ma'am, we don't see anything."

"A homeless man attacked me, and he stole my purse!" I shouted waving my hands in the air like a crazy person. "That should be good for a night in jail, don't you think!" I shouted. "I know I saw someone snooping around the place a couple of times, but. . ." I looked away from the officer who was writing down the information.

"Is this yours?" A young cop asked holding my purse in the air.

I was silent before snatching the bag from his hands. My heart raced as I began frantically searching for the cash deposit. A wave of relief washed over me when I found the envelope still in my purse.

"Where did you find it?" Officer "fat ass" asked while glaring at me over his grandpa glasses.

"It was sitting on the stoop in the corner with some papers and folders."

Perez took a quick glance in the direction the officer was pointing, then back at me. "Is everything in there?" he asked expressionlessly.

"Yes." I mumbled softly.

He rearranged his large stuffed gut in his pants. "How do

Homeless Love

you know he was homeless?" he asked, huffing and puffing as if he had run a half-mile. What a "fat ass", I thought. I put my left hand on my hip and tapped my chin with my right index finger. "Well, let's see, maybe it was that rope he had tied around his waist and that short, tight ass striped shirt he was wearing. Oh, and one more thing, he was sleeping on my fucking front stoop." I yelled.

"Calm down, Ms. Moore, we're simply asking you a few questions, that's all." Fat Ass stated.

"Maybe you should think about hiring a security guard." An officer said who was standing nearby.

I glared at both of them and rolled my eyes. "Thank you very much, Officer Perez." I said, praying that he didn't fail to catch the sarcasm in my voice. "However, I pay taxes for you to help me. And I'm receiving the same bullshit help that I received when I called a few weeks ago. Maybe you'll take me more seriously when I'm found dead."

"Ms. Moore, we're taking you very seriously."

"How, Mr. Perez? I've seen this man lurking around my place. I've seen him hiding in the shadows. For all we know he could be listening to us right now." I walked toward my front stoop and picked up my things. "I guess I'll have to take matters into my own hands," I shouted before slamming the door.

Chapter Six

❧

Franklin

"Jcan't believe you're still hanging around that woman's place," Bones said as I sipped the plain black coffee. "You're trespassing, not only on her property, but in her life. You're not supposed to be there."

I tapped my tongue to the top of my mouth. "This shit is nasty. How do you drink black coffee everyday? I need a shot of whiskey or something. My goodness."

"Don't worry about the coffee. Why you still at Nina's place? You're taking a big chance with her. If I hadn't shown up when I did, your black ass would be back doing time in prison."

I nodded. "I just sort of lost it last night. Things got out of hand, I just couldn't stop drinking."

"Why?"

"Man, I got to thinking about my daughter, my wife, and my mother." I shook my head. "What a pitiful sight, my entire family dead, and it's my fault." I tried to hold back the tears, really, I did, but they slipped out anyway. I looked into Bones' eyes, as sorry ass tears spilled from mine. I know I saw disgust pasted all over his wrinkled, worn face.

Bones was silent, and then he looked away. "Franklin, go and talk to somebody. Your past is killing you, man. Everyday you wake with that bottle clutched in your fist, you're dying. Everyday you think about your past, you're dying. It's killing you, man."

"Talking to folks ain't for me, Bones. Besides, I got you to talk to."

"I may not be around when you need me."

"Oh, hell, man," I said, trying to wipe my eyes as the bus station began to fill with people. I looked up at Bones who was staring right past me. I glanced over my shoulders to see what he was looking at. "If my past is killing me like you said." I continued. "You'll be here long after I'm gone."

"Frank, please get help!" he blinked.

"I don't need no help, man, I can do this on my own, and I sure as hell don't need no bullshit belief system. I'll stop when I feel the need."

"Then, stay away from Nina," he shouted so loud his voice traveled through the bus station like a jet.

I stared at Bones as if he said prohibition was back. "Stay away? Man, I can't stay away. Besides I have nothing but a high school crush on her." With a man size hunger.

"Franklin, you and Nina are living in two different worlds, but it can be one if you get off the booze. You're wasting your time and energy. Get off the streets, get your life back, and then seek Nina's friendship."

"You're asking the impossible from me?"

"I'm sure Nina is happier than you can ever make her in your current state."

"I hear what you saying, Bones, but you don't know Nina like I know her. Crazy Lucy is happier than she is."

Bones dipped his chicken strips into the blue cheese dressing. "Man, you must be crazy. All Lucy got is her knitting needles and a few pieces of candy. Nina got the whole world in her hands."

"Yeah, she does." I agreed.

Bones slammed his fist on the table again, causing me to jump in my seat. I looked around the station to see if anyone else was startled by his actions. "Then, do something about your drinking," he said staring directly into my eyes. "Do something about your drinking, before you die, Frank."

I almost felt the need to bust my old friend in the head, but I knew he was only looking out for me the way he's been doing for years. Because of him I still had my saxophone.

"Frank, I'm sorry," he said drawing back his anger.

I lowered my eyes.

"I just think you should take advantage of the shelters' kindness and get some help while it's free, cause when you get off the street you gonna pay for that same free service."

I stared down at my shaking hands. "I wish you would stop talking about my past," I said through clenched teeth. "Let my demons sleep or I'll end up on a three or four day binge, besides I don't see what the shelter has done for you."

Bones laughed and leaned back in his seat. "Cause I don't want to be helped, don't you know the truth?"

"What truth?" I squinted.

"God helps those who help themselves. I got all I need, Frank."

I waved him off and rolled my eyes. "What the hell does that mean? God helps those who help themselves. What the hell does that mean, Bones?"

He sat up straight, sipped his cold coffee and leaned in toward me. "Take some of those cats in the shelter. They're too young to be homeless, I mean two of them can get a job for minimum wage and bring in enough money for a one-bedroom apartment. So why are they sleeping on the streets, on park benches, and in gutters? They don't want to help themselves."

I shrugged my shoulders and looked away.

"You ain't no different. God won't help you because you won't seek him in order to help yourself. So you'll never get off the streets."

"I've gotten myself off the streets plenty of times," I said pointing to my chest.

"And you ended up right back where you started from."

"So?"

"So can't you see, Frank?"

"See what, Bones?" My old friend was really starting to freak me the hell out.

"See that you need to stop drinking so you can have Nina."

"What the hell are you talking about, I don't want Nina."

"Maybe you fooling yourself, but you're not fooling me. Can't you hear how much you've been mentioning Nina's name? It comes up in every conversation. Nina did this; Nina did that, Nina had this on; she had that on. You watch her every chance you get."

"So?"

"So. Man, she sees you in the park when she's having lunch. You say hello, she don't even speak to you Frank. You don't exist to her. How many times has she kicked you off her steps and not once has she said. 'Hey, don't I know you from somewhere?'"

I shook my head because the truth was kicking the shit out of me. "Bones, listen I don't have to take this from you."

"You don't belong on the streets, you belong in some fancy house with a beautiful wife like Nina and a few kids."

"I had that, man." I shouted. "I killed my family and that's why I'm on the streets. To punish myself for taking their lives."

"The system already did that," Bones said as if he were pleading with me.

"It wasn't enough."

"Then, stop ending up in places that she goes around town, leave her alone."

"Man, you act like I'm stalking her."

"What the hell do you call it? She gets parking tickets, you take it off her windshield and go to city hall and pay the fine. Man, that's a few nights in a motel down on University. You practically take care of Nina, protect her from the streets and she doesn't even know that you're alive Frank. You mean nothing to her."

I balled my hands into fists. "You know what? I don't want to talk about this shit anymore."

Bones grabbed my shaking hands. He looked into my eyes for a long time, then he let out a loud sigh. "Start going to church, seek the kingdom of heaven."

"Nope, that's for you, not me."

"But your situation will change."

I snatched my hands away. "Why do you put so much faith in God?"

"Because I know He can help."

"You've been praying for years, and I don't see no blessings in your life."

"He has blessed me, and I have all that I need."

"No, Bones, you've prayed to see your son or daughter for a long time. Where they at, Bones?" I shouted with outstretched hands. "Where they at?"

Bones sat still, almost petrified. His face was stone in color, and then a rose color appeared in his cheeks as tears spilled out his eyes. He lifted his hand and pointed to Lilly, the young girl who always gave us hot coffee and sticky buns or warm ham and cheese sandwiches on cold mornings.

"That's my baby girl, Frank." He lowered his head. "My son died a few years ago."

I frowned. "Lilly is your daughter?" I asked, totally surprised.

He shook his head. "I never prayed to find them, I prayed for God to allow me to accept them. I prayed for God to allow them to forgive me for the sins of my past, and he did, Frank."

"Why didn't you tell me, I thought we were friends."

"We are Frank, but I had to forgive myself for what I did to them. I wasn't ready to face my past, but I prayed for forgiveness and He gave it to me."

"I still think you should have told me about Lilly."

"I didn't tell you, because I was waiting on the Lord to heal my heart. I was a mean husband and an even worse father. The alcohol took me away from my family. It stole my dreams and robbed me of my faith, but I'm getting it back Frank." He smiled. "I'm getting it back."

"You're an alcoholic Bones?" I said in surprise.

"Yes. I never paid attention to my family. I was a functioning alcoholic. It wasn't until I lost everything, that I made a few changes in my life that I thought were useless, until I found the Lord. If He can heal someone like me Frank, He can surely do wonders in your life."

I stood, picked up my duffel bag and slung it over my shoulders. "I'm sorry about your son, Bones, but you can keep that holy crap. I don't have time." I said and turned to walk away.

"You can run from destiny, but you can't hide." Bones yelled.

I gave him the finger and headed toward Lilly to introduce myself.

Chapter Seven

Nina

J couldn't believe that I was sitting at another boring Sunday family dinner. Eating the same dry food, with the same dry people, with their same dry, fake smiles on their dry faces. I was trying so hard to look happy, and as I studied each face at the dinner table, I simply couldn't help but wonder what was I doing in this family.

The Judge, as much. as I hate to admit just how much I admired him, was one total controlling freak that I couldn't get rid of. Not to mention, I seemed to attract the same kind of controlling men. I took a deep breath and closed my eyes.

'Dear God, please send me a man who is nothing like The Judge.' I silently prayed, but, of course, I was interrupted by The Judge's heavy sarcastic voice.

"Nina."

I slowly opened my eyes.

"I've already prayed for this food," he said and sucked his teeth.

"She should be praying to help expand the family." Rachel hissed under her breath.

'Please, Lord.' I prayed again. 'Let The Judge get on his soapbox about the bloodline, so I could storm out of here.' The silence at the table forced me from my trance, when I looked up I saw that everyone was staring at me.

Alex almost fell on the floor laughing. "You were chanting, your butt off." She screamed in laughter, almost falling from her chair.

Awkwardly, my Mother cleared her throat, and frowned. "Nina, are you okay?"

My voice was low and soft. "Yes, Mother," I whispered.

"Mrs. Moore, how are you feeling today?" Maria asked as she sipped apple juice from a wine glass.

She cleared her throat again. "I'm doing much better today, dear, thank you for asking for the umpteenth time."

I felt so sorry for Maria. She was new to the Moore's way of living. If she had only asked me before marrying into this family, I could have told her to stay away from these people, but being pregnant, I'm sure, The Judge forced Harold to marry her, to give the baby a legitimate Moore's family name.

Rachel turned to face me. "So how's that baby doing?" She asked glaring at me.

"You know Rachel, I can have babies, I just choose not to give birth out of wedlock. Is that alright with you?"

"Mama and baby are doing fine." Harold shouted over Rachel's voice, as he patted Maria's bulging stomach.

"Yuck!" Alex rolled her eyes and stood.

"Where are you going?" The Judge said in such a nasty tone, I winced.

"What?" she snapped. Her voice seemed to echo. I wished I had what Alex possessed... balls.

"Where are you going?" he repeated.

"I'm getting away from all this happiness." Alex replied and went into the kitchen. Harold rose and followed her through the swinging door. Oh, shit. The movie was over too damn fast. The Judge turned his eyes on me; I now was the main attraction.

Ignoring his glare, I continued to play with the stiff mashed potatoes on my plate.

"So how's business doing?" he asked with a cold edge in

his voice.

There was a light tremor in my voice as the memory of my attack entered my mind. "It's wonderful, moving right along," I whispered.

"Heard you had a little trouble?" He shook his fork at me; a piece of dehydrated chicken dangling from the end of it.

"No trouble at all, Judge." I replied keeping my eyes on my plate.

"Hum-hum, what's going on with the San Diego office?"

I tried not to sound so cold, but I've learned to only answer the questions asked. "Nothing."

He spoke with so much authority I froze for a split second. "Permits, zone, building, everything's ok?"

I shook my head. "San Diego is great, everything should be right on schedule." My insides jumped with each question asked. I gave Alex an evil look as she and Harold strolled back into the room, each carrying a bottle of wine.

"Getting back to The Judge's question," Rachel said looking over the rim of her wine glass, "What about the trouble at your place awhile back?"

"It was nothing serious, Rachel."

"Humph." She mumbled, as she refilled her glass with my expensive Cabernet.

"What kind of trouble?" Harold asked.

"There was no trouble, I spoke to Nina about that awful rumor." Mother said.

"Your mother calmed my fears regarding Officer Perez harassing you." The Judge said as he sucked his teeth. He and I go way back, so if you can't handle him let me know." He nodded and sucked his teeth again.

Harassing me, I thought as I looked over at Mother, who smiled. She lied to him.

"Nina."

"Yes, sir." I turned to him.

Homeless Love

"If you need me to help out, let me know."

"Yes sir." I answered, grateful that Mother didn't say anything to him about the homeless Rastafarian.

"Will someone fill me in?" Harold asked, once he sat down.

"It's over with, son, just a little bad blood between me and an old friend," The Judge huffed.

"So, Maria, when's the baby due?" I asked hoping to ease the tension that sat on my shoulders.

"What's all the winking about?" Mother asked.

"Excuse me?" Maria replied.

The Judge turned to Mother. "What are you talking about, Lizzie?"

"I saw Maria wink at you." Mother said softly.

I was taken back by mother's comment. Alex must have said something to her. She's too sweet and innocent to have made such a nasty comment regarding The Judge and Maria. I needed to talk to Alex very soon, about her gossiping.

"I wasn't winking, Mrs. Moore." She said with a little nervousness hiding in the back of her throat.

Mother dropped her fork to her plate. "Oh, so now I'm stupid."

The room fell deathly silent, except for the thundering sound of Alex's ice cube hitting the bottom of her glass. We witnessed for the first time that Mother had a temper. How surprising.

Harold chuckled and kissed Maria on the cheek. "Sometimes when she gets headaches, she blinks Mother."

As if there were not enough tension in the room Rachel opened her big mouth. "Nina, now that you're expanding your business, when are you going to expand the bloodline?"

I slammed my hand down on the table. "Rachel, what the hell is wrong with you?" I screamed.

"Now, Rachel baby, don't start that tonight." Mother hummed. "Lets just finish this meal and this day. I'm tired." She groaned.

C.F. Hawthorne

Rachel sipped the last of her wine. "No, Mother, we want to know, I've given you and The Judge five grand-children. Harold's contributing his one. When is Nina going to settle down and do her duty for this family so Alex can follow?"

"My duty?" I replied.

"Yes, your duty."

I stood and put my hands on my hips. "I did my duty when I graduated from college and became an attorney."

"Yeah, with some of my dead mother's money." She snapped.

"Which I paid back!"

"Not because you had to." Mother cut in.

I turned to my frail mother. "I know, but now is the time for her to know." I said softly.

I turned back to Rachel, who continued to sip my wine. "You need to take care of your business, before you stick your nose in mine."

"My family is fine." She said under her breath, but loud enough for me to hear.

I picked up my glass of wine. "Where's your husband? I heard he hasn't been home in weeks." I said with a toast to her. The Judge beat his palm on the table. As Rachel sat speechless. "Girls, girls, this is our family dinner and the two of you are going to act like family even if it kills you; there will be no fighting in my kingdom."

I sharply turned to glare at him. His kingdom? I was surprised he didn't have us calling him God since we couldn't call him Daddy! I turned back to Rachel, who rolled her eyes as she reached for the bottle of wine sitting on the table. Mother placed her shaking hand on top of Rachel's.

"You've had enough, darling." She smiled.

Rachel jerked the bottle from Mother's grip and began filling her glass.

Harold jumped to his feet. "Rachel, if Mother said you've had enough, then you've had enough! Now put the bottle down, and don't ever disrespect her again."

Rachel held the bottle tightly in her palm. "Harold, that shit worked when we were younger, but it won't work now."

"Watch your mouth, young lady." The Judge said sharply.

Harold walked around the table. "Oh, she doesn't have to watch her mouth because she won't be in here much longer."

"And who are you?" Rachel asked as she followed Harold with her eyes.

Without a word, Harold opened the patio door, turned, picked Rachel up in her chair, and put her outside facing the pool, and closed the door.

"The wine." Alex yelled.

He opened the door, took the wine bottle out of her hand, secured the patio door and drew the blinds. The Judge became furious, but Mother demanded that she remain outside.

g

On the drive back to Riverside, my head throbbed. What a freakin' family! "Alex, I told you about telling people about my business. You know I try to keep as much as possible away from them."

"What the hell are you talking about? I never tell them anything. Not any more." She added.

"Then how in the hell did Mother know about me and fat ass Perez?"

"Nina, you were the one screaming how much you hate that man. You're the one who said that he treated you like shit because of The Judge. Anyone could have mentioned it. You know damn well The Judge has informants all over the place. So don't be getting in my face accusing me of talking shit behind your back."

"Listen Alex, I'm sorry of accusing you, I know you have my back." I said, after a long silent drive.

C.F. Hawthorne

She reached out and rubbed my arm. "No problem Nina, I understand the stress that you're under, however if that homeless man shows up again, you better believe me when I say, that I'll be calling The Judge. Those people make me nervous."

"What people?" I asked, turning down the music.

"Homeless people, they make me nervous."

"Why?"

"Because they're creepy."

"What experience have you had with a homeless person, besides what The Judge has pounded in our heads?"

She looked out the window then back at me. "A year ago I went to the Pixie Market on Town Street. This homeless man said he thought he knew me from somewhere."

I chuckled a little at Alex's expression. "What did you do?"

"I asked that fool where could he possibly know me from. He said from around town. I told him that I didn't live around town and I got the hell out of that grocery store."

"What did he do?" I smiled.

"He didn't do anything, but I could tell he wanted to hurt me, maybe even kill me." She said with innocence of a child.

"Alex, please. That man didn't want to hurt you, he wanted some change for a meal. I'm so sick and tired of you and The Judge's paranoia about homeless people, they're still human."

"Not to me!" Alex yelled.

"Yes, Alex, they are. Ever since we were kids, that's all we ever heard. How dangerous homeless people are, how a homeless man killed Rachel's mother. You and The Judge make it sound like a crime or a disease to be homeless."

"I'm not saying all that, but they do make a lot of people nervous. I'd rather not be around them if I can help it." Alex gazed out of the window and I let her have her moment before changing the subject.

"Are you staying at my place tonight or yours?" I asked.

"With you, but let's get something to eat because I'm

starving." She replied rubbing her flat stomach.

"I agree. Mother should get a cook because she's losing her touch in the kitchen." I could still taste the salty box potatoes that lingered in my mouth.

"I'm glad that Rachel showed her ass, because I couldn't eat another bite of that horrible food." Alex frowned. "She really does need to get a cook." I nodded.

g

Once we reached downtown Riverside, and I found a place to park, we began to walk the mall area in search of something appetizing. I spotted a tiny Mexican guy pushing a cart with steam rising from the top, my mouth started to water. "I'm going to catch up with that guy and get an ear of sweet roasted corn." I said.

"A what?" Alex shouted, curling up her top lip.

I yelled over the roar of someone blowing the hell out of a saxophone. "Corn-on-the-cob! That's what I want. . .." I stopped, turned in the direction of the music, and started bobbing my head. I couldn't see the musician because of the crowd, but I could feel his sweet, familiar, and comforting sounds.

I took two gasps of air as the music from the sax raced through my veins, casting a warm sensation over my entire body.

"Here." Alex shoved a large hot ear of roasted corn dripping with butter and Pico chili salt into my hand.

"Did you get a...."

She handed me an ice cold can of Coke.

I smiled. "That's why I love you so much."

"And I love you." She smiled back.

"Can you see who is working the hell out of that sax?" I asked.

"There's too many people." She took a bite of corn, moaned and swayed a little. "Oh, my God, this is so good!" She mumbled, licking the salt and butter from her fingers.

"I bet it's that same guy I was telling you about."

"You never mentioned a guy to me."

"Yes, I did, the one I told you was playing at the café."

"Oh, that guy," Alex, answered as she licked chili salt from her fingers again.

The music made me curvier. I wanted more, I needed more. "Let's get closer so I can get a glimpse of him."

"Girl, we can't get through that crowd. Here, open this." I reached for the Coke, keeping my eyes glued on the back of the crowd.

"Come on, Alex, let's just try, maybe we can get a quick look at him, he might have a CD out." I bounced on my tiptoes, trying to see over anyone's head.

"That man don't have any CDs out, if he did, he wouldn't be playing on the street."

"Let's push our way to the front." I shouted.

"Nina, what is wrong with you? You heard this man one time and now you all over him."

"Twice." I held up two fingers. "I haven't been able to get that song out of my head." I was able to take a breath again once the music stopped.

"Let's go." She cried again. "It's too many eerie folks out here and I think there's a homeless man watching us," she said looking over her shoulders.

As we walked away, I suddenly stopped in my tracks. The composition seemed to seal the air in my chest.

"That's it, that's the song." I swayed.

She gritted her teeth. "What?"

"Shush!" I held up my left hand and closed my eyes, swaying back and forth. "Do you hear it?" I moaned. "Do you feel it?"

"What?" She shouted again, this time almost bringing me out of my trance, but the music didn't allow me to leave.

"Shush!" I held up my left hand for the second time. The cold buttered corn that was suspended in my right hand quietly slipped from my fingers.

Franklin

When Bones whispered in my ear that Nina was there. My heart couldn't take it. I licked my lips because once again the reed became sweeter, and I began to love my sax as if it were her. I held her close to me. I caressed her, forcing her to come into my world, so that she could be mine without any hesitation.

I gently rocked the sax in my hands until the cool brass became warm. I rocked until my heart and the rhythm became one. I rocked until the ache left my soul and floated away. I rocked Nina, until I became dizzy. Wanting, craving, aching for a love I could never have. Just when I was about to give up, Bones whispered into my ear once again.

"She's crying man. I saw a tear Frank. One tear."

Oh why did he say that. My love began to come down like a Texas summer thunderstorm. Hard, fast and furious.
I played, until the hard brass saxophone began to feel like soft French silk in my hands. I played until the salty sweat from my brow, began to taste like sweet sugar water. I played until I almost forgot where I was and who I was. I played, until I could only hear Nina taking small gasps of air. I played my Nina's love song.

Nina

"Nina." I heard Alex softly say. But I was once again forced into a trance.

Immediately, my left hand went to my heart. I explored the outer limits of whatever I was feeling. The music wrapped me up in a warm blanket and rocked me until I felt nothing but pure, raw ecstasy. The melody melted the stress and strain from my neck, shoulders, and back. The harmony felt like warm hands caressing my breasts and my inner thighs, willing me to forget that I was out in public. My stomach trembled to the explosion of his music, and when he hit the high notes, Lord I wanted so desperately to dissolve like butter in that musician's arms.

When the sax murmured my name, I became even weaker. I felt a warm stir in the middle of my stomach that brought more tears to my eyes. My body relaxed as the melody silently slipped away. I dropped my hands to my side and breathed a sigh of relief.

"Need a cigarette?" Alex said softly.

I stumbled over to my sister and sat next to her. "What?"

With the lifting of her brows, she slowly opened her mouth again. "I said do you need a cigarette?"

I rocked my head softy. "I could use one, if I smoked." I smiled. "Did you hear him, he was incredible."

"He's okay," Alex answered. "You're the one that loves a sax. I don't, I'm a piano person, those long strong fingers frantically stroking those black keys. "My Lord."

"Okay!" I frowned. "Calm down. Damn, did you hear the sax sing my name?" I pointed to my chest.

"What?" Alex crinkled her nose. "Did I hear what?"

"He made it say my name." I beamed. "I heard it whisper, Nina Moore."

"Nina, all the women heard their names. Hell, I even heard: Alex, Alex, Alex." She smiled. "He was not playing that song for you, he doesn't even know you. So pick up that corn, throw it in the trash, and let's get the hell away from here, my feet hurt."

I was feeling so good, so light, and so free that I stayed sitting on the cold cement bench enjoying the ecstasy.

Alex continued to pull on my arm like a three-year-old child. "I'm ready to go."

"Let's stay and listen for more." I whispered.

"No, let's go." She yanked harder. "I'm tired and I want to go home."

I eased off the bench and slowly followed behind her.

"Drop me home so I can get my car," she said as her braids swung from side to side.

"Oh, my God, Alex, I felt like I was about to...."

"Have an orgasm?" She laughed.

"Yes!" I blushed "I have to hear that song again." I shuddered. "Just one more time."

Alex looked at me. "Why don't you just go up to him and say: Excuse me, sir, I was wondering where can I find your CD. I just loved your music, and I just gotta have it."

"Whatever, Alex."

"No, I'm not kidding. I'm sure he'll tell you where you can find his CD. I'm sure its right between po, broke, and hungry."

"Okay, alright! You've made your point. He's probably homeless and singing for his supper."

"Besides, The Judge would have a shit fit if you brought anything home from a homeless person." Alex giggled.

"Oh, my God, yes!" I frowned. "How on earth would that look to his associates? His successful attorney slash daughter, Woman of the Year, owner of three process service businesses, was friends with a homeless man."

"Yeah and you threw away a perfectly good white boy to marry a homeless man." Alex laughed so hard she could hardly walk.

"Alex, it's not that funny!"

"But, could you?" she asked.

"Could I what?" I frowned.

"Sleep with a homeless man."

"And have Mother's and The Judge's deaths on my hands, not if my life depended on it."

Chapter Eight

Franklin

Bones found me on the west side of the bus station counting the money.

"Frank, man." he held his side, panting like a dog. "I gotta tell you something."

"Start talking," I said passing him a few dollars and stuffing the rest into my pocket.

"Man, you ain't gotta keep giving me money like this."

"I know, Bones. You're a good friend, and you never ask for anything, but you're always giving."

"You a good friend, too, Frank; that's why I gotta tell you what I saw." He slapped me on the back. "You played your ass off today."

I tried not to smile, but I couldn't help it. "Shit, man, after you whispered in my ear that Nina was there, I couldn't help myself." I grinned even wider as we walked around the building.

"Even though I don't agree with you chasing Nina, I have to tell you this."

"Say, man, you gonna play again?" A tall, white man asked as he approached us.

I stepped back and glanced at Bones. "I don't know," I said coldly, trying to see if he was a narc.

"You were great!" He said shaking my hand, exposing all 32 of his teeth. "My wife and I will be looking out for you, do you play every Sunday?"

"Nah, not me." I answered, as my eyes widened when I unfolded the bill he pressed into my palm.

"Okay, dude you take care." He said walking away.

"A hundred dollars." Bones smiled. "Yo, my man, he play's here every Sunday and Wednesday night." Bones yelled.

"Right on, dude." The white guy shouted, displaying two thumbs up. I quickly walked away from Bones, not really upset, but mighty pissed off. When he caught up to me I had to stop and look at him.

"Man, why you give up that much information. You've been on the streets longer than I have. You know we don't volunteer information so easily."

"For a hundred dollars, I'll tell him if you playing in a baboon's butt while drinking tea." Bones laughed as he coughed up thick, brown phlegm and spit it on the ground.

"Shit, Bones, that dude could've been undercover."

"Man, cops ain't gonna give a hundred dollars to no homeless man. And did you check out his shoes and that fancy little yellow, tight ass shirt and those starched khakis?"

"Okay."

"Cops don't dress like that."

"Okay, man, you made your point. But I have to be sure, I can't go back to prison.

"I know, Frank. I got your back," he coughed.

"Cool man, now where you wanna eat tonight?" I grinned, waving the money in his face.

"What?!" Bones said surprisingly, as he followed behind me.

"I want a real meal tonight." I winked.

"How about some Bar-B-Que at Mama's?" Bones suggested.

My stomach began to ache at that suggestion. "That sounds great."

"What in God's name has gotten into you?"

"Nothing, man, I feel great, that's all." I winked.

"Why, you doing drugs?"

I skipped a few steps and turned around. "No, but I do feel high."

"What the hell?" Bones stopped and stared at me.

"Listen, man, you told me that she was enjoying my music, right?"

Bones nodded. "Yep."

"You told me she was swaying back and forth, right?"

Another nod.

"You told me she cried?"

"Uhm."

"Right?" I smiled.

"Right, right." He answered.

"That's all I need to make me high."

"So I guess you don't want to hear the other stuff?"

"Hell yeah, I want to hear the other stuff." I shouted and punched Bones in his frail arm.

"Man, I told you about hitting me."

"My fault, dude, but I haven't felt this good in years."

"Enjoy it, Frank, you deserve a little happiness."

"Oh, my Lord." I moaned when he pulled the door open and the sweet smell of the hickory smoked BBQ ribs rushed up my nose. Ham soaked Collard greens, cornbread, and candied yams followed suit all hitting my stomach like a hand grenade.

"Now, don't start spending all your money in here."

"Why not?"

"Because your black ass is still homeless."

"Well, my black ass is also hungry."

"That's great, but you should still save money."

"For what?"

"So you can get off the streets." He coughed.

"So the both of us can get off the streets." I corrected, slapping him on the back.

Bones shook his head. "Not me, man, I been here too

long, can't stand to be cooped up in a house for any stretch of time. I need to be outside where I can feel the wind in my face, but I'll come by and visit you, clean myself up and eat some of that famous spaghetti dinner you always bragging about."

"Hey, I can cook."

"I ain't never tasted nothing you cooked, so I don't know," Bones stated as he grabbed a seat near the door.

"Um, excuse me, can I help you?"

I frowned when I turned to see a beautiful young lady with rings hanging out of her face. She had two rings in her nose, one on each side of her brow, one in her bottom lip, and one right in the middle of her tongue. She had several in her ears, and even a cross hanging from her navel.

I swallowed and asked the walking jewelry store standing in front of me, "What do you recommend?" That's all I asked her. Very simple, I thought. What do you recommend?

She popped her gum a few times, very slowly. Put her hands on her hips and rolled her eyes, as she threw a few strands of red and yellow braids across her shoulders, as if I were bothering her. "I recommend you read the board and tell me what you want."

I stood shocked for a moment, before realizing that I was nothing to her. "Come on, Bones, let's go," I said as I turned to walk away. "I can't stand to be ignored or treated like dirt."

Suddenly, a powerful female yelled from the back of the tiny café, and the young witch turned and followed the sound. I pointed toward the front door and Bones began to gather our things.

"What can I get for you today, brother?" The lady said, dabbing the sweat from her brow with the back of her hand. "You have to forgive my grandchild. She doesn't like working here. Lawd knows it's hard to get this child to help me to do anything around here, but she always got her hands out for money."

I nodded as I studied the handwritten menu. I blocked out the long story about her unmanageable grandchild.

"I tell you what, let me recommend something for you and your friend." She nodded toward Bones. "It's the house special, we don't have it on the menu, it's only for a few selected people." She winked.

I turned to Bones. "Is that alright with you?" I asked.

"Yeah, man, whatever." Bones answered. "Give me a strawberry soda."

"One strawberry soda and one Coke." I said, as I handed the gentle-faced lady two twenty dollar bills.

"Make it to go," Bones yelled, as I slipped my change into my pocket. I took the drinks over to Bones and slid into the booth.

I laced my Coke with a lot of rum. "That lady sure does remind me of my Mother, God rest her soul, but no time for the past today." I sipped my drink. "Start talking, man."

"Where do I start?" Bones said rolling his eyes at my drink.

"Don't judge, Bones."

"Okay, Frank, it's your life, I'm just your friend."

"Good, now start from when you saw her swaying to my tunes."

"Oh, that part." Bones grinned.

"Yes, that part, now start talking or I'll tell the cook to make your ribs tough."

"Shit, boy I haven't had teeth since 1954. My gums are tough. I can chew anything you put in front of me. So, don't even try it."

"Man, just tell me what you saw Nina doing?"

Bones sat up straight. "This girl loves your music. I mean she was swaying to the sound of your harmony like nobody's business."

"Were her eyes closed?"

"Yep, sure were. Closed tight as a oil drum, she was so into your music she didn't even know her food fell to the ground."

"Her food?" I asked.

Homeless Love

"Yes, she was eating a corn on the cob from Jose."

"Oh, okay what else?"

"When you started to make that horn scream her name," Bones licked his chapped lips, "her face started to twist in all sorts of directions, like you were making love to her right there in the square, where everybody could see."

My eyes widened. "You're kidding me?"

"I ain't shitting you, man, I was looking right at her and that girl she was with."

"Alex?"

"What?"

"Did the girl have long blond braids?"

"Yep."

"That's her sister, Alex."

"Shit, man, you know all about this woman."

I smiled. "If only she knew how much I know about her."

"Nina was just about to walk away, until you started blowing them notes, she was yours from that point on. Alex couldn't make her move an inch. She took Nina's Coke, found a seat on the bench and waited for Nina to get finished."

"Tears? Tell me about the tears." I smiled, and thanked the girl who brought over the food.

She responded by rolling her eyes, and popping her gum several times before leaving. I shook my head and turn back to Bones.

"Oh, the tears! It was nothing man." Bones stared out the window again.

"What the hell you looking for?"

"I thought I saw someone."

"Come on, man, tell me about the tears?"

"What you want me to say about one tear that dropped from her eye. I mean she had her eyes closed, so it wasn't like she was crying a lake or something. It was one tear that escaped her heart, that's all, man, one tear."

I shook my head. "One tear." I repeated.

C.F. Hawthorne

"Yeah, Nina was all yours today." Bones added with a mouth full of BBQ beef rib.

I stopped in mid air, gripping the hot rib between my fingers. "What?" I asked. I put the food back on my plate and licked my fingers. "She was mine?" I repeated.

Bones shook his head as he continued to devour the beef rib. He licked his fingers and smiled again. "When you finished playing, Alex asked Nina if she needed a cigarette."

"Cigarette?" I repeated as a grin spread from ear to ear.

Bones shook his head again. "She said yes, if she smoked."

"Hot damn." I jumped from my seat and did a slow dance with one hand in the air and one on my stomach.

"Sit down fool, she's in love with your music, not you."

The smile fell off my face once Bones' words hit my soul. "Yeah, you right, man. She's probably one of those people who thinks singing on a street corner is degrading."

"Well." Bones sang.

"If I had a fancy car or a fat bank account," I said sliding back into my seat, "maybe she'd notice me and not my music." I stared at Bones, who only shook his head. "Maybe I should just back off."

"No time like the present." He whispered. "You won't believe who just walked in." Bones said looking down at his red beans and rice. I started to turn around and check out the scene, but he grabbed my arm.

"No, no, don't turn around, you gonna be recognized."

"Oh, hell, man, I told you that dude was undercover. Damn you, Bones." I said as I began to gather my things making a mental note of my escape.

"Calm down, it ain't the cops. It's Nina."

"Nina?" I gasped. "She's here?" I smiled.

"Standing right behind you." Bones mumbled as he continued to fill his mouth with ribs and red beans and rice, washing it down with the soda. "Come on let's get out of here," he said softly as he closed the container.

I slowly turned around as if a 400-pound grizzly bear was behind me. Nevertheless, all I saw was beauty. Her shoulder length sandy brown hair made me tremble. The red and black dress she wore so well revealed her upper back. The beautiful amber color silk skin forced me to close my eyes, but only for a few seconds. Suddenly, I saw only her in that room. If it weren't for Bones, I would have reached out and stroked her arm, just to see if she were real.

When she put both hands behind her back and I caught a glimpse of her red painted fingernails, my heart began to beat so fast, I felt as if I were out of breath. My mouth began to water as my eyes traveled from the length of her hair, to the width of her back, which lead to her waistline and round butt. My stomach began to ache. My instinct told me not to go any farther, but I did, and I saw my weakness. Her large, well defined calves, and she stood straight and elegant in those four inch red heels. I shook my head. I know I'll never get those shoes out of my mind. Nina was perfect all the way around.

"Frank?" Bones whispered.

I could hear Bones, but I couldn't answer him.

"Man, let's go, let's get out of here before you do something stupid."

"Huh." I replied, slowly. Nina's beauty was suffocating me.

"Man, let's get out of here, two cops just walked in."

Snap! I was back to reality. I licked my lips and eased out of the seat. We were out of the café and around the corner before the raggedy screen door slammed shut.

Chapter Nine

Nina

"Alex, I'm home with the food," I shouted as I walked through the kitchen door.

"Nina, I would like for you to meet Walter," she said, shoving this baldhead, dark-skinned man in my face. Good God, is what I wanted to say as I extended my hand to him.

Walter engulfed my hand in his. "Nice to meet you, Nina." He smiled, and it didn't matter that his teeth were crooked. He was gorgeous.

"Nice to meet you," I responded as I quickly released his powerful grip. "Alex didn't tell me we were having company for dinner, but if you would like to join us, I'm sure I can add a few things so we all can get a taste," I said as I turned my back to him, trying to catch my breath.

"I think that I'll take you up on that offer, but let me be the one to add a little something-something to the meal," he said taking the bags out of my hand.

"So, you know your way around the kitchen?" I asked as he followed behind me.

"You can say that. I watch the cooking channel," he smiled.

"You two go ahead and do your thing in the kitchen, and I'll set up the pool table." Alex shouted as she headed toward the game room.

"What does the WB stand for on your ring?"

Walter looked down at his hands and twisted the ring around his finger. "Oh, it's a club that I belong to." He answered and slipped his hand into his pocket.

"Oh, really." I smiled.

He shook his head. "Yeah, it changed the way I see things now."

"Well, that's great as long as it's helpful."

"Oh, it's very helpful."

§

After dinner, we played a few games of pool, but all that lovey dovey bullshit was getting on my nerves. I quietly disappeared into my bedroom with a bottle of wine and a book, leaving Alex and that gorgeous Walter alone. Soon after I heard them racing up the stairs.

Moments later, I became tense and alert to Walter's laboring sounds, which made my heart race. I closed my eyes tight and held my breath, as Alex's muffled giggles and moans seeped through the walls of my bedroom. Although I was awake, it appeared as if I were in a dream, floating above the room as the two lovers' echoes of irresistible passion for each other fought their way through my world and entered my soul.

Blood raced to my head as my inner thighs shivered. I placed the goose down pillow between my legs, willing my need to be pleased to disappear, just go away from where it came. But the desire for someone to share my bed was stronger than ever as my sister and her lover gave into the lustful gratification of their pleasure.

I quickly sat up in bed as the moonlight lit my room. I needed something to do, something to distract my thoughts. I couldn't turn on the music, which would alert them that I was awake. I was in no mood for contracts or accounting reports. The Internet chat rooms were out. There was simply nothing to distract me from my sister's lover. The preacher said on nights

C.F. Hawthorne

like this I should pray, and I know that prayer changes things, but I needed a solution and I needed it quick.

I eased back onto my pillow and took several deep breaths, my chest rose in a sea of grief as a storm of loneliness settled over me.

I tried not to eavesdrop on Alex and her lover, but the sounds! Oh, God, the sounds were slowly seeping through the walls, drawing me into their universe.

Alex's long, deep, slow breathing mixed with Walter's unyielding moans made the single bed sing a love song of their passion, and it damn sure didn't help the quivers that were dancing around between my thighs. I put my hands over my ears to block out the beckoning sounds, but it was no use. Ecstasy was near. And I didn't want to be around for the orgasmic eruption that was soon to come. I eased out of bed and tiptoed down the stairs like a cat burglar.

When I opened the patio door, the cool crisp air hit my face relieving my aching heart of its torment, and loneliness began to wrap around me until I couldn't breathe.

I went back into the house and sought out my old friend. The one I promised Alex I would never see again, Jack Daniels. I took the bottle, turned it to my lips and swallowed fast and furiously as lonely tears fell from my eyes.

A few hours later, I was awakened by light touches to my cheeks. I looked at Alex.

"Come on, big sis, I think you had too much to drink. Let's call it a night." Alex smiled.

"Where's Walter?" I asked.

"Oh, I sent him home."

I struggled to my feet. "When?"

"A few minutes ago. Put your arm around my shoulder."

"Where are we going?"

She kissed me on my forehead. "I'm putting you to bed."

As we climbed the stairs to my room, I asked, "Why didn't

Homeless Love

he stay the night?"

"Nina, you know me better than that, I don't want them to stay. I get what I need, then I move on."

"What about . . .?" I mumbled as I climbed into bed.

"What?" She asked as she crawled in next to me and put her head on my shoulder.

I cleared my throat. "Don't you want love?"

"Nope, already had some and it made me sick! Don't like the taste it leaves in my mouth." She looked at me and brushed my hair from my face. "Is that what you're looking for?"

I was quiet, I knew what she wanted to hear, but I knew what my heart was crying for.

"Well, honey, if that's what you're looking for, you better stop, cause you never gonna find it."

"But, that's what I want, I want love to go along with my bed, my home, and my children."

"Nina, that shit don't exist." She shook her head. "And if you don't stop wasting your time looking for love, you're going to be alone forever. Shit, take what you can get and move the hell on. Men don't love anymore, girl. You might have to lower your expectations."

"If I lower my expectations any more all I'll be expecting them to do is breathe."

"Well, that's all I expect them to do." Alex smiled.

"Yeah, but you want them to breathe hard," I said making loud grunting sounds.

"Stop making fun of Walter."

I smiled. "Who said it was Walter? I was just grunting."

"You sound like him."

"That's not my problem." I grunted again. "What does Mr. Noisy man do for a living?"

"He's a record producer," she responded.

"A what?"

"A record producer."

"So he says." I added.

"I don't care what he does, as long as he takes care of business. He can be one of those homeless guys living on the street, the man rocks my world." She snapped.

"I wouldn't go that far."

"I guess you're right." Alex laughed and snuggled next to me just the way she did when we were kids.

Chapter Ten

Nina

Remarkably enough, I was at the office the next morning hugging my savior, the coffeepot. My head ached, and my stomach burned from the BBQ pork and wine from last night's dinner, not to mention I had to get a restraining order against my old friend, Jack Daniels.

"Nina, you have a call on line three." Alex shouted from the other room.

I pushed the intercom button. "Can't you speak a little softer?"

"You have a call on line three." She whispered.

"Who is it?"

"Matthew Lawless."

"Oh, shit!" I didn't want to be bothered with his simple ass this morning. "What does he want?

"I don't know, but he's sounds pissed."

I wanted to scream, but I knew that my pain and anguish wasn't his fault. "Why?" I asked softly, while holding my head.

"I don't know."

"Can't you do your job and find out?" I hissed.

"No, you find out."

"Alex, you're supposed to be the receptionist."

"And?"

"And, find out why he's upset so I can at least have some lame excuse."

Homeless Love

"But he's upset with you, not me."

"I don't care, find out or I'll fire you."

"You can't fire me."

"And why not?"

"Because you love me."

"Alex, just do it, and I'll take the next angry caller."

"Promise?"

"Yes, I promise." I smiled and pushed the button. I searched my bottom drawer for Tylenol. I popped four into my mouth and washed them down with an ice-cold glass of water, which made me feel sicker.

The buzzing sound was driving me crazy. "What, Alex, dang!" I rolled my eyes and put my hand on my forehead.

"He said his papers didn't get picked up and some documents didn't get to the bankruptcy court. Now his clients are screaming economic failure or some shit like that. He wants to speak with you, now!"

"Do we have anything for him?"

"No, and we didn't have a request for a pick up from him either."

"Did you check the night drop?"

"Yes, and I also checked the night phone messages. There's nothing"

"Oh, hell, Alex, I get most of my clients from Lawless. What in God's name is going on here?"

"I don't know, Nina, but something is stank."

I started searching through the piles of papers that were on my desk. "What about drops for this morning?"

"We have a few drops for criminal court, but nothing for family law and nothing for Orange County."

I took a deep breath. "Okay, give me Lawless and let me see if I can put out this fire."

"You can put out his fire." She chuckled through the intercom. "You know he wants to sleep with you."

"Alex, pass the man to me please."

"You got it, sister, here he comes." She sang.

I took another deep breath and held it in for a while. "Hello, Matt. First of all, I don't know what's going on right now, but I'll get to the bottom of this as soon as I can, and I'll credit your account on this one." I said before he had a chance to shit on my grave.

"I'm sending people your way and they're not getting what they're paying for." He said almost shouting in my ear.

"I know, Matt, but I'm barely staying above water."

"Nina, you have an excellent reputation. That's why we chose to go with your company in the first place."

"Matt, all I can do right now is offer you my apology and pray that my reputation will not be tarnished by this little mishap."

"This can't keep happening!"

"I know, Matt."

"Do something, okay. I trusted your father when he told me I would't have any worries. Your father has a spotless reputation."

"I stand behind my work, Matt, you know that."

"I want this straightened out by the end of the week or I'll take my business, and those I brought with me, someplace else."

"I'll straighten this out, but if you feel like you want to go someplace else, remember the door is always open." I placed the phone in its cradle and took a deep breath. Perhaps Matt had me confused with someone who could be easily intimidated, by non-family members.

By the time I finished putting out a dozen fires from irate people and pissed off attorneys, I was tired and hungry. "You want to get something to eat?" I asked Alex.

"No, thank you. Walter is coming by and I'm taking him back home so he can finish eating what he didn't finish last night."

I raised my eyebrows. "Don't be too late Alex, you have to finish those papers for the San Diego office."

"Don't worry, I'll hurry back as soon as he's finished eating," she winked.

Homeless Love

❧

Two hours later, Alex walked through the door with a grin on her face and half dozen yellow roses in her arms.

"I told you not to be long." I snapped.

"Nina, calm down, I wasn't gone that long."

"Two hours is too damn long, Alex. What if everyone takes two hour lunch breaks, I'd have total chaos on my hands."

"They do take two hour lunch breaks, you said we could if we really needed to, just make up the time the same day."

"When did I ever say something as stupid as that?" I shouted, almost two minutes from choking the shit out of her.

She put her hand on her bony hip. "When The Judge told you it was a stupid thing to do and you couldn't run a business like that. You set out to prove him wrong."

"Everyone, in my office now!" I shouted and slammed the door behind me.

Before I could catch my breath, there was a light tap on the stained glass window. I counted to ten until I could steady my breathing and calm my nerves. I straightened my spine. "Come in." People began to pile into my office with serious faces.

I cleared my throat and got down to business. "It has been brought to my attention, that I have allowed two hour lunch breaks, if needed." I noticed shoulders dropping and heads lowering. "That's going to change. I'm going run this office just like any other office you've worked in." Disappointed groans echoed throughout the room. Complaining Stanley raised his hand.

"Yes, Stanley."

"Does that mean I have to take a lunch break at twelve or one?"

"That's exactly right." I nodded.

He raised his hand again. "I'm not able to do that."

"And why not, Stanley?" I asked sarcastically, folding my

arms across my chest.

"I have to pick my daughter up from school at two and take her to my mother's house. When you hired me you promised that you'd be able to work around my daughter's schedule."

"You'll need to make other arrangements. Any other questions?" I asked as quietness filled the room. "Good, lets get back to work."

&

Later that day, as I walked through my office, I could feel a distant, unfriendly sensation in the air. The normally cheerful attitudes that always filled the rooms were gone. But what could I do, things were rapidly getting out of control.

When I returned to my office, I locked the door for the rest of the day, and tried to figure out what had happened. The time ticked by slowly, I thought I was going to lose my mind, as loneliness began to creep back into my soul. I made a call to an old friend then prepared to go home. I was hoping that night would end up a little different.

Franklin

"You look like hell." Bones laughed once I made it to the bus station.

"Feel like it, too." I mumbled as I poured my breakfast into a paper cup.

"How can you drink that stuff so early in the morning?"

I shrugged my shoulders. "I just can."

Bones shook his head. "Another nightmare?" he asked. I nodded and swallowed some of the warm whiskey. "Man, I think I'm going crazy. All night I felt like someone was staring at me."

"That's your past, Franklin, you gotta let it go." Bones

mumbled. "Just let it go."

"I don't know, Bones. I thought if I filled my blood with booze, the demons would leave me alone." I shook my head. "They keep attacking me."

"Attacking you?"

"Literally standing over me." I dropped my head on the table. A loud thud echoed through the empty coffee shop.

Bones tapped the table. "Give it to God."

I lifted my head, which felt like a brick and squinted. "What?"

"You heard me. Give it to God."

"Man, you have to be out your mind, I ain't got time for no fake and phony stuff like that."

"It ain't fake and it ain't phony. It's real, I mean the Man can help, but you just gotta trust."

"What in the world has happened to you?"

"I've been going to church."

"Church!?" I exclaimed.

"Yes, Frank, church. You used to go, and you need to go back."

"Oh, hell no." I waved my hands in the air. "I don't have time for that crap."

"Now, listen to me, Frank, go to God on your knees, He can help you."

"Help me? What can He possibly help me with? What else can He take from me? My life?" I shouted. "The only man I go to is Jack Daniels."

"You need to surround yourself with Christians."

"I am surrounded by Christians." I smirked and patted my duffel bag.

"In there?" He frowned.

"Yep, I have the Christian Brothers right where I need them." I patted my duffel bag again, as Bones walked away. "It's only my life, Bones. What do I have to lose?"

Chapter Eleven

Nina

J just hung up the phone with another irate client when Alex peered around the door. "How are you on this fine Wednesday morning?"

I looked up from the pile of paperwork and smiled. "I feel like I'm on a slow drop to hell, but thanks for asking. Come in and have a seat." I said waving her into the office. "You know I'm a little jealous."

She sat in a chair that was in front of my desk. "Of what?"

"Of Walter, he's getting all of your time." I winked.

"I'm sorry, Nina, it's just when we're together, we disconnect from the world."

"You don't have to apologize." Little did she know I was really speaking the truth. I envied all couples that crossed my path.

"What's wrong, big sis? You look so sad."

"You really need to hurry up and move in with me, then maybe you can save me from myself." I looked down so she wouldn't see the embarrassment that was on my face. I bit my lip and closed my eyes in order to keep in the tears. "I did something so stupid last night, it makes me sick."

"I've done a lot of stupid shit in my life, and you've always been there for me, so it's about time you start doing stupid shit, and let me bail you out for a change." Alex crossed her legs. "So, start talking."

I tapped on the glass desktop. "I feel so stupid that I'm allowing loneliness to consume me the way it's doing. I'm too successful to worry about not having a man in my life."

"Nina?"

I took a deep breath. "On Monday night I called Calvin. He couldn't meet me until last night. I knew you were going to be with Walter, so that was perfect."

"Who the hell is Calvin?" She frowned.

"Calvin Gaston, the attorney I was seeing for a hot minute."

"Oh, yeah, I remember him, that really red brother with the green eyes. The Judge was so excited, he thought he was going to finally get some white blood in the family." She laughed and slapped her thighs.

"Anyway, he came over for dinner and a conversation, so I thought." I took another deep breath. "After dinner we sat on the couch to look at a movie he brought over . . .." I stopped and wiped the tears from my eyes. Alex waited for me to continue.

"I don't know what happened, but he started attacking me like a wild man, I mean he tore at my blouse and he kept saying that's why I called him over."

"Oh, my God, Nina, what did you do?" She asked as her hands covered her mouth.

"I tried to get him off of me, but he wouldn't budge. So I picked up that fertility doll and bashed him across the head with it."

"Nina!" She shouted and jumped to her feet. "Where did you hide the body?" That doll is made of marble. You must have killed the man."

I laughed and wiped my nose. "I didn't kill him."

Alex dropped back into her seat. "Oh, thank goodness." She laughed, holding her chest.

"But, he has a nasty gash to take home to his wife." I smiled.

She sat up straight. "His what?"

I shook my head. "His wife."

"You tramp! How could you screw a married man?" She grinned. "That's my job."

Franklin

I hadn't taken a bath in two days, nor had I eaten. I could no longer fight the evil spirits that pursued me. I tried to wrap myself up with the image of Nina enjoying my music, but the drink was the only antidote that kept the demons at bay. As I stumbled around in a daze, I found a nice place under a tree and wrapped the old tattered coat I found in a dumpster around my body. I was sinking lower and I couldn't come up for air. I thought about Bones and his God, but how could I allow a God who permitted this to happen to me, back into my life? I frantically searched for the whiskey that I'd wedged deep into my coat pocket. I didn't want to think about my past or that God Bones has been preaching about.

A sigh of relief came over me when my fingers felt the tip of the bottle. I began to shake as the strong fragrance filled my nostrils, but panic gripped my soul when I realized that the bottle was empty, and all the money was gone. I leaned my head back and closed my eyes, trying to slip into my comfortable safe place called black out.

Moments later a loud scream jolted me from my slumber. And I roused just enough to take a peek. Two homeless guys were fighting and the cops were surely going to be called. I struggled to my feet, picked up my gear, and headed in the direction of Nina's place.

By the time I made it to her front stoop it was late, and I was sober. The light was still on in her office, so I quietly walked to the rear of the building and took refuge behind the

Homeless Love

dumpster. The night air held something that I couldn't put my finger on.

I tried to find the alarm clock in my duffle bag, but the light where Nina parked her car was out. So I took the coat and made a pillow with it as I tightened the rope around my waist. I held down the tiny striped shirt that kept rising above my navel. I closed my eyes and waited for the squealing of Nina's wheels, so I could go home and smell the sweetness she left behind. But moments later, as I settled down on the ground, I heard a scream followed by a pitiful, weak cry for help.

I opened my eyes and listened closely for a second noise; something to tell me it wasn't my imagination. Many times in my drunken stupor, I here agonizing sobs in my head, but this was real.

The hoarse whisper, mixed with muffled cries, chilled me to my soul. I jumped to a squatting position and peered around the dumpster into the parking lot. Nina's car was still parked in the same place, but there were folders and papers scattered all over the ground.

Suddenly, my heart fell into my old shoes, I spotted Nina in the horrific grip of the man I've seen lurking around her window a few nights ago. Using the greenery for a shield I scampered behind this fool. I knew I had to take him down fast and hard. With one quick movement, I managed to wedge my arm around his neck, grabbed a handful of his crotch and twisted, I know that brought tears to his eyes, but I held on until he released Nina and she fled toward the building.

With the knife he was holding, he sliced the top of my hand. I released him and he fell to the ground on his knees. I kicked him in the chin, sending his head back. After a nice ass whipping, I pushed his face down to the ground and tied his hands behind his back with the rope from around my waist.

I could hardly lift my voice above a whisper as I stood in front of Nina, wanting so much to gather her in my arms and calm her fears. "It's okay. You can open your eyes now." I said feeling silly that I was holding my pants up with my left hand and the attacker who was breathing hard and bleeding even harder, with my right. "Where's your cell phone?" I asked.

"It was just turned off yesterday." she whispered so frightened and frail I wanted to kill that son of a bitch for causing her grief.

"Let's go inside so I can call for backup," I said, walking toward her.

She stepped back. "I'm not letting you inside my place," she said shaking her head.

I took two steps back. "Listen lady you can do this my way or the hard way, it's your choice."

She gave me much attitude and looked away.

I shrugged. "If I let him get away, the police will never find him, and you'll never know if he's stalking you again. So what it's gonna be?"

She held up both hands. "Okay, I have to find the keys," she shouted and stormed off toward her car. She returned breathing hard and shaking like a leaf. She dropped the keys several times before she was able to unlock the door.

Once I entered her space, I hoped she couldn't see how nervous and excited I was to be inside a building that I had called home for so long. "Do you have a place I can put this punk?" I said, violently shaking the attacker.

She took a seat next to the fireplace and pointed toward her office. "There's a storage closet behind my desk."

As I entered her office, I closed my eyes taking in her aroma. I tried to remain calm as hot waves of passion raged thorough my body. I slapped the attacker a few times on the right side of his head and whispered in his ear as I secured the rope tightly around his wrist.

"You attacked the wrong woman, and you better pray that Riverside Police Department keeps you locked up."

"Whatever, man," he replied calmly.

Homeless Love

Without thinking I slammed his bloody face into the wall before shoving him into the tiny closet.

After the attacker was secured, I cleaned my wound in her bathroom sink, placed a call to the police department and waited for the siren. I knew it wouldn't be long.

I took a deep breath and opened the door. My heart pounded something furious in my chest. I stared into her beautiful, tear-stained eyes before she turned away. Soon the sirens began to cut through the night. I headed for the front door. "Well, my work here is done," I said as I held my bleeding hand wrapped in toilet paper to my chest.

With shaking hands, she pointed toward her office. "You're just going to leave me alone with this freak?"

"I'm sorry, ma'am, but I have to go."

"You're not going to be a gentleman and wait until the police get here?" she asked as she wrapped her arms around her shaking body.

"I wish I could stay, but I really must be going. You'll be safe until they arrive."

"Asshole." She whispered under her breath.

Nina's bitterness echoed in my soul and broke my heart. I let out a long, audible breath. "I don't have any obligation to you, you told me to stay off your property, remember?"

"And did you?"

"I was simply passing by."

"Well get the hell off my property!" she screamed, pointing toward the front door.

Nina

My heart stopped as the Rastafarian closed the door behind him. Not only was I alone with the man who had just attacked me, but the Rastafarian was right, he had no obligation to me. I picked up the phone to call Alex, my only true friend at the moment.

After several rings, the answering machine picked up. "Alex it's me." I said trying to control the trembles in my voice. "I'm at the office, I was just attacked, and. . ."

Before I had a chance to go into details, three officers exploded into the foyer shouting and screaming. "Where's the officer? Where's the officer?" One officer walked up to me. "Are you alright?" He asked, staring into my eyes.

"Yes, I'm fine." I answered, just as another asked.

"Where's the officer who's hurt?"

I frowned. "There's no officer." I said as sat on a nearby chair. "There's a man tied up in the closet." I pointed toward my office.

"In there?" One of the policemen asked.

I nodded.

"Ma'am, please follow me," another policeman ordered, taking me into the kitchen where I answered question after question. I told what happened to several officers before Fat Ass Perez wobbled into the room, he sat my things on my lap and dropped my keys into my hand. He stood gawking down at me, as if I were the criminal.

"You're not supposed to report officer down, unless there is an officer hurt," he huffed out of breath.

"I didn't." I replied in a nasty tone.

"Who called in the attack?"

My eyes darted between the two officers. "The homeless man."

He held up his fat stubby fingers. "We've never received calls regarding homeless people attacking law-abiding citizens. However, we receive calls all the time that a homeless person has been attacked, even murdered." He said, raising his bushy brow at me.

"Excuse me."

"Ms. Moore, I went through this with your father when I was in San Diego. I don't want to go through this with you.

First, the homeless man attacks you, now he's helping you. Which is it Ms. Moore?" He turned to the officers that were standing next to him. "Her father has problems with homeless people." He smirked.

How in the hell, could he compare me to The Judge? I didn't have a problem with all homeless people. Just one. "I don't give a shit who my father is. I know what I saw." I was just about to get a little deeper in this man's ass when another officer came into the room.

"The dispatcher said it sounded like another male police officer."

I shook my head as nervous, angry tears started to form.

"Do you know police codes?" Perez asked patting his stomach.

I looked away. "No, and it wasn't a cop. It was the homeless Rastafarian I reported to you guys last week and the week before that."

"Can you please describe this homeless Rastafarian to us?" Fat Ass asked as if he didn't believe me the first time.

I didn't answer him. What could I say? The man I feared was the one that came to my rescue. The man that asked for help was the one I needed help from.

"And you don't know who this guy is?" the officer asked for the third time.

"No I don't." I snapped. "Like I told you numerous times before, he sleeps on my doorstep."

Another officer entered the room and handed Perez a note pad. Fat Ass cleared his throat and licked the beads of sweat from his top lip. He whispered into the officer's ear and licked again.

I stood to my feet. "Do I have to stand here and watch you lick sweat from your top lip all night?"

Officer Fat Ass looked at me then back at the tiny paper. "No Ms. Moore, you're free to go. We have all the information we need."

"Good, I'll be in my office waiting for you to leave." I said as I turned to walk away.

He cleared his throat. "One more thing, Ms. Moore."

I turned to face him, with one hand on my hip. "What?"

"The alleged attacker fits the description of a man who's been stalking and raping, both men and women, leaving them with something far worse than the violation of being raped."

"What?"

"He's HIV positive and pissed off at the world. He's on a mission to infect as many as he can."

From the corner of my eyes I saw an officer shake his head. I felt sick to my stomach.

"You were very lucky." He said softly.

I could almost detect a trace of sincerity in his voice, which frightened me.

"This mysterious homeless Rastafarian saved your life." Fat Ass pointed to me. "You need to find the man and thank him, you could have been handed a death sentence."

I took a deep breath. I needed to get away and think, I needed to let the stars realign in my favor. I needed a fucking drink.

My heart raced as terror began to rush through my blood. I walked out of the kitchen, through the front door, and down the sidewalk toward my car. The yells of the police officers were slowly fading away. My life was falling apart right before my eyes.

I slid behind the wheel of my car, started the engine and slowly drove away. I kept driving until my family's six-bedroom cabin in Big Bear came into view. I took a deep breath and slowly walked up the five flights of wooden stairs. I removed the key from the lock box and slid it into the lock.

The cabin didn't have the closed-up, musty smell so someone had been here before me and I didn't care who, my life was going to hell and I didn't want to worry about someone else's problems.

I searched the cupboards for tea and whiskey as I played and replayed the entire incident in my head, and the more I thought about it, Fat Ass Perez was right.

Chapter Twelve

Franklin

J sat nestled in a dark alley next to another urine infested dumpster. My bloody hands were shaking when Mark, a homeless man handed me the bottle of Scotch. I took several big swallows of the liquor, allowing the alcohol to burn as it slid down my throat. My eyes closed involuntarily as numbness spread throughout my body. I sank further into my resting place, without any understanding of what was in store for me.

I just wanted to forget about my past, and forget about Nina, but her beauty in the fluorescent light of her office seered my soul. She was more beautiful face-to-face than the moonlight had portrayed her to be. I tried not to stare but she captivated my soul. Even her spitfire attitude was cute to me. I wanted to stay and protect her. I wanted her to know that I was her watchdog, even if she didn't want me to be.

The vision of her well-rounded hips made me shiver, especially when she positioned her hands on them, which made her nice firm breasts stand out. I took pleasure in that thought for a few moments before the great darkness descended over me. I wanted to think of Nina as a woman I could love forever, but the screams of my child began to echo in my head preventing Nina's soft voice from being heard.

I snatched the bottle from Mark's hands and swallowed the rest of the Scotch as fast as I could and waited to pass out into the darkness...but I didn't. Instead the Scotch took me back to that night when my daughter lay dying in my arms. I began to bang my head against the dumpster until blood ran down my neck. The pain of my life was so great I didn't see the need to keep living.

"Have mercy, Lord." I cried remembering Bones' words. "Have mercy, dear God." I shrieked again as if something had touched my soul. "Father, I don't want you to help me to stop drinking, because I can't. I need you to do it for me. Please don't leave it up to me to stop this painful addiction. Send someone to help me stop." I prayed as I twisted and turned, wallowing in my vomit. I began to cry for all the times I couldn't cry. For all the times I wanted to cry. My heart ached and burned as I began to cry for my family. I stumbled around in the murkiness of the night, with the weight of my cross on my shoulders. I prayed until I slipped into a sweet silent darkness.

Nina

I sat calmly on the sofa listening to nothing, sipping my third cup of tea, wrapped in the blanket that my Mother knitted.

I lowered my head and begun to say a short prayer, when the vision of the Rastafarian constantly pulling down his striped knit shirt, which was several sizes too small, invaded my space. I began to laugh softly at first, and then the laughter turned into hysteria. I spilled the warm tea all over my legs.

As I stood to get a towel, a loud furious banging on the front door startled me and terror raced through my veins. I stood frozen in my stance.

"I know you're in there, so open up."

I exhaled as Alex's voice echoed through the door.

"Nina, dammit open this door or I swear I'll call The Judge and tell him where you are!"

C.F. Hawthorne

I removed the chair and unlocked the door. She flew into my arms and hugged me tight. I couldn't breathe.

"I was so scared when I got to the office and didn't find you there. Are you alright?" Alex asked touching every inch of my body, even the palms of my hands.

"Alex, I'm fine."

"Do you want to talk about it?" She asked releasing her grip.

"Not now." I walked into the kitchen and grabbed a towel. "How did you find me?"

"This is the farthest place you can go without leaving the planet," she replied, walking into the kitchen behind me. "I also called the hotel and you weren't there."

I walked back into the living room. "I guess you're right." I whispered after firmly securing the door by placing the chair back under the knob.

"The officer said you ran away like a bat out of hell."

"I needed to get away,"

"Well, the family is furious."

I dropped my shoulders. "Oh, Alex, why did you call them?"

"Even Rachel came."

"Rachel?" I repeated.

Alex raised her well-arched eyebrow. "Yes, Rachel, and she was genuinely concerned."

"How could you tell?" I asked, plopping down on the couch.

"She was asking a lot of questions?"

"Like what?"

"Oh, hell, Nina I don't know, I can't remember, she's just concerned."

"Who looked after all those kids?"

"Her stupid ass husband was home for once in his life, so she left the demons with him."

"How's Mother?" I asked praying that this ordeal didn't upset her too much.

"Okay, but not happy, and The Judge wants to close the

place down. He thinks the homeless man had something to do with all this."

"What? How in the world did he come to that conclusion?"

Alex shook her head. "I don't know, leave it to The Judge, he'll always find a way to blame everything on homeless people. And, he was madder than hell. I couldn't get one word in, so I just let him rant and rave until he finally calmed down."

"Then what?"

"Then, I took them to your house."

"What?" I shouted.

"The Judge said they were not leaving until you came home and explained to him what happened. You know he got the cops looking for you."

"Where's the damn suitcase?" I asked. "Because I'm not going back until Monday morning."

"It's in the trunk of my car. I also made a few calls and told everyone not to come into work tomorrow, so they'll have the weekend to calm down."

"What did Harold have to say?" I asked

"He said he understood, and he was going to try and get the folks to leave, but he wasn't promising you anything."

"He wasn't promising me anything! That's my damn house."

"You know Harold, he won't argue with The Judge. He lets that man walk all over him, that's why he ended up leaving his first wife."

"The Judge didn't tell Harold to leave Yolanda, so don't start with that shit."

"No." Alex cooed. "He didn't tell Harold to leave Yolanda, he just kept nagging him about a grandson and that damn bloodline."

"So, he's always nagging us about the bloodline, he's an old man. He wants a legacy to leave behind."

"Bullshit!" Alex shouted. "He wants control and he's running out of people to manipulate."

"He has Rachel's kids if that's what he wants." I smiled.

Alex put her hands on her hips. "Girl, ain't a damn thing you can do with those demon possessed kids. Shit, Satan ran them out of hell."

"Don't speak that way about the family."

She rolled her eyes and sucked her teeth. "Anyway, alls I know is, the ink wasn't dry on the divorce papers before he rushed off and married hell cat Maria. Now The Judge is getting a grandchild, and we're stuck with the devil bitch from the burning pit of hell." Alex looked away. "Harold only married her because she was pregnant. I can't stand her."

"Why?" I shrugged.

"I know Maria and The Judge had something to do with the breakup of Harold and Yolanda."

"You're misdirecting your anger," I said as I brought the large black blanket up to my chin.

Alex put her hands on her hips again. "What?"

"Yes, you should be mad at Yolanda."

"Why?"

"She's the one that lied. Yolanda knew that she had a botched abortion and that led to her being sterile. She's been in this family long enough, she knows how important the bloodline is to The Judge."

"That doesn't matter. They were married three years and doing great until The Judge insisted they have that stupid test. How did he get a copy of those medical records anyway?" Alex shouted. "Yolanda damn sure didn't give them to him."

"God only knows Alex, he has connections."

"Maybe The Judge is in the mob." Alex said as her eyes narrowed. "He can make anything happen just by one phone call."

"He's a Judge, Alex, he can't have any criminal connections."

She shook her head. "Like I said, Yolanda didn't give those records to him."

"I know that." I said rubbing my eyes.

"Seems like shortly after Yolanda and The Judge got into that big ass fight, up pops her medical records. She can't have kids and now she's out of the family and replaced with devil bitch Maria."

"Maria is not a bad person."

"Whatever, I just can't get next to her." Alex shook her entire body. "She's the devil like The Judge, and do you see how she's always looking at him."

"You only feel that way because you liked Yolanda."

"No, Nina, I got my eyes on that ho', I think she's up to something."

"The girl is pregnant and in love. What can she be up to Alex?"

"I don't know, but Mother should say something about Maria always grinning at The Judge."

"She smiles at Mother, hell she smiles all the time."

"Not like that." Alex shook her head. "What's up with all the smiling and grinning all the damn time? That's a sign of a sneaky woman." She marched into the kitchen mumbling as she poured half the bottle of whiskey into a glass.

I threw my hands in the air. "Oh my Lord, Alex, that's so stupid."

"It's not stupid. I'm only stating what I see. I know when a woman is after a man, I've chased enough of them my damn self." She pointed to her chest as she walked back into the living room.

"That's not what you see. Besides Harold really loves Maria, they're having a baby and everybody is going to be happy."

"Well, I don't know how he loves her when he's cheating on her."

"You're lying!" I shouted and threw the blanket over my head. "And I'm through talking to you."

Alex fell down on the sofa next to me and pulled the blanket off my head. "No, I'm not." She smiled.

I folded my arms across my chest. "How do you know?"

"Harold told me."

"He never told me."

"That's because you would have a fit."

"Does Maria know?"

Alex sipped her drink. "Hell no, she doesn't know."

"How does he get away from her? She seems to always be walking in his shadow."

"He uses me." She winked and licked her lips.

"You?" I frowned.

"Yes me, he tells the devil bitch he's coming up to hang with me, and he goes over to his friend's house."

"Who's his friend?"

"I don't know, he won't tell me that."

"Oh, that ain't right." I shook my head in disgust. "That ain't right."

"I know, but he's family, remember?"

"That still doesn't make it right." I threw off the covers and walked over to the picture window, peering into the darkness. "The Moore men are something else."

Alex walked over to me and cupped my face in her hands. "Now that we got all the crap out of the way, you mind telling me what happened with you and this homeless man, back at the office."

I turned and walked over to the mirror in the hallway. I stared in disgust at my reflection. "How in the world did I develop so much contempt for a man that I don't even know? Is it because he has no money, no car, no job? Is that why I rejected his plea for help?"

She walked up behind me. "Nina, I ain't gonna lie to you, that's exactly why. He ain't got shit to offer you."

I shook my head and closed my eyes as the memory became so clear. "But he's still human." I nodded as tears spilled out of my eyes. "You know just the other day, I saw a homeless man begging for change. I walked right by him in my brand new pair of Gucci boots.

"That's life."

"That's not life, that's bullshit." My stomach began to feel heavy as a stab of guilt burned in my chest.

"You're really tripping!" she shouted when I grabbed my chest and doubled over in pain.

I screamed and rocked back and forth. "A woman asked me to buy her some food to feed her kids. I told her I didn't have time to go back into the store." I closed my eyes. "I didn't have time Alex."

"Why didn't you just give her some change Nina?"

"All I had in my wallet were hundreds."

I heard Alex suck her teeth as if she didn't care. "She probably didn't have any kids and wanted the money for drugs." She said.

My eyes widened. "Oh, she had kids, they waved at me, but I rushed passed them. I was on my way to meet with the phone company again that day. This is not life, Alex, we have to change the way we treat people."

"Are you cracking up? Are you on the edge of a nervous breakdown? The Judge will make your life a living hell. You can't help these people--just leave them alone. Give money to the shelters and move on." She shouted. "But leave them alone."

"But, this guy saved my life. I have to do something for him."

"No, Nina, don't bring those kinds of people into our lives." She shook her head. "Leave them alone."

"Alex, the man needs help. I have to repay him for his kindness."

Alex folded her hands across her chest. "You don't mean that literally, do you?"

I stared back at the reflection that stared at me. "I don't know who I am." I whispered.

"Nina, please don't lose sleep over this homeless man," she pointed toward the front door, "or none of those asses out there for that matter."

Another stab of pain hit me in my chest almost taking

my breath away. "I told the man I wasn't responsible for him, yet he became responsible for me. I didn't even ask him his name and he saved my life." I slid to the floor sobbing into my shaking hands.

The thought of what could have happened if the Rastafarian had felt that he wasn't obligated to me made me shiver. I felt the whiskey turning over in my stomach as I cried uncontrollably from the pain that was bouncing off my internal organs.

She slid to the floor next to me. "Nina, there's nothing you can do now."

"Yes, there is!" I said as Alex tried to hug me.

"What?" She screamed.

"I can find him and apologize to him, offer to put him up for a few nights in a motel or let him live in one of my rental houses, give him money, buy him a coat. There must be something I can do."

"You can't do anything, Nina."

I brushed my tears away. "And why not?"

"Whatever you do, The Judge will undo, right before he has a heart attack, and you know what that means to Mother."

I stood and stared into the darkness once again.

Alex stood next to me and wrapped me in a cocoon of love; I allowed it, because I needed it. "Why do you always stand in this same spot every time we come to the cabin. You've been claiming this spot ever since we were kids."

I leaned my head back and rested on her shoulders. "I can see the forest from here."

Alex looked over my shoulders. "How can you see the forest for all those damm trees?"

"From where I stand, all I can see is the forest." I smirked and continued to gaze out the window. "I'm no different than The Judge. How can I hate him, when I'm just like him?"

"You're better than The Judge, and he knows that. That's

why he gives you so much shit. But please Nina, don't go near that homeless man. The Judge will make your life a living hell."

I threw up my hands. "He's homeless, Alex, not a danger to society, and surely not a danger to me."

"Please stay away." She said, almost trembling in her three inch heels.

"The Judge has instilled the fear of homeless people in us for far too long. Look at you, you're literally shaking."

Alex held up three fingers and with tears in her eyes, "He attacked you three times. Have you forgotten a homeless man killed Rachel's mother."

I closed my eyes for a moment and took a deep breath. "He didn't attack me," I whispered.

"Excuse me."

I chewed on my lower lip, looking down at my shoes. "I thought that's what he was going to do. Attack me."

She placed both hands on her hips. "So, he never touched you?"

I shook my head. "Not even once."

"But, he screamed at you."

I shrugged my shoulders. "He did appear to be a little intoxicated so maybe he was only talking loud, and I mistook it as screaming."

"What?"

"He was drunk and talking loud, begging me to let him sleep on my stoop. He said he could protect me, and he did."

"Protect you from what? The alcohol bandit."

I raised my eyebrows and looked into her cold eyes. "From something like tonight."

She shook her head. "Well, isn't that a nice little convenient coincidence. Someone comes to attack you and the homeless man is there waiting in the night. It sounds like a setup to me, my dear."

"It wasn't a setup. He saved my life, and I'm going to find him and apologize."

"For what?" She screamed, almost hysterically.

"For being so rude-for being an ass like The Judge." I pointed in her face. "If he doesn't want anything I have to offer, I'll allow him to sleep at the office."

"Oh, hell no." she said, kicking over furniture. "Have you lost your fucking mind? What in the world would The Judge say? Not to mention our friends? What would they say if they knew you were offering your doorway? Ain't there shelters for people like him?"

"Aren't there shelters for people like him?"

She stopped her tantrum and turned to face me. "Hell, I don't know— that's what I'm asking you?"

"No, Alex, you're supposed to say, Aren't there shelters for people like him."

"What?" She frowned. "I can't believe we're in the middle of a crisis and you're giving me a fucking grammar lesson."

"Never mind. Yes, there's shelters for the homeless."

Alex shook her head, brought me in her arms, and hugged me. "Nina, I think you've been traumatized and you need to talk to someone other than me. You're losing your mind."

I pushed out of her arms. "He saved my life, and I'm grateful, and I will repay him."

"Give him some money, that should be payment enough. He's homeless, he's a drunk. Better yet give him a few bottles of that expensive wine you had imported from France, but not your office doorway."

"He's homeless Alex and that translates into he needs a place to sleep. Besides he's going to do it anyway, now it's going be with my permission."

She put her hands on her hips. "Your permission?"

"Yes, my permission." I repeated as I walked toward the master bedroom. "And The Judge will know nothing about this." I shouted and slammed the door in her face

Chapter Thirteen

ᘓ

Nina

Early Monday morning, I tried to follow Alex down the winding mountainside as she drove like an evil spirit from the pit of hell, but I had to give her the space she was longing for. I gently coasted down the hill as if I had sense. When I exited the 91 freeway and turned left onto Market, I felt sharpness in my chest forcing me to take small gasps of air as I waited for the pain to subside.

I know I can do this; I've worked too hard to let some ass come in and take it from me. I know that fear would destroy everything I've built. I took another deep cleansing breath and rounded the corner toward my office. Another sharp pain hit me, when I spotted a crowd of people standing in front of the building.

It seemed as if I jumped out of the car before it came to a complete stop. When I approached the mob, they parted like the Red Sea. I spotted Alex standing next to a very large wrought iron gate.

"What the hell is this?" I asked staring the gate, as if it would magically open for me.

"I don't know, I didn't do it, but it's a great idea." Alex beamed.

"How in the hell are we going to get in? Who has the keys?" I shouted. "When did this damn thing go up?" There was a quiet hum around the building; no one had an answer.

"Maybe The Judge knows." Richard said, pointing toward the chestnut Jaguar rounding the corner.

Homeless Love

I walked to the edge of the crowd and saw Satan's chariot pulling up in front of the building, stopping right along with my heart. When The Judge opened the car door and stepped out, his slicked, greased hair glistened in the morning sun. He slipped one hand into the pocket of his starched khakis and walked slowly around the front of the Jaguar. I could tell by the expression on his face he was through with me, and I was feeling the same about him.

He handed me a box. "Here are the keys and remote controls for the gate. He smirked, and adjusted his Ray Bans on the bridge of his nose.

Reluctantly I took the box and handed it to Richard, who was standing next to me. "Open it." I commanded without taking my eyes off The Judge.

"I can't believe I still have to protect you," The Judge said smiling as he began to walk away.

I stared at his back, visualizing an ax sticking out the back of his head. "Judge." I called out as calmly as I could. He continued his stride. I ran to catch up to him. "How dare you take it upon yourself to secure my property and lock me out of my building!" I said to his back.

The Judge snatched his shades from his face and turned to face me. The same red eyes that held me in bondage as a child, kidnapped my soul once again. "Nina!" he shouted.

I took a deep breath. "You have to mind your own business and leave us alone."

Before I knew what happened, Satan was in my face. He grabbed me by the arm and brought me into his chest. "Now you listen to me," he snarled like an animal. "You need me."

I don't know what took my mind, but I jerked away from The Judge, which sent the crowd into a complete silence. I had no idea silence could be so damn loud, but I stood my ground. I didn't have a choice. "No, you have a sick wife in that car." I pointed. "She needs you. I'm grown; I can handle whatever is sent my way. Now leave me the hell alone." I turned and walked back toward the building feeling liberated and scared.

"Nina Marie Moore. I will always protect what's mine."

I clutched my hands into a fist and slowly turned around. I wanted to tell Satan to go back to the pit of hell, but the face of an angel, my Mother appeared in the lightly tinted window. Her frail beauty willed my mouth shut.

I knew she was going to hear that demon yell all the way back to San Diego. I shook my head and closed my eyes. "Just go and take care of Mother." I said as I turned and walked back toward the building.

Franklin

As Bones and I sat at our usual place in the bus station coffee shop, I wanted to drown my disappointment in the first bottle of anything I could get my hands on.

"I don't know why you're pissed at her, Frank, She did what she had to do and that was protect herself."

"How hateful can she be?" I shook my head. "That dude was going to slit her throat."

"And you expected what?" Bones asked.

I held Bones' gaze. "I expected her to. . ."

"To what, Frank, shake your hand, give you a medal."

I was quiet. That's exactly what I expected her to do, or at least thank me for saving her life. I lowered my head. "This is a mean ass world Bones."

"No, it's not, you just have to know the rules and who's playing in the game."

Staring blankly I asked. "What game?"

"The game of life, Frank. It's the haves against the have-nots. And you're the have-not, my friend, and you're losing the game. If I were you I'd stay away."

"Why would I want to do that, she's the only beauty that

I see in this world!"

"Rich folks don't pay attention to homeless folks until something happens, then they can give a complete description of us."

"So, what you saying?"

"What I'm saying is you better watch yourself and stay out of that girl's way." Bones shook his head and coughed. "Believe me, she gave the police a very good description of your ass."

I lowered my head as a police officer walked past us. "I had nothing to do with that attack. Hell, I stopped it." I said under my breath.

"That's what you say, but is that what she told the cops, you said she was ungrateful. She could have told them anything in order to keep you off her property."

"She's already taken care of that little problem when she put up that big black gate. I'm too old to climb over a fence."

"See what I mean, man, if she was so grateful, she would have offered you a place to stay, so you could be her watchdog and continue to protect her." Bones laughed.

I closed my eyes for a moment to seal the pain of rejection from my heart.

"Maybe she thinks that's the last time she's ever going to be attacked in her life. You know how many times a person can be attacked in a lifetime."

I listened to what Bones was throwing at me and even though I didn't understand why Nina would be so cruel, I had to face the fact, I was a homeless man and that's how America treats the homeless.

"If I were you I would start looking for another place to call home and never go around her again. If she hasn't already given your description to the cops you better believe me it's on her mind to do so." He shook his finger at me. "And the very next time she gets mugged, your face will become her attacker, and you and I both know you don't want to go back to the clinker."

C.F. Hawthorne

I nodded as I picked at the sticky bun. "You know something Bones, you haven't, up until now, made much sense. But I think you got something, and I'm going to take your advice and find me another place. I hope that iron gate can protect her."

"So where you gonna go, man?"

"I don't know, I found her place, and I can find another one."

"Why don't you come to the shelter with me?"

"Damn, man, I already told you I can't deal with the shelter life. All those guys coughing and hacking in my face. I've been quite healthy sleeping outside under the stars. I don't want to mess around and catch something I can't get rid of. No, thank you."

"Frank."

"I'll see you around, Bones." I stood, shook Bones' hand and grabbed my duffel bag. I tapped the table and started to walk away.

"Frank."

I turned slowly toward Bones and tried to hide the tears that were in my eyes. "I've tried praying." I said softly.

"I know man, I know it's hard when you've lost your faith." He threw me a tiny Bible that had seen better days. "Just read the words, man, just the words."

Chapter Fourteen

Nina

J was sitting in my office late Thursday afternoon keeping one eye on the clock and one ear on what was happening on the other side of the door. I was going to leave with everyone else.

"Nina," Alex called from the intercom.

"Yes, Alex."

"The guys are here from the fence company, one of them wants to talk to you."

"Okay, send him in." I said, as I rehearsed the speech that explained why I didn't need the fence The Judge ordered.

I heard two small, simple knocks on my door. "Come in." I rose to greet the tall, handsome, dark-skinned man with sparkling black eyes who walked in like a king.

"Nina Moore," I said shaking his warm, soft hand.

"Wow, what a grip," he smiled.

"Please have a seat, Mr. . ."

"Jon Banks, but please, call me Jon."

"Okay, Jon, what can I do for you?" I asked taking a seat behind my desk.

"Well, I'm a little concerned that you want to remove the security gate, my work is guaranteed."

"I'm sure that it is, Jon, however I don't want it, I don't need it, and I didn't order it."

"I understand that, Mrs. Moore, but I also know that you've

had a few problems around your property, one as recently as last week. Now if you'd had the security gate…"

I held up my hand. "You're right Jon, however if you can remove the gate as fast as you put it up for my father without my permission, you'll have another happy client on your hands."

Jon nodded with a smile. "I walked right into that one, didn't I?"

"I'm afraid so."

"Well, Mrs. Moore, I'll leave you to your decision, but if you ever need protecting, just call me, here's my card."

"It's Miss Moore, I'm not married, and if you ever need a divorce you know where to find me."

"I won't be needing a divorce because I'm not married," he smiled and closed the door behind him.

Alex ran in shortly after Jon walked out the front door. "He was making a pass at you." She beamed with excitement.

"A what?"

"A pass, I heard everything. The man was telling you to call him."

"Alex, just because you think every man wants you, doesn't mean they want me."

"That man was saying call me if you need me."

I stood and walked over to the window. "Girl, go back to work and leave me alone. That man was worried about his money and not about picking me up." I watched as the men began working to remove the security gate.

Alex looked over my shoulder. "Why are you removing the gate? I think it's a big mistake."

"I will not let The Judge control this business. It's bad enough that he controls us."

"It's your call, Nina, but I still think it's a big mistake."

"Good, let it be my mistake." I walked back to my desk and picked up my keys. "You want to have lunch with me today?"

"Are you buying?" Alex smiled.

I put my hands on my hips. "Yes, but I'll pick the place."

"Okay, but it better be good, you know I don't eat cheap."

I smiled, where I was taking her, it couldn't get any cheaper.

"I have to make a phone call." Alex winked. "I'll be right back."

I strolled back to the picture window. "Okay, fine call me when you're ready, I know how long it takes you to do simple things."

"I won't be long," she added before leaving the office.

I gazed at Mr. Banks as he shouted orders. My eyes traveled his muscular arms, which lead to his broad shoulders and back, which slipped into a V-shape, to his small waistline. My stomach turned into knots and I closed my eyes as I thought about the two of us in a few compromising positions.

It wasn't until the knots turned into growling hunger pains that I grabbed my purse and headed for the front office. "Are you ready?" I said as I bumped into fine ass Walter.

"I sure am, let me grab my purse." She smiled.

"Hey, is this a ladies only thing or can I join you?"

"It's a sister thing, Walter." I answered before Alex had a chance to invite him. "But, you can come by the house for dinner tonight and eat until your heart's content."

"Okay, it's a date, what are we having?"

"Spaghetti." I smiled.

His face brightened at the suggestion. "What should I bring?" He asked.

"Your appetite and you can't spend the night." I added with a giggle. "I need my sleep."

გ

"Where are we going?" Alex asked once we were in the car.

"It's a surprise."

As we drove down Market Street, Alex went on and on about Walter and how wonderful he was. I was becoming more jealous, but I couldn't let it show. So I nodded in agreement.

When I made the first right and parked the car, Alex lost

Homeless Love

her mind.

"We're eating at a park?" She cried.

"Yes, I went to the Chicken Shack last night and bought lunch for today."

"We don't have a blanket." She whined.

I snatched the blanket from the back seat and playfully threw it in her face.

"Nina, you can't be serious!" Alex said shaking her head. "I can't believe we're going to eat cold chicken in a park."

"Yes, I am serious, we haven't done this since we were kids."

"Nina." She cried. "Please."

"Come on, get out and let's find a nice place to eat."

"But I don't wanna eat outside. I wanna eat in a nice restaurant with tables, chairs, and silverware."

"Alex, we have all that stuff except the table, I brought the plates and forks, I even brought glasses. So stop acting like a baby and get your butt out of the car."

I walked over to a spot in the grass and laid down the blanket. I put the picnic basket full of chicken next to my pouting sister who was sulking as she held on tightly to the CD player.

"Why are we eating out here?" She cried and stomped her feet.

I pretended to be preoccupied with the beautiful ducks in the lake. I looked past the old locomotive and smiled at the lovers in the park.

Alex grabbed my shoulders and shook me. "Nina?"

"What?"

"Why are we eating lunch in the park?"

I glanced around me. "Because, it's nice."

She brushed dirt off the blanket and sat in front of me. "It's not nice and I don't like it, and who the hell are you looking for?"

"I'm not looking for anyone." I shook my head and dumped a mound of mashed potatoes on her plate, next to her chicken.

"Yes, you are. Your eyes haven't stopped searching this park ever since we got here. Now, who are you looking for?"

C.F. Hawthorne

"I'm not looking for anyone in particular, I'm just enjoying the serene surroundings, that's all. I feel so at peace. Don't you?" I smiled.

"Hell no, I feel stressed." Alex mumbled under her breath and rolled her eyes. "I hope you're not looking for that damn homeless man."

"No, I'm not." I answered looking right past her.

"Oh, so I guess I'm crazy? Like I don't know homeless people hang out at the park."

"Alex! I told you I'm not looking for anyone."

"Yeah, okay Nina, then put your eyes on your plate."

"Would you please calm down, you're scaring the birds."

Alex waved her chicken leg in the air. "What birds, I don't see any damn birds."

"I was just trying to say you're talking too loud." I whispered.

"We're at a freakin' park for Christ's sake. We don't have to be quiet at a park, Nina!"

"Well, I can see that you're a little upset about our picnic, so let's just go home."

She threw her chicken leg to the ground. "Fine."

I stood and headed back toward the car.

"Will you help me pick up this shit?" She screamed as she gathered the CD player and blanket.

I continued my pace for the car. "Leave it!" I shouted. "I'm sure some homeless person can use it."

Suddenly, I heard plates and forks hit the ground. "What about the Mexican blanket Rachel gave you last summer?"

I stopped by the car door and turned to Alex. "Do I look Mexican?"

"Well, no." She frowned, with her hands on her hips.

"Then what the hell do I need with a Mexican blanket."

She walked around to the passenger side of the car. "You don't have to be Mexican to enjoy a Mexican blanket you know, so calm down and think about that for a moment."

Homeless Love

Franklin

I limped toward Bones and laid my aching head on the cool Formica table, hoping the room would stop spinning, but it didn't. "Lilly, said she just finished baking these." I told Bones, who was waving at her. "I'm glad that she let you back into her life. Twenty years is a long time."

Bones lowered his head. "She was only four years old when I left them." He mumbled shaking his head.

"I'm sorry that you never got the chance to know your son."

"I know man. Lilly said he was a good kid."

I sipped the warm whiskey from the paper cup. I don't mean to judge, but how could you walk out on your wife, while she was pregnant?"

Bones chewed on his lip and which meant he was on the verge of exploding. "I had no choice." He said softly. "I had no choice after my brain burst open. I couldn't hold down a job, and the medical bills were eating my family alive. When she told me she was pregnant I had no choice. I was already taking her through so much as it was." Bones cleared his throat and continued to speak.

"I cashed in everything I had; all stocks, bonds, 401k, and other insurance policies, everything. We refinanced the house and once my disability checks started coming in through direct deposit I left. Laura Ann, my wife would find me to sign the papers in order to keep the disability checks coming in. I provided for my family until the streets claimed my soul. Then I lost contact with them."

"I can't believe all this time you've been in my shit about getting my life together, getting off the streets, quitting drinking, and you have a family waiting for you to come home."

"I had a family Frank, but I never got a second chance to

do it again." He smiled. "But now Lilly is my second chance." She smiled.

"Where's your wife?"

Bones lowered his head. "Dead."

"I'm sorry man, but why you never told me about Lilly, why you never told me about any of this?"

"What good would it have done? You can't give back my youth, my life, my wife, or my kids."

As we sat in silence, I was speechless. He was right, what good would it have done.

"Oh, man, don't look now." Bones said under his breath. "But here comes trouble."

"Who is it, the cops?" I asked without turning around, and my heart melted. I did miss seeing her, and today she looked more beautiful than ever before. I wanted so much to hold her in my arms.

"Frank, man, you staring." Bones whispered.

I couldn't take my eyes from her nice round behind. Nina had my undivided attention and she didn't know it. I was hypnotized by her grace. I wanted to soak in everything she had to offer. I didn't know when I would see her again, and the sight of her felt like new blood coursing through my veins.

My heart melted when she smiled at Lilly. Nina's presence gave me joy and my soul felt great, but suddenly a pain shot up my leg, gripping my heart, stopping the blood from flowing to my head. I felt weak, dizzy-like. "Oh, shit!" I screamed and looked into Bones' face. "Why the hell did you kick me?" I shouted.

"I was trying to get your attention." Bones whispered.

"Well next time say my name. Franklin, shit." I hissed while applying pressure to the bruise on my right leg, which I sustained from one of my many alcoholic stupors. Then a melody so soft and sweet removed the pain right out of my leg, it felt like a mother's kiss.

"Hello, Franklin?" she whispered softly.

Bones and I were so busy arguing; we had neglected to see Nina moving into our space. My jaws tightened when I slowly looked into the most beautiful brown eyes a man could ever see. Eyes, that matched her smooth, brown, silk skin. I inhaled the sweet smell of her perfume, mixed with the warm smell of the sticky buns she was holding.

I've waited for what seemed like a lifetime for Nina to notice me. Now I was speechless!

"Good morning, Bones." She nodded.

My toothless friend returned her smile, cleared his throat and said, "How did you know my name?"

"I didn't until I heard the two of you arguing," she smiled, which took my breath away.

"Pleased to meet you." Bones replied.

"It's a pleasure to meet you, my name is Nina Moore." She turned to face me and extended her hand. "And this man saved my life as I'm sure you are aware of."

I wanted to kiss the tips of her fingers as I gripped her warm hand. I was trying not to show my nervousness, but I'm sure it was obvious by my speechlessness.

"Yeah, he mentioned something about that, but Frank's a modest man, he didn't go into details." Bones replied. "Would you like to join us?" he asked as he slid over.

"No, thank you, I just stopped by to tell Mr. Franklin thank you." She gently squeezed my hand, but I was too weak to squeeze back. "Thank you for saving my life."

I cleared my throat. "You're welcome."

"What you did for me a few days ago, I really do appreciate it. I know it didn't seem like it at the time, but I do."

"So, that's how you show your appreciation by putting that security gate up?" Bones cut in.

She lowered her head and her hand slipped from mine. "It wasn't me, it was my overprotective father."

"Her father, Frank." He smirked.

"It was." she replied.

"Your father doesn't have to worry, I won't be sleeping on your property anymore," I answered, trying to calm the shakiness in my voice. I swallowed hard and looked away, then back into her beautiful cocoa colored face.

She stiffened as though I had struck her. "That's why I was looking for you." She said calmly as she licked her crimson colored lips.

My heart jolted and my pulse pounded.

"I would like to repay the favor, as long as. . . ."

Bones jumped in with his sarcastic remarks. "As long as you don't catch him hanging around your property, right?"

Nina smoothed down her hair, and a drumroll began to form in the pit of my stomach.

"No, I wasn't going to say that. I was going to say, as long as you forgive my rudeness."

"Thanks, Miss Moore, but I've found a place to live."

She nodded. "The invitation is open whenever you'd like to take advantage of it. The motel is on Seventh Street across from Sam's Food, you'll have a room waiting for you, ask for Michael."

"Thanks for the offer, but like I said, I have a place." I answered as I forced my eyes away from her mesmerizing gaze.

We sat in silence, for what seemed like an eternity before she took a deep breath, which drew me out of my trance.

"Well, I have to get back to the office," she said and extended her hand again. "It was a pleasure meeting you." She smiled, and strolled away.

"I bet she's feeling like she just won the Good Samaritan award." Bones grunted.

Nina

Later that evening after Walter and Alex finished eating dinner, they disappeared upstairs, leaving me alone once again. I picked up the phone, pushed speed dial and grabbed my glass of wine as I headed for the back patio.

"Hello."

"Richard, it's me, Nina."

"Whatcha doing, girl?" He laughed.

"Nothing, I met him today."

"Who?"

"Franklin, the Rastafarian."

I could hear the volume go down on Richard's television. "Oooh, do tell, sugar." He sang, he was truly one nosy man.

I took a deep breath. "There's nothing to tell, although it felt great to put a name with his face. He's a simple man, very clean for a homeless man. Much cleaner than I'd expected him to be."

"Some homeless people try to take care of themselves, not all are filthy creatures, you know."

"I know it now, but he should take some of that hair off his face, and oh, my goodness those dreads are a mess."

"Did you ask him to marry you?"

"What! Marry me?"

"Yes."

"Why would I do that?"

"I was just curious with the way you're going on about his appearance. I thought he was going to be your husband or something."

"Richard."

"I was only stating the facts."

"There are no facts. I was only describing him to you, that's all."

"I'm sorry, darling, go on."

"Anyway, he has very clean teeth for a homeless man."

"You were all in his mouth, girl?"

"He was talking, Richard."

"Oh, so you did speak to him?"

"Yes, briefly."

"Huh."

"I wonder what led him to be homeless, what happened to his family?"

"I thought you spoke with him? Why didn't you ask him those questions?"

"We had a quick conversation and I left."

"Why did you leave in such a hurry, did he scare you?"

"No." I said defensively. "I don't know why I left so quickly, I just had to leave." I remembered my heart was beating so rapidly when I stared into his eyes, I felt like I needed to head for safety.

"I know why," he laughed. "The Judge would die if he saw you or any of his kids having a conversation with a homeless person, that's why you left in such a hurry."

I sipped more wine as Richard's words rang true in my head. "You know he has a friend named Bones," I said once he stopped laughing. "And his mouth is full of broken teeth. Now, that's what I thought a homeless person's mouth would look like, but Franklin has nice teeth."

"There you go trying to put all homeless people in the same category. You're better than that. I know it. You look to the inner self not the outer appearance, you told me so yourself. So don't judge homeless people by their appearance."

I was quiet as I listened to what Richard was saying, but it didn't take away 35 years of The Judge's hatred for homeless people, which, he planted in our heads.

"Nina, are you there?"

I cleared my throat. "Yes, I'm here."

"Good because Rugby is on, and I want to watch the game. So this is where I say good night."

"Good night, Richard."

I hung up the phone and grabbed another chilled bottle of wine from my collection. I slid back on the couch, and picked up the remote control. An old Get Smart re-run was on. I didn't remember seeing any of it. Moments later, I felt a warm hand stroking my face.

"Alex." It said softly. "Its me." She whispered as she reset the alarm. "Why do you always sleep downstairs when Walter's over?" She asked as I struggled to sit up on the couch.

I stared off into space. "I don't know." I lied. What was I supposed to say... I become tense listening to the two of you screw, while my pillow is wedged between my legs?

"We're not disturbing you, are we?"

I shook my head and looked out the window.

"Why haven't you called Jon?" She asked.

"Who?"

"Jon, the fence guy." She said, sitting down next to me.

I wiped the sleep from my eyes. "Are you crazy, I'm not going to call him."

"Why not?"

"Because, I'm not."

"Don't you get horny?"

I stood and stumbled over to the refrigerator and took out my third bottle of wine. "Even if I did, I wouldn't call a total stranger to come over and screw me, then leave."

"Maybe you should."

I slammed the refrigerator door and walked back toward her. "I need a little more for myself than a mercy screw, Alexandra."

"Nina, I don't think that your situation qualifies as a mercy screw. It's more like a Lord-let-me-help-this-girl- out screw."

"Whatever!" I smiled as I watched her rolling on the floor laughing. I wanted to kick her in the face. "I don't like that joke." I said.

She sat up on her knees and grabbed her stomach. "How

long has it been?" She asked out of breath.

I stared at her for a few minutes before laughing my damn self. "It's been a couple of years."

"A couple, a couple is two." Alex held up her fingers. "I know it's been longer than two years."

"Oh, so now you're keeping up with how often I get laid."

"Somebody has to, you seem to have forgotten that you need that sort of shit."

"What sort of shit?"

"Sex."

"Oh, please, Alex. I'm okay. You need that sort of shit." I answered, trying to avoid the thought of how badly I needed it. Hell, the mail carrier was starting to look good and he has to be about 70!

"If you're okay, why did you pause right after you said you don't need that sort of shit?" Alex smiled.

"I was thinking."

"Yeah, about how it use to feel, before you got particular."

"Alex, I can't help it. I was about to marry a man who was only after my money and not my heart. But thank goodness you saw through that." I winked.

"I told you, I got your back. I can spot a two-bit hustler a mile away."

"I'm glad that you can, but I'd hoped you would have spotted him before he left me at the altar."

"Well, you know I didn't have anything to do with that. It was The Judge who got hold of his ass and gave him some time in the jail."

"And, that's where my heart has been ever since. Locked up!" I started to cry as the memory of that day drifted back in my mind. Jilted at the alter.

"Oh, Nina, don't cry. You gonna find the right man, I promise." She hugged me. "Please don't cry."

"I can't help it, it hurts when your heart gets broken so

many times. I can't trust anyone. Just once I pray that God would send me someone who doesn't want anything from me, but love."

Alex took my hand. "I understand about a broken heart, mine has been broken many times too, and I've searched for love in all the wrong places."

"You've had really great guys in your life, Alex."

"I know, but I've made bad choices, especially when it comes to brothers with nicknames."

"What?" I frowned and wiped my eyes.

"The Judge said, if a man introduces himself to you with a nickname, then he doesn't have a future."

I shook my head. "Why do you listen to that crazy man?"

"Listen." She rubbed my shoulders. "It really makes sense. A well-respected man wants the world to know who he is. And a De-vo, Pookie, and Lil John, dem don't have a future."

"You need to stop listening to that crazy Judge, you're starting to sound just like him." I smiled through my tears.

Alex rolled her eyes. "Anyway, you have a very successful business and you're getting ready to open the second one in a few months and the third one after that. Can't you see, you've moved on in your professional life, but your personal life is still at the altar? Let it go, big sis, and have some fun." She snapped her fingers.

"Alex, I can't love them and leave them like you, I need more than a one night stand."

"Walter is not a one night stand," she answered.

I grabbed the tissue that was on the side table. "That's only because you're not tired of him."

"No, that's not it at all, he makes me feel good when I'm with him. He makes me laugh."

"That other guy made you laugh all the time."

"Who, Rodney?"

"Yes." I blew my nose.

"He was a stand-up comedian, he made everybody laugh; that was his job."

"Oh, yeah, that's right. He did Kelly's party, right?"

"Speaking of party, you didn't hear this from me, but rumor has it that you've been nominated to receive an award from the Women in Business."

"Why did The W.I.B nominate me for one of those prestigious awards?"

"You're about to open two businesses in twelve months, if that's not something to be proud of, then I don't know what is. You're so ungrateful."

"I'm not ungrateful, however I have so much to do to get ready for the opening of the San Diego office, and not to mention, I have to find out what the hell is going on with the Riverside office. I don't want to add something new to my plate."

"You don't have to do anything, Nina, I'll take care of everything. All you have to do is invite Jon, so he can relieve you of your stress."

"I think that's a damn shame, that you're turning this event into a manhunt."

Alex walked up to me and took the glass out of my hand. "It's not simply to meet a man, it's so you can get laid, big sis." She sipped my wine while trying to suppress a smile.

"I don't need to get laid that badly," I said, retrieving my glass.

She raised a brow. "You don't think you do, but once he gets started, you won't want him to stop," she said while gyrating her hips like a stripper.

"I still think having a party to meet a man is stupid."

"What's your bright idea?"

"I don't have one."

"Well, until you get one, my idea stands. So that settles that, we're having a party the night after the Orange County office opens in December. Right here." She said patting the sofa.

"Why here?"

"So I can get you drunk and then you'll allow Jon to help you out. So good night, I'm tired and I need my beauty sleep."

Homeless Love

g

I cannot believe I woke up the next morning craving sticky buns from the bus station. I tried to wake Alex, but she wouldn't budge. I threw on a pair of jeans, USC sweatshirt and a baseball cap.

The sun had barely settled in the sky when I backed the jeep out of the garage and headed for downtown Riverside. I waved at one of my neighbors whom I didn't know.

When I made it to the main street, I drove slowly as I people-watched. Mothers and daughters were on their way to do the family's grocery shopping; fathers and sons taking care of the lawn. I smiled inwardly at a sight so many people took for granted. I pulled into the bus station parking lot, jumped out of the Jeep and headed for the coffee shop.

"Good morning, Ms. Moore."

I turned around. "Excuse me."

"I'm Bones, Franklin's friend?!"

"Oh, hi, how are you today?" I smiled and shook his rough hand.

"I'm fine," he smiled.

"Well, that's good, I'm just on my way to get a few sticky buns, would you like one?"

"No, thank you. I have one every morning. Lilly's my daughter you know."

I frowned then smiled. "That's great." I said and tried to walk away as that uncomfortable feeling began to creep over me.

"You have a great day," he yelled.

I stopped and turned back to him. "You have a wonderful day as well." I waved and disappeared inside.

I couldn't believe how crowded this place was so early in the morning. The line for the bakery shop was longer than I expected. I waited patiently for my turn as I glanced around the bus station. Then I saw Franklin sitting alone at a table looking depressed. He stood and came over to me.

"You couldn't resist the craving for a sticky bun, now could you?"

"You got me." I smiled.

"I know what you mean. I love those things."

"I can see why." I replied, feeling uneasy that I didn't have more of a conversation. "They are delicious!"

"Yes, they are." He grinned and hoisted the duffel bag higher on his shoulders.

"That thing looks heavy?"

"Nagh, it's not that bad. Besides I'm use to it, keeps me in shape." He said, taking a body builder stance.

"I see." I nodded.

We stood a few minutes in silence, until he spoke.

"Well, it's almost your turn, so I'll let you handle your business. I'm going to go and take care of mine."

"Okay, have a wonderful day." I waved as he walked away.

g

When I returned home, Alex was sitting on the sofa eating cereal and milk, laughing and talking on the phone.

"Hey, where you been?" She asked, stuffing her mouth with food.

"I went to the market, so I need your help to unload the bags, and I also got us sticky buns." I said waving them in her face.

"From the bus station?" She smiled and jumped to her feet after placing the bowl of milk on the table.

"Yep." I nodded.

"Give'em to me," she laughed with outstretched hands.

"Not until you get the food out of the jeep." I said as I left to retrieve more bags.

"Let me holla at you later." I heard her say as she

Homeless Love

approached the jeep.

"Who was that?" I asked as I took two grocery bags from the backseat.

"A friend," she winked, only grabbing one bag.

"Walter."

"No. Someone I met two weeks ago."

"But, Walter just left here last night."

"And what does that have to do with the price of a weave?"

I raised my eyebrows and shook my head. "Now do you see why I insist that you use a condom, you're sick!"

"I'm not sick, just lucky." She winked as she put the tea bags away.

"But I thought you liked Walter?"

"I do, but I like this guy as well."

"Does Walter know?"

"Why should he? I'm not married to him, I'm a free agent, I can do anybody I want." She yelled and did a little dance.

"Besides, he pissed me off."

"Well it's your life, do what you want."

"And I will, I'm not about to settle down and do a damn thing for this bloodline."

"You will one day."

Chapter Fifteen

❦

Nina

Wednesday night at 8:00, I found myself cuddled in bed, on the phone crying to my mother how sick I was of this week.

"Nina, baby," she said. "Maybe things aren't as bad as you think."

"Not as bad as I think! Trouble shot through the office like a raving lunatic."

"Oh, baby, I'm so sorry," she moaned.

"Now get this one, I received a stupid letter from the Bar Association. They're threatening to dis-bar me, and to top it off, Orange County is giving me grief about building permits. I'm losing my freakin' mind."

"You don't practice law anymore, and your father knows a few people in Orange County, maybe he can put in a good word, you know he's good at calling in favors."

"Mother, no. I can handle this." Don't say anything to him."

"Okay, okay! You sound stressed."

"You think!" I huffed.

"Nina."

"I'm sorry, Mother, but don't start on me about relaxing or having fun. Alex was already on my case about that." I cried into the phone.

"Maybe she's right, maybe you need to go out and have some fun, get a different life."

"I can't go out and have fun with all this crap swirling

around me."

She was silent for a few minutes, then she spoke. "You should take off for the weekend, then maybe you'll be able to think better."

I sighed, "You just don't understand. The Judge has always taken care of everything for you. It's just me in this three ring circus I call life."

"Nina, whatever problems you have now, they're going to be there later, so go out and have a little fun. Stress will make you sick."

I rolled my eyes. "Mother!"

"Promise me that you'll go out and have a little fun. You don't want to end up like me, with a life full of regrets."

"I'm not going to have any regrets, but I have a lot of things to do. Someone is trying to sabotage my business. I've gone over the personnel files and I can't find one thing out of the ordinary."

"Nina, you're not telling me something that I don't already know."

"How do you know?"

"Baby, just because I'm in San Diego doesn't mean I don't know what's going on with my family. I'm not stupid, I just look this way."

I chuckled at my mother's comeback line. "Alex told you, didn't she?"

"No, but speaking of Alex why didn't you go to Los Angeles with her tonight."

I glanced at the indigo clock that sat on my nightstand. I couldn't believe it was only 7:30. "I have so much to do."

"On nights like this you're usually at the office until one or two o'clock in the morning."

"I know, but I was starting to go crazy in that place."

"Good, I'm glad. Now put something on and go downtown. If I remembered right, the city blocks off the streets for its Wednesday night events. Go on. Child, you just might find a man who'll ease some of that tension."

"Mother." I grinned.

"Nina, I'm old, not dead, if a woman don't get a fix, she can get sick."

"Okay, now you're going country on me." I smiled. "What kind of symptoms would she have?"

"Headaches, fatigue, depression. Some of your symptoms, so get up and go check it out."

"I don't want to go, I have too much work to do."

"If you stay stressed, you'll end up in the hospital, then he'll run your business. So please go out and have some fun for the both of us. You can call and tell me all about it in the morning,'" She said in a soothing compassionate tone.

"Yes, Mother."

&

After I hung up the phone and surfed from one TV station to another, Downtown Wednesday Night started to sound appealing, and the thought of The Judge handling my business was the straw that broke the camel's back. I pulled out a pair of maroon and white jogging pants and matching shirt.

Before I had a chance to change my mind, I was behind the wheel of my fire red jeep, scanning the radio stations for something other than jazz. As I approached Market Street, I could tell the streets were still alive with dancing and music, as I parked the jeep in one of the antique shop's parking lots.

I grabbed my blanket and began walking toward the crowd. I could smell the hot kettle corn and roasted candied almonds mixed with Polish sausage and sauerkraut. Suddenly the engaging melody hit me. My breathing slowed, as tranquil music filled the air. I began to float in the direction of the echoing composition. When I reached the melody I saw a perfect spot just on the outer limits of the crowd, where the familiar tempo was escaping. As I spread the blanket on the ground, my body began to warm. I sat with my legs crossed at the ankles, leaning back on my elbows, allowing my head to hang between my shoulder blades. The musician took total control of my senses. My mind was completely his. This was the closest I was going to come to an orgasm tonight, so I allowed my soul to roam free as he became a life preserver in my stormy sea. I closed my eyes and enjoyed his lovemaking.

Franklin

Playing on Wednesday night in downtown Riverside was a gold mine, especially after a drinking binge. I needed more money to sustain my standard of drinking, which was out of control according to Bones. I didn't have a problem with it. Even though I claimed the streets as my way of life, Bones insisted that the streets were claiming me. I don't think he understood. When a man has nothing to live for, he dies a little each day.

I shook my head as the memory of my pathetic life floated before me. I made the sax sing my song of pain and sorrow, loneliness and despair. My heart began to ache and I squeezed my lids tighter to keep the pain from slipping from my eyes. Grown men ain't supposed to cry, but a lonely man will surely die, the sax whispered. I wanted to stop playing, but I needed the money to drown the soreness I felt deep in my soul.

When I was able to regain control of my emotions, I forced my eyes open to gauge the faces of the crowd. I enjoyed making love to them with my music. Something I'd perfected over the years.

I scattered the soft harmonious notes over them like flowers, and it lingered in the air resembling a bedspread, then I slipped in a high note that tied the spread around them and took their hearts to heaven. I held them there for a few wonderful moments, before gradually letting their hearts and memories descend back to this bitter earth. A massive sigh of tension floated back to heaven. Who needed to make love to one when I could make love to them all? I smiled.

The crowd cheered and pleaded for more, dumping $20 bills into my hat. "Encore! Encore!" They screamed.

I began to feed their hunger with a slow, soft, sensuous, vacillating overture, which made the crowd fall into a lovers' induced trance. I lured, then seduced them without their approval, planting the seeds of love and forgiveness in their hearts. I was caught up in the passion of my music when the vision of Nina swayed in my mind.

Nina

"Have mercy," my soul cried when the softness of the melody suspended me over my troubles. His music held me up for so long my spirit deteriorated when he brought me down to earth. His music spoke to me, willing me to give in. To stop worrying about what people might say or think of me, what The Judge demanded from me.

I longed to be free, free from the responsibility that bound me to this earth. I wanted immunity like the musician's songs. Salivating for more of its beauty, I slowly opened my eyes and noticed the size of the crowd had swelled sevenfold, people were standing on my blanket!

I breathed a sigh of relief and eased my limber body up from the ground, when suddenly I heard that song—the one that spoke my name; the one that made my body quiver, the one that made me warm deep in my soul, the one that was going to emancipate me from my lonely life.

The melody weakened me, willed me to stay just a little while longer, and I did. I slid back into position and crossed my legs tighter at the ankles, trying to control the shivers that were brewing deep in my soul. I was going to give in to whatever he had to offer, as the soft, sensual sound forced my head back and my eyes closed.

My heart thumped slow rhythmic beats, I parted my lips a little wider in order to breathe a little easier. My chest rose with each breath forced from my body. It was unbelievable! Unbelievable how my body began to feel so alive, my nipples peeked through my shirt, I couldn't move to close my jacket. Fearing I would explode right in front of everyone. The sensation was incredible, and I didn't want him to stop playing that song.

Franklin

In my mind, I made love to Nina with my music, I held her a little closer and rocked her a little softer. It was the only way my past would allow me to enjoy her, to savor her on my lips or feel the sweetness of her warm embrace. Every inch of my saxophone represented my Nina. From the delightful sweet taste of the bamboo pressed against my tongue, to the smooth surface of the keys when I caressed them so passionately.

The long curves of the saxophone opened up to free the sweetest music, when I stroked her just right. Oh, yes, this was indeed my Nina.

My lips began to ache and my fingers burned until they became numb, but I continued to play. I played until my heart ached for Nina to love me, so that I could love her back. If only she knew that loneliness was a pitiful, painful thing, when there's no one in your life to love. If only she knew, she could free me from my darkness, the darkness that binds me to my sorrows. I blew a little harder and a little louder making the crowd roar at the howl of my harmony, but they couldn't hear the sound of my pain. I was a lonely child in this motherless land.

My music screamed, If only I could hold Nina tonight and

kiss her gently on the lips, if only I could hear her say, 'It's going to be all right,' I would truly be free.

The pain of loneliness crept up my arms and captured my heart. My eyes closed a little tighter. Then I saw Nina reaching out for me, but when our fingers met she became the image of my dying daughter, her life slipping away from my hand once again.

The memory forced my eyes open and the sweet melody became a death march. I couldn't go on. I threw everything into my duffel bag and quickly fled the scene, leaving the crowd like a lost love.

Nina

I pressed my thighs tighter together, preparing to ride this steaming sensation to the end. When suddenly my wonderful world ceased to exist. I was drowning as the silence snatched me from the best rhythmic, orgasmic feeling I had ever experienced. I scampered to my feet and pushed my way to the front of the crowd, but found nothing but an empty space.

"This guy is fantastic!" I heard someone say as my heart began to ache.

"He should be making CDs," another replied, and I felt sick.

I snatched up my blanket and stormed away. By the time I made it to my Jeep, I was really pissed off. I threw the blanket into the backseat and screamed, kicked the tires and slid inside. As I sat in solitude, I began to hear music coming from across the street.

Like a junkie searching for the next high, I peered over the steering wheel and read the makeshift sign, "The Bar!" I drove past the hole in the wall and noticed what appeared to be Franklin slipping inside.

I made a U-turn in the middle of the street and parked in front of the dive. I stared at the tattered door and neon sign, which blinked "u weiser" because the "b" and "d" were gone.

I contemplated going inside to have a drink, just one drink! There's no way anyone in that place would know me, and The Judge would never find out. I cautiously glanced over my shoulder, and then parked in the lot next to the tavern.

I slowly unbuckled my seat belt and applied a fresh coat of lipstick. I took a deep breath and slid out of the jeep.

When I opened the tavern door, the darkness startled me at first, but my eyes adjusted and I found the bar. Once I cleaned off the bar seat and sat down, I gazed at a group of grungy men drinking beer and playing pool. A few ladies—if you could call them that—were leaning on the jukebox, where the music was escaping.

Peanut shells were scattered on the floor. My arm stuck to the bar when I tried to re-adjust my ass on the tiny stool. I was about to leave, when a hoarse voice shouted, "Now put your hands together for Ms. Eddiemae." I stopped and glared at the makeshift stage.

The small crowd went crazy, whistling and clapping as if Patty La Belle was coming onstage.

I blinked twice as a petite, feeble lady, with intense red lips, which glowed against her bronze skin, strolled onto the stage. Her grace told me she was an old pro at this game. Her big hoop earrings weighed down her earlobes and her steel gray hair was pulled back so taut, it gave her an instant face-lift. I had to smile as the two-man band started playing, and Eddiemae started swaying her tiny feeble hips and snapping her fingers, which made the glitter in the red nail polish sparkle.

I started to leave again, but when Ms. Eddiemae released that down-home Mississippi voice, laced with a hint of smooth Southern blues. I stayed.

"Whacha drinking?" A redheaded, white woman asked as she smacked on a clump of gum. Her large sun-dried breasts almost plunged out of the tight red and white-stripped blouse she had squeezed into.

"Nothing, thanks," I replied and tried not to stare at the woman's leathery breasts.

"Listen," she said clamping down twice on the gum, making tiny popping sounds, "that guy at the end of the bar," she pointed, "paid for a drink and I ain't giving the money back, so whacha wanna drink?" She smacked.

I peered into the darkness. "What guy?"
The large busted women pointed toward the darkness again. "You can have water for all I care." The lady smacked, turning up her pointy nose at me.

"Coke in a can, I'll open it."

"We ain't got no Coke in a can in a bar." The woman frowned.

"Beer in a bottle."

The busty lady put her hands on her hips. "Don't serve no beer in a bottle in this bar." She shook her head and readjusted her breast.

"What the hell you got in this place that I can open myself?" I shouted, as she insisted on interrupting my zone with Ms. Eddiemae.

"The door." The lady pointed.

"Can I get a Coke in a paper cup?"

"Nope." She smacked again.

"I tell you what, you surprise me and I'll give you a tip." I smiled, then quickly frowned when the woman turned away.

Chapter Sixteen

Nina

When I turned my attention back to Ms. Eddiemae I came face to face with Franklin.

"What are you doing here, slumming?" He smiled.

I looked past him. "No, I come to this bar all the time."

"No, you don't."

"And why not?"

"I would have seen you here before tonight," he answered with such a gentle tone. I had to shake my head. "Mind if I have a seat?"

I waved at the stool next to me.

He bit his bottom lip to stifle a grin as he took a seat. "So, what brings you to this part of town?"

"I came to enjoy the nightlife."

"What night life?" He chuckled.

"Wednesday night street scene, I love it down here!"

His expression grew still. "Oh, yeah, that's right, I'm on the streets every night, sometimes I forget there's a nightlife, other than my own." As an awkward moment of silence passed between us, I watched him from the corner of my eye, brushing off lint that wasn't there. I turned my attention back to Ms. Eddiemae, but my eyes continually kept track of his movements. I wondered how he became homeless; it's obvious that he was somewhat intelligent. I thought as I cleared my throat. "A few weeks ago when you saved my life…"

"I didn't save your life, I just stopped you from getting hurt."

"No, Franklin, the officer said, that fool is the lunatic with AIDS whose been raping and infecting everybody he could get his hands on." I took a deep breath and tried to relax. "He has some sort of vendetta against the world. He'd been stalking me for a while."

"Wow!" He shook his head, then sipped his drink.

"That's something, isn't it?"

"Yes, it is." Franklin mumbled softly.

"So that's why I say you saved my life, if you were not there," I looked away, as the pain stabbed at my heart, "I would have been sentenced to death."

"Well, don't worry about it, I just did what I thought was right." He winked.

"If you would accept my apology, I would be ever so grateful."

Franklin looked away and slowly sipped the brown liquid that lingered in the glass. He hesitated, then his jaw tightened. "Apology accepted." He said stroking his long stringy beard. "I told you that already."

I stared at him. "Thank you, Franklin. Again." I smiled.

He repositioned himself on the barstool. "Nice smile," he said as he glanced at Ms. Eddiemae.

"Thank you." I blushed and quickly regained my composure. "Now, do you mind explaining that 'officer down' stunt you pulled at the office on that dreadful night?"

"What?" he smiled again.

"Officer Perez said you knew just what to say in order to get them there in a hurry."

He passed a hand over his salt and pepper beard and stared down into his glass. "Well, I'm not a cop if that's what you're thinking."

"I'm not thinking anything, but you did know what to say."

"When you're homeless, you have a lot of time on your hands, so I read up on the California Penal Code."

"So, you want to be a cop?" I asked raising my brows.

I watched as he gazed down at the small amount of fluid that was left in his glass. He closed his eyes tightly and threw back the rest of the whiskey, and then he ordered another one.

"No, I don't want to be a cop; I'm a homeless man, that's what I am."

A warning voice whispered in my head, but I continued to ask questions. "Are you planning on being homeless all your life?"

"Are you planning on running your business for the rest of your life?"

"Well, yes, but that's different."

Franklin sat his glass on the bar. "How is it different?"

"I don't know." I shrugged.

He rubbed his bearded face again. "Listen, I have to make a quick run; stay right here until I get back. Alright?"

I shook my head. "Okay."

"I'll be right back, don't go anywhere."

I watched him as he whispered into the large breasted woman's ear. Then my attention was drawn back to Ms. Eddiemae, before I could get into her melody, Franklin reappeared with an even wider smile.

"Okay, Ms. Nina," he clapped his hands, rubbing them together as if he were trying to warm them.

"Would you like to grab a table?"

Instantly, I agreed.

"How about another drink?"

I glanced back at the bartender "I'm still waiting on my first one."

He turned toward the bar. "Cora, can you please bring the lady her drink?" He shouted over Ms. Eddiemae's voice, as he led me toward a table.

"So tell me more about you, Franklin."

"Nina, I'm sorry, but there's something you have to understand about homeless people, we don't trust anyone. Everyone is out to get us and we're not inclined to tell our life's history. Now, once I get to know you and trust you, then it's another story all together."

I nodded. "I understand, but I don't want to harm you." I pointed to my chest.

"Well, I don't know that, now do I?"

"No, I guess you don't." I replied softly as I sat in the seat he pulled out for me.

"But, I tell you what, you can ask me one question every time you see me," he said with a warm smile.

I made a quick involuntary appraisal of his features. The long graying beard and out of control dreadlocks made him appear to be about fifty or older. To old to be on the streets. I held up two fingers. "What if I see you twice a day?" I asked playfully.

"Then, I guess you get two questions."

"What if I see you three times a day?"

"Then, I'm not doing a very good job at keeping out of sight, and I would need to work on my disappearing act, now wouldn't I?"

"Why do you hide?"

"Is that your question for the night?"

I thought long and hard. Why would a homeless man's life be of interest to me? But curiosity got the best of me. Franklin was the first homeless person that I'd had a conversation with.

"I nodded. "Yes, that's my question."

"Very well." He said, wetting his lips with his drink. "If I don't stay out of sight I'm harassed, made to feel ashamed. Society thinks I'm invisible. So I stay invisible."

"I don't understand?" I frowned.

He took a deep breath. "Before our lives were thrown together you would not have given me the time of day."

"Franklin, I..."

"No, Nina, I've seen you in the park, and I've slept on your doorstep, for months."

I looked into Franklin's eyes. "What do you want me to

say? I was a different person back then."

"What can you say? You're part of the society that doesn't see homeless people. We come from two different worlds, suspended in the same universe. Your world allows freedom to live as one sees fit, my world demands that I go undercover and only come out when the need arises."

I shrugged. "I'm so sorry."

"Are you apologizing for society?"

"Well, no, but I have to apologize for my father's beliefs."

"There's no need, I'm sure that he has his reasons for his beliefs."

"If only you knew."

"I'm sure your father is a great man."

"I don't want to waste time talking about my father. Tell me something, is it hard living on the streets?"

"I don't have many worries, except for food."

"And shelter," I added.

"No, I can find shelter anywhere, it may not be the best, but it helps out on rainy nights. It's almost like camping. Do you camp?"

"In a cabin?" I laughed.

When he joined me in laughter it felt calming. I can't explain it, but it did.

"That's not camping, I mean sleeping outdoors, under the trees."

"No, thank you, too many bugs and creepy things." I shrugged.

"I take it you don't like bugs."

I shook my head. "I get my house sprayed every three or four months, I can't stand them."

We started laughing as if we were old friends, and it could have continued into the next day, but the bar was closing and big-chested Cora wanted to go home. So Franklin walked me to my Jeep and watched as I drove away. I never did get my drink.

※

My normal route didn't seem so mundane. The long stretch of street that was lined with trees seemed so passionate in it's picturesque world. The night air that chilled my body and blew through my hair seemed to refresh my soul, until I pulled into my four-car garage and realized that I was still alone.

As I opened the kitchen door and stepped inside, a screaming Alex, leapt into my face.

"Where the hell have you been? I was just about to call The Judge."

I threw my keys on the counter. "For what?"

"I didn't know where you were?"

I took the pink paper from the refrigerator and gave it to her. "I left a note."

She snatched it out of my hand and threw it to the floor. "I read the note, Nina, and I went downtown, I didn't see you."

I bent down to pick up the note. "Hold on, we're both adults here, and I can go and come as I please." I squinted.

Her expression changed and she became almost somber.

"But you never go out," she pouted.

"But I can go out, you're not the only one that has a life you know."

She grabbed my shoulders and hugged me tightly, almost choking me. "You right, I'm sorry."

I patted her back. "That's okay." I said as I pulled out of her arms.

"I got a little scared," she smiled.

"I understand."

"Who did you go out with?"

Her question caught me off guard. "What?"

"Who did you go out with?"

I said the first name that popped into my head; "Jon," I couldn't even remember how the man looked.

She shot me a twisted smile. "Who's Jon?"

I began wiping down the kitchen counter and rearranging the well-placed canisters. "Jon, the fence guy."

"Really?" Alex beamed. "So, you took your little sisters'

advice and called him?"

My heart took a dangerous leap from my chest. "Yes, I did."

"Do you like him?"

"It was our first date, Alex." I smiled and left the kitchen as fast as I could.

She followed me up the stairs asking question after question, for which I had no answers. I stopped right in front of my bedroom door and I turned to face her. "You really should mind your own business."

She stepped away from me. "Why are you being such a bitch?"

"Just stay out of my business." I slammed the door in her face, clutching my chest with both hands as I tried to steady my racing heart.

Around four a.m., I found myself tapping lightly on Alex's bedroom door. "Alex, are you sleeping?" I asked as I opened the door.

"Yes." She mumbled.

I eased the door open and stuck my head in. "I didn't mean to slam the door in your face, but there were too many questions for me to answer at one time, so I lashed out."

"I understand, stress is a bitch," she said, raising the pink satin comforter so I could crawl into bed next to her. "What's your problem, Nina? Why you tripping? Yes, I love you, and yes The Judge loves you too, he's just a little overbearing at times," she said in a half sleepy voice.

"This is not about my insecurity. I need you to promise me that you won't tell anyone what I'm about to tell you."

"In other words, don't tell the world." She huffed.

"Pretty much." I mumbled.

"Is it that bad?" She yawned.

I shook my head. "I think so, Alex."

She yawned again. "Okay, I promise."

"I wasn't with Jon tonight."

She repositioned her body next to mine. "You weren't?"

"No, I was with Franklin."

"Who's Franklin?" She yawned, for the third time, making me yawn.

"The homeless man."

There were a few moments of silence, and then she quickly sat up in bed. "You went out with a homeless man?"

"Yes."

"Tonight, Nina?"

"Yes."

"The one you were going to hunt down and apologize to?"

"Yes," I replied softly.

Alex turned and clicked on the bedside lamp. "Are you out of your mind?"

"Alex, he's a very nice man."

"I'm sure Jack the Ripper was a nice man." She leapt out of bed and clicked on the main light. "Hell, The Judge's a nice man and as you see, he acts like a damm fool."

"Alex."

She began to pace back and forth. "What has gotten into you, you must be losing your mind. Do you know what The Judge is going to do to you when he finds out you're seeing a homeless man." Alex shouted, flailing her hands in the air. "Out of all the freakin' men in the freakin' world, you had to go out and find a homeless man. Hell, you could have gone out with Reg."

"Reg who?" I frowned.

"Richard's friend, the dude that works at the Bar Association. He's the one that's keeping Richard informed about your license with the Bar Association."

"You mean Reggie Raper." I motioned with my hand.

"Yes."

"Alex, Reg is three feet tall, what am I going to do with a man who's only three feet tall?"

"A whole hell of a lot more than you can do with a broke ass man, that's for damn sure."

"Alex that's ridiculous."

"The Judge is going to kill you."

"The Judge can't do a damn thing to me, Alex, I'm a grown ass woman, I pay my own bills, and I sure as hell can see who I want to see," I shouted.

"Oh, yeah, well let's just call him and find out just how grown you really are," Alex shouted back as she picked up the phone.

I jumped out of bed and wrestled the phone out of Alex's hand. "Wait, wait I have to think before you call him."

"Well, you better think of something good, girl, cause you have lost your mind, that man ain't got shit to offer you."

I put my hands out in front of me to calm my nerves; I closed my eyes for a few seconds. "Father help the day. Alex, remember when you made me promise not to tell The Judge about the two abortions you had?" I asked holding up two fingers.

She put her hands on her hips. "Yeah."

"I never told, never said a word."

"Nina, this is different, you need help and I think The Judge is the one to give it to you, he'll get that fool out of your head, real quick."

"There's nothing to get out of my head. I ran into the man a few times. Damn, can't I say hello to folks without you running to report it to The Judge?"

"First of all," she held up one finger, "I've told you I won't tell him anything, but there is always the first time for everything." She looked away. "I just don't want you to get caught up in no bullshit."

I made her face me. "I'm okay."

She shook her head. "You may think that you're okay, but you gotta watch your back with The Judge, not me, I'm okay. I can handle my shit with the man, he don't scare me."

"Yeah, right."

She plopped down on the bed. "He doesn't scare me!" She huffed, crossing her arms and legs.

"If you can handle The Judge, why did you allow him to

run you out of San Diego?"

"He didn't run me out, I left."

I sat next to her. "Liar."

"The Judge don't scare me, I just can't be around him for very long."

"You know damn well he kept showing up in every club you went to and made a big ass out of you."

"No, he didn't."

I raised both my brows. "I guess you forgot about Humphrey's, Chicago, and the Sinclair Club."

She was quiet and tiny frown lines appeared in the center of her forehead. "No, I didn't forget about those clubs. I can't believe that man, he actually came in there screaming and yelling at me."

"And why did he lose his mind in the grocery store?"

Her shoulders dropped, as I'm sure her memory became clearer. "He didn't like that cashier I was dating." She shook her head.

"So if he didn't like that cashier you were dating, or the bartender at Sinclair Club what do you think he'll do to me if he finds out I was with a homeless man? And I only had a conversation with the man."

Her frown lines were back. "He'll wait until the grand opening to embarrass you, Nina, not to mention the shit he's gonna cause in your life."

"Exactly, so that's why I'm asking you to just be patient with me. Franklin and I are just friends, that's all."

"You promise, just friends." She frowned.

With a wink I said. "Yes."

"Okay, but please be careful, don't get in too deep with those people."

"I would never get in too deep with a homeless Rastafarian." I closed my eyes and kissed Alex on the cheek.

"Thanks, little sis."

"No problem mon, now tell me bout Mr. Rastafarian

Franklin!" She smiled.

I took a deep breath. "There's not much to tell; I mean, what can I say about a homeless man. He doesn't have a car, he doesn't have a any money, he doesn't have a home and he doesn't have a job."

"Then, what's so interesting about him, if he ain't got shit?" she questioned.

"He has personality, charm, and he can hold a great conversation without including any sexual innuendos."

"Why would the brother waste his time, I'm sure he knows it ain't no way in hell he's gonna get some ass."

"It's not about sex, Alex."

"Then, what the hell can it be? You got me all twisted in the head."

"It's friendship, girl."

"Friendship, oh, hell Nina, with your money you can buy all the friends you need."

"That's just it, people have always been in our faces because of The Judge, this man don't know me from Adam and don't care about the Moore bloodline. Franklin is only looking for a friend, it can be lonely living on the streets."

Alex made smacking sounds with her mouth. "Well, enough about that bullshit, how does he look? Is he all dirty and stinky, does he have horrible teeth and bad breath?"

"No, no and no."

"Then, what kind of homeless man are you seeing?"

"First of all, I'm not seeing him, we're just friends; and second of all, I don't know what kind of homeless man he is. He has beautiful white teeth and nice clean hands. Soft, too."

Alex jerked back. "You touched them."

"I shook his hand when we said good-night."

"Okay, Nina, none of that touching shit." She rolled her eyes and shook her head. "I've disobeyed The Judge all my life," she mumbled, "but this tops anything I've done."

"I don't know why I told you."

"I can't believe you've actually talked to a homeless man, The Judge is truly gonna have a shit fit when he find out about this." She laughed.

I raised an eyebrow. "He won't find out right?"

"Don't worry, I ain't gonna tell, but let me ask you this, what the hell you gonna do when he does find out?"

"There's nothing to find out. We had a few drinks and a few laughs. I didn't break the law."

She nodded. "Were you scared?"

I thought about it for a moment. "At first, then his smile helped to loosen things up. He's very nice and polite; it's hard to believe he's homeless. I was more comfortable with him, than with most of the men I've been out with."

Alex seemed almost disappointed in me. "What?"

I looked down at my hands. "Franklin knows he can't get anything from me. So, he takes what I have to offer."

"I'm shocked," she mocked sarcastically.

"You know, Alex, I'm sort of surprised myself, before that incident I would have walked past him like a stranger, now I'm listening to music with him in a seedy bar. It felt sort of like I was rebelling."

"No, stupid. I'm shocked that he would think he had a chance with you."

"What!"

"Never mind." She waved me away. "Tell me about this seedy bar."

I held up my hand. "Lord, girl you don't want to know."

"Are you gonna see him again?"

"No, it was just this one time." I threw my hands in the air. "I'm through rebelling for the year." I smiled.

"Good, now I don't have to worry about that crazy ass father of yours. You know he just needs one more push to get back on that 'run the homeless folks off the planet' campaign."

"I know Alex, trust me I know."

Chapter Seventeen

Nina

On Friday afternoon, I was sitting alone in the back of the Street Kar Café, trying to read the Orange County contract. Instead I ended up musing over Wednesday night; the music, the madness and Franklin… when suddenly he appeared.

"Good afternoon, Ms. Moore," he said with a big smile on his face that said he was excited to see me.

"Franklin, good afternoon." I nodded.

He repositioned the duffel bag on his left shoulder. "And why you sitting in the back? There's a lot of room up front."

"Oh, I'm sure there is, but as you can see," I pointed to the thick contract, "I have a lot of reading to do."

He lifted his novel. "It's a nice day for reading in the park."

I was going to accept his invitation, but the face of The Judge appeared before me.

"No, thank you, I really have to read this thing before I sign it, and the park would only distract me." Our eyes met and I quickly looked away. "Were you on your way to the park?" I asked.

"Yes, I'm meeting with my friend, Bones."

"Oh, yes, Bones." I nodded remembering the weather beaten, toothless, old man. "Tell him I said hello."

"I will, Nina," he smiled. "Will I be seeing you at The Bar again?"

"I can't say, that was very spontaneous of me."

"I understand, you have a nice day," he said before heading

out the back door.

"Franklin," I yelled and looked around to see if anyone heard me.

He almost ran back to my table "Yes."

"Have you eaten today?"

He smiled. "Thank you, I have, Nina."

I returned his smile with a nod.

"Well, I gotta go," he said, "I'll see you later."

"Okay, take it easy."

He tapped the table a few times before he turned and walked away.

ჰ

By the next Wednesday night, I found myself walking the streets of downtown Riverside. I was nibbling on an ear of hot buttered, roasted corn-on-the-cob. I was hoping to find last weeks' musician, so I could release the tension that had built up in my body from the days before.

"Nina! Nina." I heard a voice shouting over the crowd. Surprise siphoned the blood from my veins when I saw it was Franklin.

"Fancy meeting you here," he grinned.

"I finished reading the contract, so I decided to come back and see if I could...."

"Find me." He smirked.

I stepped back. "No."

"Well, I came back to see if you were here."

"That's nice, Franklin." I said, looking around me, fearing that someone who knew the Moore family might spot me with this homeless Rastafarian. "I actually came back to get this hot buttered corn," I continued. "Would you like some?"

He placed his duffel bag on the ground. "Sure would," he replied and swiftly snatched the corn from my hands so fast I didn't have time to object.

My eyes widened.

"Man, I love roasted corn, and you got just the right amount of black pepper, and lemon salt on it," he added, gnawing zealously at the corn.

When he finished, he handed me the bare cob and we laughed at his silliness. "You can't offer a homeless person a bite to eat."

"Well, I didn't think you would actually take it." I answered, throwing the cob into a nearby trash can.

"Don't offer anything unless you intend to give it away forever." He winked.

"I'll keep that in mind." I smiled.

"Good, then you never have to worry about getting your feelings hurt."

"Well, I guess."

"Hold that thought. I'll be right back," he said, grabbing his life's possessions, and leaving me standing in the middle of the street.

An uneasy feeling began to creep into my soul, and suddenly I became paranoid, thinking everyone was staring at the homeless man and me. I was about to deny my friend, when he reappeared with a chocolate chip cookie that was big as my face.

"You have to try these cookies, they're delicious!"

"Oh, no, thank you, I need to stick to this diet. The corn was a treat."

"A what?" He frowned.

I tapped my hips. "Diet, I have to lose a few pounds."

"Maybe in your dreams. Girl, you look fine!"

"No, I don't."

"What, your husband told you to lose a few pounds?"

"I'm not married."

He raised an eyebrow. "Oh, so your boyfriend." He smiled.

I shook my head. "Don't have one of those either."

Homeless Love

Franklin shoved the cookie in my face. "Then, eat your cookie before you waste away."

I took the cookie, but not before glancing around the crowd. "Let's go someplace else, there's too many people here tonight," I suggested.

"There's always the library, it's right on the corner."

"That's great," I said thinking there was no way anyone that I knew would be in the library on a Wednesday night. All the information they need is at their fingertips surfing the net.

We walked inside and went to the second floor. After we were seated in the back, and I could breathe easier, I just blurted out. "Is it hard being homeless?"

He looked away.

As soon as the question left my lips I knew I had hit a nerve. "I didn't mean to offend you."

"You're not offending me, I don't know how to describe my life. It's not hard being homeless, it's less stressful. The one thing I hate about being homeless is how everyone denies your presence; I hate being ignored. Say hello or something, but don't ignore me."

"I understand." I nodded, trying not to allow guilt to tiptoe back into my life, but I found myself there, feeling almost rebellious. I cleared my throat. "Have you found a place to sleep? If not, I can put you up for a few weeks."

"At your house?" His eyes widened.

"No, at a motel, I have a few connections."

"That's okay I can handle it, but thanks anyway."

"Don't forget, if you prefer to sleep back at the office, you have my permission."

"Nah, that's okay, I got my eyes on another great place, no one lives there, so I'll have it for awhile, besides it's going to start getting cold, so I'll need a little more shelter."

I felt so bad that he was refusing my help, but all I could do was make the offer. I broke a piece of the cookie and slid it between my lips. "This is good," I mumbled.

Franklin whispered. "You are not supposed to eat in a library!"

I nervously folded the plastic over my cookie. "I haven't been in a library in so long I must have forgotten."

"That's one great thing about being homeless, you have a lot of time on your hands to enjoy the little things in life, like reading."

"I guess you're right."

Franklin passed a hand over his locks.

"Why the dredlocks?" I asked.

"It's easier, do you like them?"

I raised an eyebrow. Now was not the time to be honest.

"If you like them, I love them." I smiled.

"I try to keep my hair as clean as possible. Go ahead touch them."

I shook my head.

He slumped back in his chair. "I understand."

I made a gesture with my hands. "What about the facial hair?"

"What about it?"

"Why so much?" I asked touching my hand to my chin.

He smiled and said. "Nina, I'm homeless, I can't shave everyday."

"Oh, sorry, I just don't understand the state of homelessness. There's so much you can't have being homeless."

"It's just the way the dice fell for me." He took a deep breath. "Listen, I don't want to talk about me. Let's talk about you for a change, besides you've used up your one question."

I nodded. "You got me. What do you want to know?" I winked.

"What do you like to do?"

"I like reading, painting, skating, and . . .."

"You like to skate? I love to skate!" he said with so much excitement a few people cleared their throats.

"Yes, I do, my sister and I used to go to the rink on Magnolia by the Galleria mall, all the time."

"Used to?" he frowned.

I looked up toward the ceiling. "God, I haven't been in years."

"I go skating on Saturday mornings."

Homeless Love

"Really?" I nodded.

"I used to go at night, but people didn't take too kindly to a homeless man skating with their kids. So the manager said if I didn't mind coming on Saturday mornings, I could skate for free."

"Free?" I repeated.

He shook his head. "Skating keeps you fit." He patted his flat stomach.

"If that's the case, I just might see you Saturday morning."

"Really?" He beamed. "I'll be. . . "

I sprung to my feet when I spotted one of The Judge's golf partners with his family. "You know, Franklin, it's getting late and I have to get up early, maybe we can continue this another time."

"Was it something I said?" He asked, jumping to his feet.

"No, not at all I just have to go."

"What about Saturday?"

"Yes, that will be great." I whispered. "Let's say around ten in the morning." I didn't wait around for his answer.

§

On Saturday morning, I nervously waited for Franklin to show up for our skating session. I really wasn't going to show up, but every time I saw him, he reminded me of my promise. I don't know why I told the man I could skate. I hadn't been on skates since I was a child. Fear began to knot up inside of me when I spotted him crossing the parking lot. The long trench coat hung so loosely around his body, I thought it was going to slip off. I looked away as he hoisted the duffel bag higher on his shoulder, almost falling. When I turned back, he had taken off the dirty white cap and freely tucked it into his pocket.

His mere appearance wanted to make me run for cover, until I spotted a cluster of wild flowers drooping from his fist. I wiped my sweaty palms on my jeans and anxiously waited for him to enter the building.

When he entered, I panicked, as the fearful images of The

Judge's anger ran through my mind.

"Well, hello, Nina." He smiled and gave me a handful of wildflowers.

"I picked these in the field I crossed. I know ladies like flowers."

I could hear the nervousness in his voice when he spoke. I took the flowers and brought them to my nose. The strange surge of affection I felt frightened me. Then a warm glow streamed through my soul. How odd I thought, as my mood suddenly went from threatened to buoyant. "Thank you, Franklin." I blushed. "It's been awhile since a man gave me flowers."

"I know they aren't roses, but they are pretty."

"Yes, they are." I blushed again. My face then became stern when I noticed a young mother gawking at us as she held her toddler tight in her arms. The uneasy look on her face told me I must have been doing something wrong. My stomach began churning with anxiety. "Are you ready to skate?" I asked as I walked past her gaze.

"Are you ready to skate?" He asked smiling like a school boy.

I looked at all the mothers holding their little people's hands, teaching them to skate, and I smiled.

"I think so." I nodded.

We walked over to a circular bench and he helped me strap on my in-line skates. When I stood, I simply could not comprehend the theory of balancing on four wheels in a row.

"Okay, just hold on to me," he said, offering his arms for support.

I tried to take a quick glance around the room before grabbing his arms for support. "Maybe these things are broken," I said nearly collapsing to the floor as my knees buckled for the second time.

"Just hold on to me, you're going to be alright."

After several attempts to master skating, the floor and I became well acquainted. I knew it was time to give it up when a six or seven-year-old boy swooped by, skating backwards.

"You need some help lady?" He asked showing a toothless smile.

I looked him right in his tiny light beady eyes. "No thank you, I think I can get up."

"Just hold on to the wall, okay." He grinned and skated into the disco light. If he were a few feet taller, I would have kicked him.

I frowned up at Franklin. "These things must be broken."

"They might be." He winked and offered me his arm again. "Let me help you to a seat," he said. "I'll get someone to come and take a look at them."

I flopped onto the bench with a grateful sigh. I felt happiness coiled within me as he walked away. If The Judge could see me now, he would die of a heart attack, right here on the skating rink floor. A satanic smile spread across my lips as I envisioned The Judge's face.

"Hi, I'm Jake, Frank's friend." He said offering his hand.

"Hi Jake." I smiled, and shook his hand.

"Frank said there might be a problem with your skates?" The young blond kid said as he knelt down next to my feet.

I nodded when he made a few minor adjustments to the skates.

"I think I fixed the problem." He winked. "Stand up and try them out."

When I stood, it was like magic. I didn't wobble once. "Franklin, look," I shouted and held up both hands. His smile broadened in approval as he walked over to me.

"Very good. I thought you might want a drink, after your little floor exercise."

"Thank you, but I think a pillow would be softer." I said, before sipping from the cup he extended to me. I don't think he could help himself, because he burst into laughter.

"If I had one it would be yours, because you hit the floor quite hard this last time.

"You know you're right, but I'm ready to try again, now that the problem is fixed."

"Just be careful."

"I'm not worried, you'll be there to catch me when I fall," I said and turned away not waiting for a reply.

Franklin

I continued to marvel at her as she took the paper cup and brought it to her lips. Nina made me feel as if I could do anything thing. I guess fear makes me a prisoner of the bottle. I was so nervous when I handed her the flowers, but when she brought them to her nose and closed her eyes, my heart melted and the nervousness slipped away.

Several slow songs came and went; still my nerves didn't allow me to ask for one dance. When the instrumental version of *Brown Sugar* came on, I gently took Nina's hand and led her to the center of the skating ring. I skated backward so that I could see her. I tried not to stare into her eyes, but I couldn't help myself. I wanted so much to hold her in my arms, but for now I'll take anything she gives.

It didn't even bother me that she continued to look over her shoulders to see if anyone was watching us. Today I had Nina all to myself, and maybe into the night, if I can get up the nerves to ask her to the movies tonight. I let go of her fingers and continued to skate backwards as she skated toward me. *Brown Sugar* seemed to be a lot longer than I remembered. I glanced up and saw Jake in the D.J. booth smiling.

"What's so funny?" She asked with three tiny frown lines in the middle of her forehead.

"Life." I winked.

She smiled. "This is true, how funny is this?"

"What?"

"Us."

"What about us?" I asked as a small electric shock wave continued to attack my heart.

"You and me, here, right now."

Homeless Love

"What's so funny about this?" I asked, skating around her.

"Franklin, we're from two different places, how do you explain something like this. How do you explain to your friends that you went skating with me, and how do I explain it to my friends?"

"Maybe, some things can't be explained."

"Everything can be explained." She winked.

"This is true, but does it make sense?"

"If it can be explained." She smiled. "It makes sense." She added grabbing hold of me for support.

"Not really." I smiled noticing how relaxed her fingers felt entwined in mine.

"Like what?"

"Like bees for instance, they make honey by throwing up."

"So." Her eyes widened.

"So, we eat the honey."

She frowned and nodded. "Good one, you win the argument, Mr. Franklin."

"Why thank you, Ms. Nina." I skated around her a few times just to hear her laugh. "Would you like to sit, I don't think Jake's gonna stop playing *Brown Sugar* anytime soon." She nodded and we skated back toward the yellow and orange booths. Once we were seated, I swallowed and blurted out. "I don't have much money, but would you like to go to the movie theater on University Boulevard?" I asked, regretting the question as I watched her smile fade and she turned away from me.

We sat in silence for a long time before she slapped her thighs and stood. I jumped to my feet, leaving my heart on the red Formica table.

"It's getting late, and I have a lot of things to do. So I must be going." She said reaching out for my hand. "What time does the movie start?"

"Nine." I said trying to hold in my excitement.

She smiled and tried to skate away.

Chapter Eighteen

Nina

As I prepared to go the movies with Franklin, my stomach was in knots. I breathed a sigh of relief when I heard the garage door go down. I could always count on Alex to get her party on. I grabbed my purse and shivered at my secret rendezvous. As I hurried downstairs, imagine my surprise when I saw Alex stretched out on the sofa with a bowl of chips on her stomach, watching something on TV. I dropped my purse on the stairs, took a deep breath and walked up to her.

"Where you going?" She asked, gawking at me.

"Nowhere, I heard the garage door close, I thought you were going out."

"I was but I changed my mind, so I let it down."

"Alex, it's a Saturday night." I said nervously. "Don't you have to go to some new club to meet Walter?"

"Nagh; I'm cool." She smirked. "Beside you've been gone or too busy to hang with me for the last month. So I decided to take some time to spend with my big sister." She winked, and slowly placed a chip into her mouth.

By this time I wanted to scream. "You really should be with your man."

She sat up straight and put the bowl of chips on the table in front of her. "I don't want to be with my man. I want to kick it with you and do some sister stuff."

"Alex, there'll be plenty of nights once you move in here for us to do some sister stuff." I answered as I pried her off the sofa and grabbed her shoes and purse. "Here, take my car." I handed her the keys as I pushed her toward the door.

"The Beemer?" She screamed with delight.

"Yes, the Beemer, lil sis." I opened the door and shoved her out. "Now go and have some fun, you crazy girl."

My heart skipped a beat with excitement as she headed for the car. Then, suddenly she stopped, turned to me, and dropped her shoulders. "Oh, hell no, what's up, Nina?"

I gave a forced smile and with an adventurous toss of my head, I said, "Nothing's up! But I know when you start hanging around me, that usually means you're contemplating dumping your old man for a new man, and you'll need me to tell you that it's okay to do so. I don't want to go through the drama with you. Not right now." I shook my head.

"Nina, I am not dumping Walter."

"Oh, I know you're not dumping Walter, because I'm going to put a stop to that. He's a great man," I said I as opened the garage door.

"I just want to spend some time with you," she whined.

"I don't need you to spend any time with me, I'm a big girl. I can handle being alone," I stated as I pushed her toward the newly washed car. "Did I ever tell you how stunning you would look driving my sea green BMW with the top down?"

Her face lit up. "Really?"

I shook my head. "Yes girl, you look stunning."

"Nina, are you sure you alright?"

"Yes, now go. I bought new CDs, they're in the backseat. Help yourself." Hell! I would have given her my firstborn just to get her out of the house.

It was a tad past one in the morning by the time I made it home.

"Why didn't you call me, Nina?" She screamed before I had a chance to get out of the Jeep.

"I was too busy, besides I'm a big girl, I think I can go out by myself."

"What were you doing?"

I walked past her and went into the house. "I had things to do, Alex. Didn't we have this conversation before?"

"Nina."

"Is Mother alright?"

"Yes, she's fine, but The Judge called, he tried your office and your cell phone."

"My cell was turned off again. What does he want anyway?" I asked.

Her bare feet made clapping sounds as she stormed in behind me. "He wanted to remind you about that stupid Sunday dinner."

I grabbed a Coke from the fridge and turned to face her. "Oh, damn! Is it this Sunday?"

"Yes. Where were you?"

"Out. Did you say anything to him?"

"No, but I should have."

"No, you shouldn't have and don't be telling him my freakin' business, Alex. I can take care of myself."

"I know you can, Nina, but you're always home, and when you're not, I get worried. You look after me, and I look after you. Right?"

"Yeah."

She walked up to me and took the soda can out of my hand. "So, whatcha up to?"

"I'm not up to anything, so drop it. Let's prepare to go and see Mother, The Judge and the rest of that crazy family tomorrow." I began to walk away from her; I guess that's why I don't practice law; I loathe all the prying.

Homeless Love

"Were you out with that homeless man?" She shouted.

I stopped and turned to face her. "Alex, I don't question you when you stay out all night."

"Yeah, but that's what I do. I party. You work."

"Well, maybe I want to start partying now."

She inhaled. "You were out with him, weren't you?"

"Alex."

With both hands on her hips, she walked past me. "Is he the one who's been taking up all your time?" She crossed her arms across her chest. "I'm surprised that you even set time aside to have dinner with the family on Sunday."

I walked up to Alex as close as I could get without stepping on her toes. "What I'm doing with my time is my business and if you're going to start questioning my every move, maybe we should reconsider your moving in with me once your lease is up." I pointed toward the upstairs. "I can have the carpenter stop the expansion on the bedroom."

She waved both hands in the air. "Nina, don't get stupid."

"I have The Judge and Mother monitoring my every move; I don't need you to join in with them as well." I said through clenched teeth. "Now I'm tired, I want to take a shower and go to sleep, if that's alright with you," I snapped as I headed toward my not so lonely thirteen stairs.

Alex grabbed my arm and stopped me. "Nina, can't you see what this man is doing to you? He's turning you against me, you've never spoken to me like this, so why you starting now?"

"There is no man, Alex, and you've never given me a reason to speak to you like this, but if you keep this up you'll be out on your ass."

"Oh, so all of a sudden Mr. Homeless man comes into the picture and now you want to throw family into the street."

"I'm not throwing you in the streets, but you're headed that way, and for the last time there is no man! Homeless or otherwise."

"I know when there's a man in your life."

"You heard me, Alex." I said as I continued on my journey.

"Are you going to dinner on Sunday?" She shouted up the stairs.

"Yes, Alex." I yelled. "Didn't you hear me."

"Can I ride with you?"

"Yes, Alex."

"I love you, Nina."

"I love you too, lil sis." Then I closed my bedroom door.

Franklin

"Who's that?" I asked when I came upon Bones at Fairmont Park, leaning against a tree, thumbing through a small photo album.

"Oh, shit, you scared me." He said, as he hurried and closed the book, slipping it under the blanket, that was covering his leg.

"Who are those people?" I asked reaching for the album.

"Can I have some privacy?" Bones snapped.

I stood in silence, shocked at Bones anger. He then took a deep breath, lowered his head, and took the 5x5 photo album from under the blanket. He held it tight with both hands.

"This is all that's left of my family Frank." He mumbled. "This is all I have."

I didn't ask him to peek into his long forgotten world.

"My little girl gave this to me." He said as tears fell from his eyes. I've never seen Bones cry.

I allowed him his time to grieve for his family, for his past. Once he was finished, he looked up at me.

"Where the hell you been?" He shouted as if nothing had happened, "I've been baby sitting this damn thing all night." He said pointing toward my duffel bag.

Homeless Love

"I met her again." I smiled like a schoolboy. "She's so beautiful, Bones. We went to the movies. It was like heaven on earth."

"Man, you need to slow down, you have some things you gotta take care of."

"You act like I'm gonna ask her to marry me or something. She's just a friend."

"Shit, I ain't worrying about you marrying her. I'm worrying about you falling in love with her and getting your heart broken. Then, you never gonna get off the streets. That's what I'm worried about."

"What's up with all that anger?" I asked staring down at him.

"This is what's up with all my anger!" He shouted shaking his photo album at me. "You gotta clean up yourself up before you fuck up her life, like I did my family, like you already did your family."

"Oh that's a low blow Bones, but I understand that you're feeling sorry for yourself, so I'll let you have that one for free."

"Whatever Frank."

"It's not whatever Frank, you act like it's a crime to have a friend in the other world? I ain't gonna fall in love with the lady!" I said shaking my head, knowing that I was already in love with her.

"I ain't saying you can't have a friend in the other world, but you should see what I see."

"What you see, man. Huh, what the hell do you see?" I shouted.

"I see that you have a different look in your eyes every time you see her. You're eating more, and you've been down to the shelter almost everyday taking a shower."

"I can't take showers?"

"Yes, you can, but when a man gets to taking a shower everyday and he don't have to, you better believe it's a woman involved, and it's serious."

I waved him away. "You don't know what you're talking about."

"You know it's true. You know if that woman gets one whiff of you, it's over. She'll never give you the time of day."

Bones' words hit home. I lowered my head, unable to meet his gaze. "But this woman sparks something in me that makes me want to put down the bottle, get off the street and start a family."

"Then do that Frank, start a family."

"How in the hell am I gonna start a family? Tonight she asked me if I knew this saxophone player that plays on Wednesday night. I couldn't tell her, that I'm the player she's searching for."

"Why not? If she's your friend as you claim, you should be able to tell her anything"

I shook my head, and took my duffel bag from Bones.

"Not now."

"Then when?"

"When I've cleaned up. I don't want her to see me begging for money on the streets."

Bones stood to his feet. "Frank you don't beg for money. You play hard for the little money you receive. But I have to agree, you have to clean up, before you get too deep into that friendship shit and she just happens to stumble across you one day, in one of your drunken stupors."

"Bones please."

"No, Frank I already told you man, you don't belong here."

I scratched my head. "I'm thinking about it, because it's been a long time since I laughed."

"Don't think, just do it!" Bones pleaded.

"I don't know, even if I do get off the streets, what's to say I'm not going to end up right back here."

"Cause you gonna have Nina and she ain't gonna let you fall, man."

"You need to wake up, I'm never going to have enough to give her, she's twenty light years ahead of me." The truth tasted so foul in my mouth. "You and I both are fooling ourselves if we think any differently."

He shook his head. "She's not twenty light years ahead of you, Franklin, she's just around the corner on Sober Street, where you need to be." Bones spit on the ground. "Forget about friendship, forget about everything, go for the brand new life." He coughed.

"Even if I get on Sober Street, this woman has a mansion, a BMW, a fire red Jeep. She's talking about opening franchises all over the state. What do I have? Not a damn thing."

"Why are you so focused on the material things? Why you gotta be the one to bring home the bacon, why can't you be the one to cook it?"

"Cause that's what a man does, we bring home the bacon and the woman cooks it."

Bones stood to his feet. He grabbed his head. "You better wake up, women are bringing home the bacon and cooking it too, they don't need a man to do that for them. Hell, they don't even need a man. They want a man, and believe me there's a difference."

"I'm not going to lay up on a woman and let her take care of me."

"She ain't gotta take care you, y'all can take care of each other."

I took the bottle out of my side pocket. "Nope, can't do it." I said as I swallowed the Black Velvet whiskey.

"Frank, listen. I know you; you're a decent guy. Broke, but decent, so why can't you take care of her, be her strength when she's weak."

"Man, I ain't got nothing to offer her, shit I got a duffel bag full of junk and a saxophone. That ain't worth shit."

Bones grabbed my shoulders and shook me. "You got heart, that counts for something. Get yourself together, get off the streets and live the life you were supposed to live."

I was silent as I stared down at my hand, gripping the whisky bottle. "Maybe you're right, but getting off the streets means I gotta stop drinking and you know I can't stop drinking,

C.F. Hawthorne

not yet." I took another swallow.

"Oh, bull, Frank, lots of people stop drinking, you ain't no different, you just gotta wanna stop drinking."

"I just gotta wanna stop." I chuckled.

"Yeah man, you just gotta wanna stop." Bones repeated with a deep throaty laugh, and spit on the ground again.

"Are you alright Bones?"

"I'm fine, you just do what you gotta do."

"I have to think about it." I said rubbing my head.

Bones shrugged his shoulders. "What's there to think about?"

"Putting down the bottle means cleaning up a lot of stuff and . . .."

"And you don't wanna clean it up."

"Not yet."

"Not even for Nina?"

I looked up into the trees, and pressed my lips together, squeezing my eyes tight in order to hold in the pain. "That's your second low blow." I mumbled, fighting back tears.

"Yes I know." He smirked. "But you can do it Frank!"

Chapter Nineteen

Nina

By 11:35 Monday morning, my mind was aching for a good conversation. Thank goodness, I was meeting Franklin for lunch.

"Did Rachel mention she was coming to the opening?" I asked Alex who was sitting in front of me, wearing an orange and white designer mini skirt, with matching knee high boots, staring at her reflection in her Gucci hand-held mirror.

"I guess you didn't see how that witch was gawking at you when The Judge mentioned the opening night."

I sighed. "I saw her," I said as I lowered my head. "I guess I was hoping for something different."

"Well, you ain't getting nothing different than any other time, so stop hoping."

"She does have a hard life. Mother said Harold had to pay all her bills this month. Is her husband working?" I asked.

"On that pipe." Alex huffed.

"Alex."

"I ain't lying, that boy is grabbing that pipe so much he shoulda been a plumber." She leaned in close to me. "Mother said Devlin. Rachel's baby boy, told her that his daddy threw all the food in the front yard. You know that baby boy kinda slow, so Mother didn't pay too much attention to him when he told her that." Alex laughed. "But it was true."

I shook my head. "What did The Judge have to say about that?"

"You know, Nina, that's the strangest thing, he never brings it up. I've questioned Mother about that and she doesn't want to talk about it either. I want to know why Rachel can get away with so much?"

I raised an eyebrow. "What the hell, no one told me anything!"

Alex leaned back in her chair and crossed her legs. "You don't like gossip, and especially not about the family."

"This is not gossip, this is information. I feel so sorry for her."

"I don't, that bitch is crazy."

"Alex." I snapped. "That's your sister."

"And I can't have a crazy bitch for a sister?" She rolled her eyes. "Lots of people have crazy bitches for sisters."

"We know she has problems, but she's still our sister."

"Whatever, Nina. The Judge didn't look pleased to hear that the San Diego office was going to open on time."

I nodded as the disappointed face of The Judge flickered in my mind.

"I wonder why he kept looking over at Rachel." Alex's smile turned into a chuckle. "Rachel was twitching like her G-string was to tight." She sucked her teeth. "She's psycho you know. Are we sure her Mother wasn't crazy?"

"I don't want to talk about Rachel anymore, I want to talk about you and how proud I am of you."

Her brows flickered a little. "Me, for what?"

"Walter has been around longer than anyone of the thousands of guys you've been with."

She sat up straight, all the while trying to suppress a smile. "I haven't been with thousands of guys."

I cocked my head slightly to the side. "Oh, really?" I smiled. "Damn near, I was thinking about buying some condom stock."

Alex crinkled her nose. "Was I that bad?"

"I'm not one to judge, but you're the female version of Wilt

Chamberlain."

Alex rose and stood next to me. "I just wanted to thank you for being there for me, and for always getting on my case about using a condom, there were many times they didn't want to, but I always heard you say that you didn't want to lose me to some stupid disease."

I stood and hugged my baby sister. "And I don't." I said squeezing her tighter.

Alex pulled away from me. "Did you see how Maria was hanging all over The Judge last night?"

I rolled my eyes. "Alex, that's enough."

"Nina, I'm just stating what I saw, and it wasn't in my head."

"That's not what you saw. You don't like the girl, so you criticize everything she does. If she blows her nose, you complain it's too loud."

"It's too damn loud. Nina, we can't hear ourselves think when she starts that shit at the dinner table. Even her sneeze is ridiculous."

"See what I mean. The poor girl can't get a break when it comes to you."

"I just don't like her, she's too damn nice to Mother for me, and she's too damn sneaky."

"Everybody is sneaky to you. The Judge is sneaky; Rachel's sneaky; everybody's sneaky. You don't want anybody to come between you and the people you love."

"I don't." She grunted. "Besides, Rachel is the result of The Judge being sneaky, so I rest my case." She started counting on her fingers. "Harold is screwing around on Maria, Rachel is hiding something I don't know what, and I don't think Mother has bleeding ulcers."

"You think Harold is screwing around on Maria?"

"Oh, hell yes, big time."

"You really don't think Mother has bleeding ulcers?"

"Nope." Alex shook her head. "She goes to the doctor once a week and when she gets back, she's too sick to do anything. I think it's something else."

"See what I mean. You're suspicious of everybody."

"Yes, I am, including you."

"Me?" I said in surprise. "I have nothing to hide."

"That's what you say.

"I told you that my life is an open book. I thought we went over this on the ride to and from San Diego."

"Yes, we did, and I apologized for accusing you of hanging around that homeless man."

When she said homeless man, I stiffened. I had come to see Franklin as more than a homeless man. He was becoming something to me that I could never admit to anyone, not even to myself.

"Come on, Nina, tell me."

"I'm not hiding anything." I shook my head.

She tapped her long orange and white fingernails on the edge of my desk. Lord that girl knows how to make good money look bad. I shook my head. "So why did I find a pair of skates in the Jeep."

"You found them because you're nosy."

"That's not the point." She tapped again. "Who are you skating with?"

"I skate alone, I heard it helps you to lose weight."

Alex put her hands on her hips. "The pool stick?"

"I like to play pool and skate, and neither of those sports requires a partner."

"I still say you're hiding something."

"Well, I still say that you're crazy as the rest of the Moore family." I stood and walked over to the filing cabinet. My heart was pounding so loudly in my chest I thought she could hear it. "What are you hiding?" I asked as I leaned against the cabinet, closing the door with my back.

She shrugged her shoulders. "I have nothing to hide, my life is an open book."

"Good, open your book and let's discuss the San Diego office, before I head to Orange County." I took my seat in front of her.

Alex opened the ledger. "See." She pointed. "I have a record of everything that I did, I have notes and everything."

"Okay, what's first?" I asked.

"Well, first things first." She smiled. "You have to call the Lamont building inspector in San Diego."

My shoulders dropped. "For what, I'm due to open in two months."

"No, girlfriend, you're due to open next month." She said softly.

"Next month?" I whispered in confusion.

She nodded. "Yes, next month."

My lips began to quiver. "What happened to two months, Alex? We had two months left?"

"I know, Nina, but you left a message to move the date up. So I did."

I grabbed my chest. There were so many things going on in my life, every conversation began to bleed into the next one. "Why didn't you confirm the changes with me?"

"I left the new date right here." She rose to check my cluttered desk. "I promise."

My head started to spin. "Well, I never got it!" I shouted, pushing her away.

"I left it here, right here." She pointed again.

"Go and ask Sabrina, if she saw the notes?"

"Why her?" Alex frowned.

"I saw her coming out of the office a few days ago. Maybe she picked up the notes by accident."

Alex stopped moving papers around on my desk and looked up at me. "Why would she be coming out of your office?"

"According to her, she was putting files into the cabinet." I pointed toward the window, where the filing cabinet was standing.

"Yeah right."

"Don't start on her."

"Why can't I start on her? She's sneaky and evil."

I held up my hand. "I don't want to hear it Alex. I just want

Homeless Love

to know what are we going to do about the opening? I need office supplies, office equipment, hell I even need an office manager."

Alex fell back into the chair and crossed her long legs. "We can call a temp agency and fill the vacant spots, and if we like them, we keep them. If we don't, we let them go and get someone else."

I leaned back in my chair. "That's one smart thing you've thought of. Now what about an office manager? I can't have just anyone over my new company."

"I'm sure you can find a competent person to do the job."

I nodded. "I have."

"Who? Not Sabrina." Alex squinted.

"No, you are going to work the San Diego office until I can find a competent person and someone I can trust."

She sat up straight. "I can't."

"I can't have the San Diego office, on Red alert like the Riverside office."

"But I can't." She cried again.

I started straightening up my desk. "And why not?"

"Walter asked me to go to Bermuda for two weeks."

"Two weeks! What about the opening?"

"Nina, he just gave me the tickets when he came over last night, I thought I had everything under control. We're leaving the day after the opening. I'll work the San Diego office the week it opens, and that depends on how much shit I can take from The Judge."

"You're going to leave me high and dry for a man?"

"He's not just any man, Nina, I think he's the one. Besides, I don't want to miss out on an all-expense, paid trip to Bermuda, with the man of my dreams. Please don't ask me to do that." She frowned.

"I can't leave the Riverside office to look after the San Diego office, and no one else is ready for that position, not yet."

"What about Richard?"

I shook my head. "Nope, he's office manager for Riverside."

She covered her face with both hands and screamed. "I

can't make it down there with The Judge, please Nina, I'm begging you, just being there on Sundays drives me insane."

I leaned back in my chair, and tapped my index finger on my chin a few times. "You better make sure that the San Diego office is up and running to full capacity, before you leave or you'll have to find another place to work."

"You know I got your back, sis, I won't let you down." she smiled and stood.

"Don't worry about letting me down, don't let yourself down."

§

After Alex left my office, I was preparing to meet Franklin for lunch when a soft tapping on my office door, made my shoulders drop. "Come in." I said softly, trying to play off my irritation, but I was hoping this was not going to take long. "Hey, Richard, what's up?" I asked, as I smiled at his light pink suit with matching shoes. "I'm on my way to start those dreadful Monday afternoon meetings in Orange County."

"I didn't know you had a meeting today." He frowned.

"I just received the call and I'm going to be late. What's up? What do you need?"

"Did you close the Papers Plus account?" he asked, as he set a pile of files down on my desk.

"That account isn't closed, ask Alex."

"She just left."

"To go where?"

"I don't' know, she said her head was hurting."

"Listen, I'm going to be late for my meeting. Find out what's going on with the account, and we can discuss it when I get back? I know you got my back on this one." I smiled.

"I would, if a brother could get a little help around here."

"Isn't Sabrina helping you?"

His mood veered sharply to anger; his nostrils flared with

fury. "That child doesn't know anything. She's always reading or re-reading everything she gets her hands on. She's no help, just a pain in my ass."

"Okay, calm down, get the company on the phone, and I want a manager, not some store clerk." I walked over to the file cabinet. "Also, get the phone number for their district office just in case I don't get anywhere with the store manager."

His voice drifted into a hushed whisper. "Nina, there's something else."

I leaned against the cabinet. "What?"

"Papers Plus is not going to reopen the account. They said we placed a large order."

"A what?"

"We supposedly ordered a lot of office supplies and haven't paid for it, so they want the money now."

I turned and strolled back to Richard. "Pay them." I said as I picked up my briefcase, irritated that he couldn't handle something as small as that.

He propped back on one leg and said. "Sugar, it's a lot of money, over $20,000. I don't think we should pay them until we can find out who ordered this stuff, and where the supplies are." he said as he waved tons of papers in the air.

I glanced down at my watch praying that he would let me out of here so I could meet Franklin. "If they said we ordered the supplies, they must have an inventory sheet."

"I'm checking our stock and I can't locate any of the things they said we ordered. Someone is bringing over the stores purchase slip, because I can't find ours."

"Listen, I'm going to be late for my meeting. Can you handle this little problem and let me know the outcome," I said and patted him on the arm as I hurried out the door to my secret rendezvous.

§

I walked into the dimly lit pool hall, my pool case in hand. I tried not to choke on the funky, musty air that entered my lungs. I spotted Franklin leaning against a pool table in the back. The balls were racked and ready, waiting for me to break them. I removed my jacket and threw it across my arm, feeling relaxed and confident as I maneuvered my way in and out of the rows of pool tables until I reached him.

I cleared my throat and threw my jacket on the nearest chair, as I unzipped my black and red case and threw it aside as well. Franklin's eyes widened. I smiled and sucked my teeth just like The Judge, as I slowly screwed the two pieces tightly together.

"I know that you're a pro at skating," I said smoothly as I strolled toward him. "I also know that you had Jake fix my skates so they wouldn't roll back."

He smiled. "Nope, wasn't me."

I made one smooth nod and walked to the table. "When it comes to pool, I'm the pro." I winked as I powdered my hand and gently slid the pool stick through my fingers. "I'll show no mercy."

Franklin smiled and licked his lips. "Well, bring it on, Ms. Pro," he said as he shook my hand. "I don't lose many games and especially not to a girl."

I can't explain it, but there was something in that simple handshake that soothed me. I was by no means, attracted to him. However, his touch did make me smile. "The first time is always the best time for a Nina Moore butt kicking." I winked, as I bent over the table. I looked over my shoulder at him. "Don't take this personally, but this game is going to be over real quick," I said matter-of-factly, as I sent three solid balls running for cover in the left and right corner pocket.

I stood and arrogantly strolled around the table. I could feel his eyes on me and I had no mercy for him. Two more balls slipped into the middle and lower pockets.

"Man, you weren't kidding." he cringed.

I stood and leaned against the table. "No Mr. Franklin, I

Homeless Love

wasn't kidding," I winked "but I'll let you break the next game." I smiled as I turned around to finish what I started.

"My goodness Ms. Lady, you know how to make a man run for cover." He winked and racked the balls for another butt kicking.

I had no mercy on the second, third or fourth game. After he was sick of me kicking his butt, he soon cried uncle.

"Ok, Nina you got me." He said placing his pool stick on the table and lifting his hands in the air. "I did have Jake tighten your skates, but you didn't have to beat me that bad."

I leaned against the pool table. "Why did you have him tighten my skates?"

He lowered his head and tapped his feet on the gray torn carpet. "I didn't want you to keep getting hurt." He mumbled so softly I could barely hear him.

As we stood and stared at each other, in that weird moment of silence, I had no response to his answer. At that very moment, a waiter wedged himself between us, and I was glad for his rudeness.

"Frank your food is ready." He said stepping between us.

"Thanks, James." Frank said, slapping the man on his shoulders.

"Not a problem." He said and walked away.

"Lunch, I thought we were going to play pool."

"I wasn't going to miss the opportunity to feed you." He winked. "So if you please, follow me."

I unscrewed my stick and tucked it into the bag, I picked up my jacket and slowly followed him into the back room, trying to shake off a fear that I didn't understand. My eyes fell on a table sitting in the center on a dance floor and one dilapidated candle burned in the middle of the table.

Nervously I asked. "What's this?"

He walked me over to the table. "These are french fries, and these," He pointed. "are catfish nuggets, you do like catfish don't you?"

"As matter of fact I do."

"Then have a seat Ms. Lady." He said pulling out my chair.

When I returned to the office almost two hours later, I realized that Franklin had left a burning imprint on me. When was the last time I'd truly enjoyed myself with a man? He truly understood how crazy my father was, he even understood my fight to break away from him and the struggle was not going to be easy. My smile faded a little when I looked up and saw Alex staring at me.

"A penny for your thoughts?" she mocked.

"They're worth more to me, than you."

Her eyebrows arched mischievously. "Oh, do tell."

I shook my head. "Like I said, it's not worth anything to you. How's your headache." I asked changing the subject.

She took a seat. "Oh its fine, hey, Walter wants to know if you want to have dinner with us."

"When?"

"Tonight."

I looked away hastily. "Where you guys going?"

"Steak and Stack."

I picked up a few files. "In San Diego or Irvine?"

"In Irvine, he's meeting a client out there."

I opened a folder and pretended to be reading it. "No, you guys go on, I have too much work to do. Maybe next time." I said as Franklin's smile kept slipping through my thoughts.

"Are you sure?" she asked, gawking at me.

"Yeah, I'll be fine, besides the opening's in a few weeks, so I have to fine tune everything." I opened another file. "Did Richard tell you about the Papers Plus account?"

"I'm working on that, but I haven't ordered any supplies for the San Diego office. I don't have a clue as to what he's talking about."

I nodded. "What time are you leaving for Irvine?" I asked.

She stood. "Right after work."

"You guys will be right in the middle of traffic."

She shrugged her shoulders. "That's fine, as long as I don't have to drive there or back, traffic don't bother me."

"What time is dinner?"

"Eight. What's up with all the questions?"

"I'm sorry." I blinked.

She put her hands on her hips. "I'll be home late tonight."

"That's fine." I smiled.

Chapter Twenty

༄

Nina

Ꮢd been spending so much of my free time with Franklin, the opening just crept up on me, but now I as stood in the doorway of the second Moore Legal Assistant Group in San Diego, I was still secretly praying that I could be with him.

"Nina, can I speak with you?" Richard whispered in my ear, interrupting my fantasy.

I jumped at the sound of his voice, and immediately I was pissed. "No bad news, Richard, not tonight," I spat. But my mood lightened when I saw him in a three-piece, medium blue suit; a light blue starched shirt and blue tie. I smiled and shook my head. He raised his pant leg, so that I could partake of his baby blue socks and blue alligator shoes, then he playfully pushed me into the vacant office.

"No, I have good news, girlfriend." He smiled as he closed the door behind him.

Clenching my teeth, I said under my breath, "Where in the hell did you get that gold tooth from?"

"Oh child, its fake." He grinned even wider.

"Then, why in the hell do you have it in?"

Satisfaction pursed his lips. "My friend likes it."

"Richard."

"Nina, folks in the South sport gold teeth." he smiled again.

I cringed, but tonight I was not going to allow others' problems to concern me, after breakfast I was heading back to Riverside. "Whatever turns you on." I answered.

"Whatever turns my friend on." he smiled. "But that's another story. I came in here to tell you that we found the San Diego supplies."

"You did, where?"

"They were shipped to a few schools throughout California."

Shock and anger laced my voice. "What?"

He held up a manicured hand. I was beginning to wonder about this boy. "Don't worry, it's a nice little charity tax break. I'm still puzzled as to who signed your name to the authorization slip," he said, shoving a stack of yellow faded slips into my hand.

I stared down at the papers. I counted five sheets. "This list of supplies will take care of all the public schools in Southern California for the rest of the school year." I glared at Richard with heated eyes.

"Exactly." He grinned showing off that damn gold tooth.

"This is my signature, but I never signed this."

"I know." He continued to grin.

"But I don't want to donate $20,000 worth of school supplies to these freakin' bullshit schools." I screamed as the names of the schools stood out at me. "I want my money back and an investigation started."

"I know you do, Nina, but the donations have been made. The kids are writing you their tiny little thank you notes."

"I want my money, Richard."

"The editors of Book Matters Magazine and Lawyer Expression Magazine want an interview." He shouted, knowing those two magazines were my favorites.

"Oh Richard." I dropped my shoulders. "That's $20,000."

"Nina, think of the tax write-off." He said patting me on the back as I bounced my head off the wall.

"Twenty thousand dollars," I repeated.

"Well, you can't pull out," he snapped.

"Where the hell is the good news?"

"That was the good news. Their little sabotage backfired. All this publicity is really going to pay off. So you don't have a problem." He said with both hands in the air. "Thank God, the Riverside office could spare a few supplies, so everything worked out."

"Why didn't you tell me this earlier, like yesterday?"

"I wanted to have something in my hands to show you before I came with the good news."

I looked down at the schools once again. I threw my hands in the air. "When life gives you lemons, you make lemonade." I kissed him on the cheek.

He stroked my face. "The article came out in the Lawyers Post regarding this office and the Orange County office. You're on your way, girlfriend. So cheer up, you've accomplished a great deal."

"Then why am I so sad?"

"You have to ask yourself that question." He said and walked out of the office.

I shook my head and walked behind Richard who was truly showing off tonight. I went over to the bench where my mother and Aunt Louise were sitting. I kissed them both as Mother reached for my hand. I kissed her again, on her baby soft face.

"I love that wonderful playroom you built for the kids."

"Thanks Mother." I smiled.

"But I don't understand why you put these comfortable chairs and the smoked glass table in the foyer."

"So my clients can fill out forms and keep an eye on their children."

"Brilliant Nina." She said with a wink. "Now let's see what fault your father can find."

"Thanks Mother, and where's The Judge anyway?" I asked as I searched the crowd. "I just saw him a few minutes ago."

My mother pointed, with shaking hands, toward the corner of the foyer. "He's talking to those guys."

"Who are they?" I asked.

"I don't know, sugar."

I felt a knot forming in the pit of my stomach; I knew if The Judge sent one client my way he would own this place, just like he thinks he owns the Riverside office. "I don't want The Judge to have anything to do with the San Diego office."

"I understand."

"If he sends one person, . . ." I stopped as I realized my mother and I agreed on the same thing where The Judge was concerned. I was just about to sit next to her and give her a big hug, when she tightened her grip around my hand.

"What's wrong?" I asked, looking in the direction of her gaze.

"Who got a thong on?"

"Aunt Louise, I asked Mother what was wrong."

"Oh my bad." She chuckled.

"Aunt Louise, you need to stop watching BET." I hissed.

"What you betting on now child and I want in."

I didn't bother to reply, as I glanced down at my watch, and my guests began to leave, I was grateful that the evening had come and gone without incident. Alex and Walter were in one of the offices playing on the phone. Harold was talking to a very expensively dressed woman, and Maria and The Judge were walking toward us.

My mother's painful squeeze made me wrench. "What's wrong?" I asked as I continued to survey the room for something out of the ordinary.

Her hoarse whisper broke my heart. "Nothing, baby, it's just the pain."

"Do you want to go home?" I asked looking down at her wet eyes.

"Who got a bong?"

"Aunt Louise." I hissed.

Mother kissed my hand. "No, sugar, I'll be alright."

"I thought this was not going to open up until much later, there would have been a great deal more people here." The Judge said, standing right behind me.

I slowly turned around to face him. "I had no choice, Judge, things got out of hand, so I just went with the flow."

"Well, it still turned out nice. I'm going to take Maria home, she's not feeling well," The Judge said as he bent down to kiss Mother on her cheek.

"Why can't Harold take his wife home?" Mother said turning her cheek away from him.

"He's talking to Sherine Guin who owns a large PI firm in Los Angeles. I don't want to take him away from his money. He has my grandson to support. She pays well!" He winked.

"You always seem to have an answer for everything, don't you?" Mother snapped.

"Mother Moore, I can wait until Harold is finished, it's no big deal." Maria said, rubbing her stomach.

"I'll get Alex to drive you home," The Judge said waving Alex toward him.

"No." I said pulling his hands down to his side. "You don't want to do that, I'll drive Maria home."

"You can't leave your party to take Maria home, she lives almost 30 minutes away." The Judge said gawking at Mother.

"Just take the girl home, Harold, and stop all this bullshit!" Mother shouted, which caught Alex's attention. "Judge, take Maria home and get back here as soon as you can."

He stared angrily at Mother. "I'm not coming back over here, so come on, and let's go." He said, under his breath, almost snatching Mother from her seat. It seemed he didn't care if he hurt her or not.

"No, Harold," she shouted, and gave him an evil glare. "You do what you have to do. I'm sure I'll be home before you."

I was shocked when I saw so much hatred glowing in my Mother's eyes.

"Go!" she shouted, which momentarily silenced the entire room and brought Alex running toward us. I looked around for

Harold to take his wife home, but he and Ms. Money Bags, Sherine Guin, had disappeared.

"Oh shit!" Aunt Louise said, sliding away from mother.

I watched in disgust as The Judge and Maria slipped out the door.

"Mother, are you alright?" Alex asked, kneeling down next to her.

"I'm fine." She snapped, which made Alex flinch.

"Where's The Judge?"

I dreaded answering her, but what could I do. "He took Maria home." I whispered.

"Where's Harold?" Alex asked.

Walter, who simply didn't know to keep his mouth shut, pointed toward the exit sign. "I saw him go in the back with this lady."

I turned and glared at him. "Mind your business." I sneered through clenched teeth.

He quickly stuck his hands in his pockets and looked down at the floor.

Alex stormed in one direction and Richard managed to hurry the rest of the onlookers in a different direction.

"Aunt Louise, please stay with Mother."

"I don't smell no burnt rubber!" she said, sniffing the air.

"Okay, Aunt Louise." I smiled and turned to Walter. "Keep an eye on them, please."

Franklin

As I stood in a dry bar with men and women, both past and present alcoholics, the thought of being sober as a way of life scared the hell out of me. It took everything I had not to drink when Nina was around, now these AA fools were telling me I couldn't drink at all. That's some scary shit! The thought of giving up my security blanket made me ill. As long as I had a little something in my stomach and something in my duffel bag, I was okay.

After Nina told me she wouldn't be able to meet me until Monday or Tuesday, I felt my world crashing down on me. I found myself walking around in a daze; my body aching for something to drink, and the pain of the past was near.

"Franklin!" Patty, a silver-haired, white woman, shouted.

I looked up. "Yes?"

"You're mumbling and we can't hear you, please speak up."

Uneasiness slipped back to grip me. I slid my hands into my pockets and cleared my throat. "I remembered the night I prayed to God to send someone into my life to help me stop drinking." I chuckled. "I think God is a comedian. Why would he send me Nina?" I shrugged my shoulders and shook my fist at heaven. "Why her? I was fine just the way I was, I was doing great. Now here she is. I didn't want a woman." I shook my head. "And I especially didn't want Nina. I wanted to be clean and sober before she came into my life."

"You prayed, He answered." Patty smiled.

I looked down at my tattered shoes. "But I need a drink more than I need Nina."

"No, you need Nina more than you need the drink." She corrected.

"You don't understand, I have demons, bad demons from my past."

"We all do. That's why some of us drink." A three-month, sober Stanley said.

I shook my head. "You don't understand."

"Have you told Nina about your past?" Pam, a mother of three and sober for five months, asked.

"No!" I stated. "My past is not for her to know."

Pam walked over to me. "If you don't tell her, your past will kill your future with her."

I picked up my duffel bag. "I can't do this. A clean and sober life is not for me," I said as I headed for the door and the nearest bar.

Nina

I was glad to be pulling into my garage. The solitude of the evening was going to do me some good. As soon as I entered the house I kicked off my shoes and dropped an armload of papers, folders, and books to the floor. Staying the night at my parent's house would have been devastating to my health.

The only thing I wanted was a nice chilled glass of wine, soft music and my fireplace, along with a good book. A man would do, but I didn't have one at the moment.

A few minutes later I was seated in front of the blazing fireplace, bobbing my head to the soft melody of Miles Davis. I sipped the Muscat wine and breathed a sigh of relief.

"Yep, all I need is a nice handsome man to ease the kinks out of this old body," I mumbled, as I let my head hang off the edge of the leather couch.

The house seemed exceptionally quiet now that I knew Alex wasn't going to pop in at any minute, screaming my name. I lifted my head off the sofa and glanced around the large living room. Even though the silence was soothing to my soul after the last few days, I wasn't enjoying it at all. I refilled my empty glass and strolled slowly onto the patio, enjoying the night as it covered the land. I leaned against the railing where I could view most of Canyon Crest and some of downtown Riverside. "I'm sitting on top of the world!" I yelled with outstretched arms. Then I dropped them to my side. "But I'm sitting here alone," I mumbled softly.

When I turned, I caught my sad reflection in the patio window. I let my ponytail lose and my hair cascaded over my shoulders.

I sipped more wine, unable to see the pretty woman that Franklin saw. I tried to gather the strength to suppress the need to find him, but he made my sprit so happy, I simply couldn't resist the urge to spend a few hours with him. It was 11:20 when I walked back into the house. My footsteps thundered as I ran up the 13 steps, taking them two by two. I was in and out of the shower in 10 minutes flat.

I pulled my hair into a much neater ponytail, slipped on a pair of gray jogging pants with a matching short-sleeved, gray shirt and headed for the Jeep.

As I flew down the winding hill, changing the gears faster than the Jeep could keep up with me, my heart fluttered each time I thought about Franklin's wonderful smile. It was almost midnight by the time I made it to University Avenue. The streets were deserted. I drove around for a few minutes searching for Franklin's tattered white cap.

There was no sign of him or any homeless people for that matter. It still amazed me that they could just fade into the darkness.

I circled around the block a few times; staying away from Fairmont Park, as instructed by Franklin. But I was running out of places to look.

As I drove down Seventh Street behind the bus station, I spotted many dirty white caps, but none belonging to Franklin. Sorrow began to creep into my spirit and brought self-pity along for the ride. Suddenly the familiar sense of loneliness tiptoed into my soul as I sat in front of the bus station. I didn't understand what I was feeling as I rested my head on the steering wheel.

I allowed the pent up tears to flow, when suddenly the sound of a saxophone lured me into an underlying sensuality that captivated my heart. My ears began to search the night air for the sound when my eyes fell on another old seedy bar called The Music Box.

Without thinking, I turned the Jeep around in the middle of the street, stopped in front of the door and jumped out. This was my chance to find the man behind that breathtaking music, I thought as I entered the dimly lit room.

My mouth fell open and my breath lingered in front of me when I saw that it was Franklin blowing the hell out of that sax.

Homeless Love

I watched as his fingers gently embraced the keys and stroked them so softly. His shoulders were rising and falling with each note, and his melody pulled me roughly, almost violently to him. I was standing right in front of him. His eyes were closed so tenderly, it gave me a sense that he was playing only for me.

I couldn't believe Franklin, the homeless man, was behind the music, which lingered in my heart. The musician that I had been searching for, the melody that haunted me in my dreams was right in front of me. I licked my lips and tried to pretend that his melody didn't affect me, but I lost my breath as his erotic, enticing music forced my body to sway to the rhythm of his engaging purrs. His music was magnificent, I didn't want it to stop; Franklin projected an energy and power that sent a delicious shudder of excitement though my veins. My soul was on fire, and he spoke a universal language that calmed the fears of The Judge's thundering voice. For a long time I felt as if I were floating on air, lifted by the unbelievable power this man had over me. Chills ran up my spine when he licked the reed, wrapping his moist lips around the mouthpiece making it scream notes I'd never heard before. I wanted to cry, the way he made me feel with his music. Lord help the day.

"It was you all the time." I whispered as the music floated over, around, and right through my body. "Oh, my God." I gently exhaled. "But The Judge," I said as one tear escaped from my heart and slid down my face. I released the stress that held my body captive for so long and cried, as I enjoyed my homeless lover's music.

Chapter Twenty-One

Franklin

When I opened my eyes and saw Nina sitting in front of me with her lids closed so sweetly. I repositioned my saxophone between my thighs, slowly and enticingly I massaged the keys, making the sax hum just a little longer. I wanted slowly and seductively to caress Nina's body, to ease her pain, and chase away her fears.

When I hit the high G, and Nina's head rocked back and forth, I started to tingle with excitement.

I teased each note so tenderly until Nina was almost rising out of her seat. Her head dropped oddly forward as if she were drunk from my sweet, sultry melody. I continued to entice her with my harmony, begging Nina to give me a chance. Pleading with her to help me as her beauty tortured my soul. If only she knew that she could save me.

My music had Nina twisting in her chair, arching her body, trying to seek freedom from my musical embrace. I had to fight an overwhelming need to cross my legs, but I didn't move, I had Nina just where I wanted her, vibrating in her seat.

I took the harmony to a light, low hum. Making Nina shake her head at the sensation that flowed through the tiny dim room. If only I could hold her or even touch her, if only I could feel the warmth from her body and the heat from her lips.

I forced the melody to a rolling high pitch, then back again to a pulsating quiver. The intense passion in which I played, made Nina gracefully rock in her seat; I could tell her body needed just what I was giving her. With the low drift of my sax, I softly pleaded with Nina to help me. The yielding, sultry, arousing moans of the sax forced the oxygen out of her lungs. I sighed, as tears fell from her closed eyes to the sticky table.

I played a few more notes, bringing the crowd that came in from the streets to a peaceful calm. With my eyes still on Nina I placed the sax in its stand, and watched as Nina's shoulders dropped.

Nina

"How are you tonight, Nina?" He asked in a voice that carried me up thirteen stairs and gently laid me on my bed.

"Fi . . ." I cleared my throat. "Fine and you?" I managed to answer as my cynical inner voice cut through my thoughts. If only he wasn't homeless, if only I could present him to the family, if only. . .

"Well, I could be better, but I made it through another day, so I'm not going to complain," he said smiling as if he knew what he had just done to me.

I was caught in a weird and wonderful position when two tall gray haired men slapped Franklin on the back. "Good job, man."

"Yeah, that was wonderful, brought in a lot of customers, never heard you play like that."

"I never had a reason," He winked at me, which made me blush.

Once the graying old men were gone, I nodded. "That was great."

"It was nothing." he replied, softly.

"It was nothing?" I frowned.

"The juke box is broken, had a fight in here the other night some guy was slammed against it, his head went right through the front of the darn thing." Franklin said, pointing in the direction of the jukebox.

"Did anyone get hurt?" I mumbled, still gawking at the thickness of his fingers.

"Nope, but I'm sure he had a hell of a headache." Every time his gaze met mine, my heart turned over in response.

"Oh yeah, that's right. Men don't get hurt."

"Yes, we do hurt." Franklin replied.

I turned away from him. What was I thinking? He's homeless, he has nothing, and how in the world would I tell The Judge that I think I've fallen for a homeless man who plays for his supper. I shuddered at the thought of The Judge's anger.

"What's wrong, Nina?" He asked touching me on my arm, sending uncontrolled shivers through my body. "Are you cold?" he asked with a frown.

"No."

He touched me again, and again I vibrated. "You're shaking."

"I'm okay, really." If he didn't stop touching me, it was going to get quite embarrassing.

"Excuse me, are you going to play again tonight?" A pale-faced young lady asked.

"No, I'm calling it a night," he said with a smile.

"Bring out the karaoke!" One of the bartenders shouted.

I stood. "Well, it's time for me to go."

"Do you have to go home so early?"

"I don't have to go home, but I have to get out of here. I can't stand bad music." I winked toward the karaoke.

"Now, wait a minute, some of these folks might have a little talent."

"I'm not an agent and I don't have time to wait for that one good person to show up. Besides I already heard good music for tonight." I patted him on the shoulder.

"Well, thank you, ma'am." He bowed from the waist.

"Let's get out of here!" I shouted over the two people imitating Captain and Tennille's *Do It To Me One More Time*.

"I have to settle my bill, can you wait for me?"

"Sure, go on." I said as I walked outside and got in the Jeep, which was illegally parked. "What in the world am I feeling?" I asked the reflection in the mirror. I must be crazy. "Am I that desperate that I'm picking up homeless men in seedy bars?" I screamed and buried my face in my hands.

"Are you okay?"

I jumped at the sound of his voice. "Oh, yes, I'm fine. Where're we going?" I asked, as I started the engine.

"Going?" He repeated, sounding shocked.

"Yeah, I thought we could go and get a bite to eat."

Franklin looked down at the wad of money in his hand. "Okay, but it's my treat," he said, placing his duffel bag into the backseat.

"But you treated last time." I smiled as he jumped into the passenger seat.

"And you drove last time."

I shook my head. "I'm really hungry, what do you want to eat?" I asked, trying to dismiss The Judge's anger, which was replaying over and over in my head.

"Spaghetti, with lots of garlic bread."

"And lots of butter," I added.

"And a big salad," Franklin said laughing.

"I love cooking spaghetti."

"You can cook spaghetti?" He asked, turning to face me.

"Just like an old Italian Mama." I winked.

"No way."

"Yes, I'm telling you I can. Hell, I'm a wizard in the kitchen."

Franklin pointed to his chest. "I can cook a mean pot of spaghetti, it's one of my favorite dishes."

"My spaghetti is da bomb, but it's too late for me to show off my skills in the kitchen tonight. So what else do you want to eat?" I smiled with a wink.

"Meat loaf." He grinned.

"Meat loaf it is." I answered, as I turned the corner toward the freeway. "Why didn't you tell me you were the musician I was looking for?" I asked once we was safely on the 60 Freeway.

"Nina, it's a long story, but the bottom line is I was just too embarrassed to let you see people throwing money into a brown paper bag at my feet."

"That's crazy, Franklin." I said as I took the Heacock Boulevard exit making a left onto Sunnymead Boulevard. I spotted Denny's on the left-hand side of the street.

"You sure did drive a long way just to eat at Denny's." He frowned.

"I like driving, you don't mind do you?" I asked as I pulled into a parking spot and hopped out of the Jeep.

He grabbed his duffel bag from the back seat. "Oh no, I don't mind. It was wonderful riding and not walking for a change."

"You can leave it in the Jeep." I pointed to his bag.

"Habit." He smiled, as he placed the duffel bag back on the seat.

"I understand." I said and walked through the front door he held open for me. A milky skinned waitress, who eyed Franklin as if she was seeing something new, greeted us. He looked down at his wrinkled clothes.

"Restaurants makes me nervous." He whispered softly as he stuffed the dirty cap into his back pocket, and smoothed his dreads.

"Why?"

"I feel out of place."

"Well, you look fine to me." Even if your hair does look more matted than dreaded, I thought.

"Two?" The tiny, frail looking waitress asked holding up two bony fingers. I shook my head and giggled when Franklin looked behind him.

"She's smart," he whispered.

I elbowed him in the stomach and ran to catch up with the waitress.

Homeless Love

"Do you really want meat loaf?" I asked once we were seated in the far back.

"No. Hey, they have spaghetti."

"No, thank you." I wrinkled my nose and stared at him trying to imagine him without the massive mound of hair on his face and head. I couldn't see anything but the homeless man.

"What's up, Nina?"

"Excuse me?" I blinked.

"What's up, you're staring at me?"

"I have to know, Franklin."

"Nina."

"Franklin, we've been meeting every chance we get. Every time Bones tells me to meet you somewhere I'm there. You know everything about me, my entire family, even the trouble I'm having with my company."

"Yes, I do, and I still say it's an inside job."

"Yes, I've heard your theory." I smiled. "But there's no one on my staff who would benefit from all the shit I'm going through."

"You never know, Nina."

"Franklin, don't change the subject, I just want to know about you."

"I thought we weren't going to talk about my past right now?"

I lowered my head. "I know, but I just have to know. I mean I . . .."

"It's not drugs, if that's what you're thinking."

"I don't want to accuse you of anything?"

"I'm clean." He pulled up both sleeves. "Ashy, but clean," he smiled.

"Yes, you're very clean for a homeless man, that's what's so confusing to me."

He took my hands in his, and I realized I was okay with that. "Does it bother you that I'm homeless?"

"No, not really." I looked down at the menu.

"Not really?"

His touch was overwhelming. I cleared my throat and pretended not to be affected by him. "I don't know."

"Would it be any different if I met you at a club, or a grocery store, would I be more worthy of your time, if I were a clean cut white collar worker."

My shoulders dropped as pain spread across his face.

"Franklin, I'm not here to judge you."

He tapped the tip of my nose. "Good answer."

I turned toward the plate glass window and stared at my reflection. Now I felt very rebellious; as I counted how many heart attacks The Judge would have had by now, just seeing me with this homeless Rastafarian. I smiled inwardly and thought, why not go for a full cardiac arrest.

"How about you come over to my house this Friday night for a taste of my famous spaghetti."

When I turned to face Franklin, he seemed to be glowing. "You mean I get to see where you live?"

My heart was hammering in my ears. "Yes, why not?" I smiled.

Franklin sat speechless as he stared at me.

Chapter Twenty-Two

Nina

Richard was dumfounded as he hung out in my office, on Monday morning, wearing a black and white glitter open shirt suit, still sporting that damn gold tooth. "Honey, I can't believe you invited a homeless man to your domain this Friday for a spaghetti dinner, you go girl!" He screamed.

"I know, Richard, I know." I shook my head and pressed my fingers to my lips, hoping that he would get the hint and sit his ass down before the entire office rushed in. "I offered to put him in a motel and help him get off the streets," I said, adding another level of excitement to Richard's life. "But, he keeps refusing."

Richard slipped into the chair and crossed his legs. "Homeless pride. Some people don't know how to accept help, but at least he'll get a home cooked meal." He winked.

I nodded for a few times. "I, Nina Marie, invited a homeless man over for dinner and a movie." The phone rang calming my panic but raising the fear that was stirring up inside of me.

"Well, you can't turn back now, sugar." Richard grinned and snapped his fingers.

"I know, Richard, but remember you're sworn to secrecy."

"Honey child, my lips are sealed," he said as he sauntered out of my office.

"Yes, Sabrina." I said as butterflies turned in my stomach.

"You have a call on Line 3."

"Can you take a message?"

"I tried, but she insisted on speaking with you."

"Who is it?"

"It's the Williams & Hopper Law firm."

"Okay, I'll take it."

I took a deep breath to still my shaking voice. "Beverly Williams. Hello, Long time no hear." I tried to speak calmly, but it wasn't coming out that way. "What've you been up to?" My stomach ached at the sound of her voice.

"Just fighting crime as usual."

I settled back into my seat. "Fighting crime, I thought you were a divorce attorney."

"In Orange County divorces can be criminal," she laughed.

"Girl, you're something else."

"Me? You're the one," she sang. "I heard a rumor." She said, almost sounding pleased with her little hidden information.

Suddenly, I was anxious to escape from this disturbing phone call. My heart stopped, as Franklin flashed in my mind. "Hold on Beverly, let me close my office door, this sounds like its going to be juicy," I said as I pushed the hold button and bit my bottom lip. I stood up so the blood could circulate and make it back to my head. Damn, damn, damn. I made it a point to keep him a secret. I was about to kick the trash can, but the painful memory made me resist the urge. I inhaled as a salty taste filled my mouth, I couldn't think for the ringing in my ears.

Taking a few deep breaths before picking up the phone, I wiped my forehead free of sweat and sat down. "Sorry it took so long, I had to stomp out a fire." I closed my eyes and shook my head. What the hell was she going to tell me?

"Are you sitting down?" She giggled. "Because I just can't believe it."

I swallowed. "Yes, I'm sitting, go on, don't keep me waiting too long." I replied with a little annoyance in my voice.

"Patricia Hall called me."

I shivered uneasily at the sound of her name, but I calmly managed to say. "Oh, really?" As if Pat's name didn't mean a damn thing to me.

"Yes."

"Gossiping Patricia, who should have been a reporter instead of a lawyer?"

"Yes, that Patricia!" Beverly repeated.

"Okay, let me have it." I said as I licked the sweat from my top lip. My defense attorney attitude skipped to red alert. "What do you guys have on me?"

"Honey, you know how Patricia is always sticking her nose where it doesn't belong?"

"Yes, don't I know that?" Bitch!

"Well, she was down in Riverside last Wednesday evening and guess what she saw."

Oh, hell no, my brain screamed as my palms dripped with sweat and my nerves exploded through my body like a lighting storm. "Get to the point, Beverly!" I shouted. "You're driving me crazy."

"She saw an article in Judge Jean's chambers that said you had opened an office in San Diego and were opening one in Orange County."

I breathed heavily into the phone.

"Are you alright?" she asked.

"Oh, yes, I'm fine," I said as my heart rate returned to normal, and I loosened the death grip I had on the phone.

"Anyway we wanted to call and congratulate you on your success and invite you to lunch today."

"Today?" I repeated.

"Yes, today, we're on our way to Riverside for a meeting. Afterwards we wanted to take you for a quick bite. Nothing fancy, just a congratulatory lunch."

"Well." I hummed as I searched my mind for a out of the way place to eat.

"Oh, come on, Nina, it would be just like old times."

"Okay, that would be great and I have just the place."

Homeless Love

"Oh, don't bother, Patricia has already made reservation at some little warm, quaint café. I have the directions, so I'll be at your office around oneish."

"One is fine, but I'll meet you there, you can give my secretary the information."

"Okay, see you then."

I hurried and transferred Beverly to Sabrina right before I threw up into the trash can. I had nothing to worry about; Franklin only played within walking distance of the park, and knowing Pat nothing around here would suit her taste.

⅋

I leaned against my car, and watched as my three college friends strolled across the parking lot, the same way they use to stroll across the college campus. Arrogant and good looking. "I didn't know this café took reservations?"

"They don't," Patricia answered, throwing her Giorgio Armani scarf over her left shoulder, and kissing me on both cheeks. I hugged Beverly and Phyllis as we giggled like school girls.

"You know Patricia, she hates waiting." Phyllis chuckled, the same way she use to do in college.

"So how did you manage to reserve a table?" I asked rushing to get in front of them.

Pulling down her Ray Bans, Patricia answered. "I have my ways."

"And daddy has a fat checkbook," Phyllis laughed.

"That too," Patricia winked. "Let's go in."

I grabbed Patricia's arm. "Wait! Can't we eat out here?" I shouted as panic, like I'd never known before surged, through my soul.

"On the streets?" Beverly said almost screaming, as she smoothed down her silk firm fitting dress.

"Yes, it's a beautiful September day, and I haven't seen you guys in ages. It's much too noisy in there, anyway." I said looking toward the brown café door.

"No, I reserved a table and I want to eat at my table, and

C.F. Hawthorne

not on the street like some vagabond. Besides, it's hot as hell out here," Patricia, added, storming into the café as if her heels were on fire. Beverly and Phyllis followed suit as they have always done. Now I remembered why I didn't keep in touch after college.

As we sat at one of the largest tables in the café, with a starched white linen cloth and two candles burning in the center, I felt like a mad dog on the verge of biting the hell out of somebody this afternoon.

"Nina, how's that handsome private investigator brother of yours?" I faintly heard Beverly say.

I could barely disengage my view from the door. "Fine." I smiled and turned my sights back to the entrance.

"Are you waiting for someone?" Beverly inquired.

"No, why?" I asked.

Beverly grabbed my forearm. "Well, honey, if you stare at the door any harder it's liable to fall off the hinges."

I looked away. "Was I staring?" I questioned almost out of breath.

"Hum." Patricia breathed.

"Are you ladies ready to order?" A young blond girl asked.

"I'll have the potato soup with garlic bread and raspberry ice tea, two lemons." I said quickly.

"Well, I guess you come here often?" Beverly mumbled, raising an eyebrow at Patricia.

"Not at all, I glanced over the menu, while you guys were gossiping about folks." My voice trailed off when I spotted Franklin walking through the door. Ours eyes met and a smile ran across his face. I hesitated, torn by conflicting emotions; I turned away and looked down at the floor, then back at him.

Franklin walked past the table wearing a long green trench coat, an army bandanna tied around his head—looking like a black Rambo—and his duffel bag slung over his right shoulder. I tried not to stare as he disappeared in the back.

"Judge Howard said nothing about this place being crowded with vagrants." Patricia gasped.

"Oh, my goodness, and you picked it, Patricia, so it's no

one's fault but your own." Phyllis chuckled.

It seemed as if I was being held under murky water, I couldn't breathe, I couldn't see, I couldn't hear. My world as I knew it, was over. Franklin hated to be ignored; now I was forced to treat him as if he were a common stranger on the street, as if I didn't have any feelings for him. As if he never touched my life. I had a much stronger guard up than I realized.

When Franklin emerged from the back with his sax, I wanted him to play a death march. That's what betrayal felt like when he placed the stool practically in front of me and winked. "He winked at you." Beverly spat. "The homeless man winked at Nina." She sang in Patricia's ear.

A warning voice whispered in my head, but did I pay it any attention: "Nooo. He winked at the table." That alone set an alarm ringing in my head.

My heart skipped a thousands beats. When I gazed into Franklin's face, I saw something flickering far back in his eyes.

Franklin

I lowered my gaze to my sax as I tried to swallow the pain of a friend ignoring me. I knew she regretted what was said the moment the words left her lips. I know she wasn't ready to let the world know about me. But I did have a glimmer of hope. Just thinking of her rejection sent my nerves on edge and to top that off, I dropped the damn mouthpiece.

I watched it roll under the table where she sat. When I bent down to pick it up, I felt a soft tap on my shoulders. I turned to see an overly, expensively dressed woman, offering me a $20 dollar bill.

A strange surge of hatred raced through my veins. "You can put it in the jar if you like my music." I uttered sarcastically. "I'm a working man." I said sharply, glancing at Nina.

I seductively licked the reed to moisten it and watched

faces contort. By the end of my second song, everyone at Nina's table was screaming for more. My jar overflowed with dead presidents, but I never, not even once looked into Nina's lovely brown eyes.

Nina

My soup sat cold in front of me. Lost in a trance as I heard his voice so smoothly escape his lips.

"Wasted talent," Beverly whispered into my ear. I blinked softly and turned away.

Franklin made the sax mimic his words, and I felt as if everyone knew he was singing about me. I flinched at the tone of his voice.

"You ever thought you had a friend?" He sang as the sax repeated his words. "But suddenly that friend wasn't there, and you found yourself standing alone." The sax rumbled low. "Then you realize that your friend was just your imagination, a true friend would never leave you standing alone."

Hitting the notes much higher than I had ever heard him go before, forced tears from my eyes. I had hurt him. The shame of not being able to call Franklin a friend forced me from my seat and I hurried toward the door.

The paused note stopped me. I know he wouldn't do that, he wouldn't play my song. But he did, he started with high, but soft notes causing me to take a deep breath. The sounds drifted into a hushed whisper.

I didn't understand what I was feeling, but my heart begged to be released.

I was too embarrassed by the world he represented, to proud to enjoy the gift that God had given him. I walked out the door without looking back, leaving my friend to stand-alone.

After thirty minutes of laying my head on my cool glass desk, beating myself up, because I walked out on a friend that brought me so much happiness, the knots in my stomach were finally beginning to loosen.

Then Beverly's and Phyllis' silly laughter coming from the foyer made me want to throw up all over again. I pushed the intercom bottom. "Send them in." I said before Sabrina could call me.

Of course, Beverly came in first. "Why did you get up and leave in such a haste?"

"I'm glad we drove our own car," Phyllis said as she gawked at my many achievements displayed on the wall.

"That homeless man was wonderful." Beverly laughed, shaking her head slightly. "You missed the entire show. I know your father loathed homeless people, but I had no idea that he passed that hatred on to his bloodline."

"Oh, the bloodline." Beverly smiled. "I forgot about that. Is The Judge still on that kick?" She turned to the others. "Remember she had to keep her male friends a secret just to have a date on the weekend."

"Oh, yeah, I remember that." Phyllis giggled.

"Is that why you ran out, because you couldn't be in the same room as a homeless man?" Beverly smirked, pulling down her Coach glasses.

I rose and walked over to the file cabinet. "Beverly please, my pager went off, and I needed to make a call." I shrugged my shoulders. "That's what happens when you have your own business, you're always eating on the run. Who do I owe for the soup?" Beverly clapped her hands together. "Don't worry about it, we were taking you out to lunch."

"Speaking of lunch, it's over and we need to head back to Orange County before the traffic gets too bad." Phyllis added with one of her stupid giggles. "I have to be in court later today."

"Yeah, sometimes there's a lot of traffic heading back to Orange County," I said as I rolled my eyes and practically pushed them toward the front door.

"Let's keep in touch, Nina, are you ever going to practice law again?"

"No I don't think so."

"Maybe we can do some business once your Orange County office opens up." Patricia winked.

Yes, that would be great," I said as I walked them out of my office and down the stairs. Ignoring Patricia, I kissed the air on each side of Beverly's and Phyllis' cheeks, waved them goodbye, and prayed that I never saw those three bitches again in life.

Slowly I walked up the stairs with my arms folded across my chest and my mind heavy with the vision of Franklin's face, I knew I had to go back and apologize. Again.

As I drove down Seventh Street I spotted Bones and another man going into the bus station, I crossed the center divider, almost jumping the curve. "Bones!" I shouted through the window. "Have you seen Franklin today?"

"No, he's been spending all his time with you," he smiled. "Why, is something wrong?"

I got out of my car and walked up to him. "I was so mean to him today, Bones, I just can't believe it, now he'll probably never speak to me again." Anger knotted up inside of me. The bitches were right, The Judge had really done a job on us. "I ignored him in front of people that I didn't even care about, how stupid."

Bones broke our gaze and stared at the ground. "Frank's a pretty cool guy, Ms. Nina, I wouldn't worry about that, he'll come around," he said with such a critical tone in his voice, it frightened me.

"When?" I questioned.

"Well, I don't know, I can't answer that question." He chuckled with a deep rattle in his chest and throat.

"I know, Bones, I know." I sang as I walked toward my car, I reached in and took out my wallet. "Take this money and do me a favor."

"Like what?" he questioned.

"Search for Franklin and tell him that I'm truly sorry, I didn't mean it."

"Ms. Nina, I'll do that for nothing." Bones smiled.

"Take the money." The other man nudged.

Bones shook his head. I handed the money to the other man.

"Thanks, Ms. Nina, I'll give him the message." The thin young man replied.

"Thank you." I answered as I slid behind the wheel of my car.

"You could have saved him, Ms. Nina," Bones said as he walked away with his head hanging down. His words cut my heart in two.

By the time I arrived home; I was so miserable that I had hurt Franklin, I felt like Judas, but Franklin wasn't Jesus, and there was no way he was going to forgive me. Being ignored was his number one pet peeve.

The answering machine flashed four messages; I pushed the button and listened as Harold begged to spend this Friday night with me.

I laughed to cover my pain. "Whatever Harold, I'm sure that I'll be alone," I said to the machine as I descended up my thirteen stairs to my lonely ass bed.

Chapter Twenty-Three

Nina

Tuesday morning was business as usual. People, problems and concerns. I closed my office door and told Sabrina to hold as many calls as she possibly could. I was bound and determined to prove to myself that I was immune to Franklin, to his kindness, his gentle voice and playful disposition.

As morning turned to noon, I realized nothing was getting accomplished. Around three o'clock my soul began to crave Franklin, like a sinner pleading to be saved. I pushed the intercom button and waited for the sound of Sabrina's professional voice.

"Yes, Ms. Moore."

"Sabrina, I'm going to leave early, is there anything on my agenda that can't wait until tomorrow?" There was a brief moment of silence, not the normal grunting that Alex made as if I was bothering her.

"No, there's nothing."

"Great. Have you seen Richard?" I asked as I gathered things to take home, I wasn't sure if I would even be in tomorrow.

"He went to San Diego, didn't you check your messages?"

"Oh, shit. That's right. Well, never mind. I have to stay and lock up."

"I can do that for you if you really have to leave, all I need is the code."

"All right, I'll give it to you before I leave."

"Ok Ms. Moore." She said so professional.

I made a few phone calls, signed a few forms, and ignored the problems stacked on my desk.

"The code is 1107, make sure you shred it once you're done." I said handing her the code on a sheet of paper.

"I will, Ms. Moore, and you have a wonderful evening."

"Thank you, I will." As soon as I left the office, I began searching for Franklin, in every dive and hole in the wall that he had taken me to. No one saw him. The sense of urgency to find him was driving me crazy. I fought hard against tears that I refused to let fall.

I felt powerless to resist what my heart was telling me. My entire body, mind and soul were engulfed in despair. I felt drained, hollow and lifeless. I didn't intend to allow myself to fall for him, but shit happens. With an exhausted sigh, I drove home to drink away my pain.

Chapter Twenty-Four

Nina

That dreadful Friday slipped in like a thief and was going out like O.J. Simpson. Pointless. I was not able to get anything accomplished, and bad attitudes were hovering around the office like a plague. Especially mine.

Richard was constantly complaining about Sabrina, and I failed to see what the problem was, so I let it fall on deaf ears.

I was surrounded by mounds of closed accounts and denied loans. Phone calls were unanswered and paychecks unsigned. I was losing control of my life and The Judge's condescending words rang in my ears. "You're moving too fast Nina, you need to settle down, find yourself a good man and let him run the show." I shook my head and popped four Tylenols.

I spent the entire week searching for Franklin and not even Bones could find him, and he could get into places that I couldn't! Acquiring information from a street person was like finding Jimmy Hoffa's body. It wasn't going to happen.

Sabrina's soft voice sliced through my pain of losing Franklin like a machete. "Ms. Moore."

I pushed the intercom button. "Yes."

"The contractor from Orange County is on Line 1, he doesn't have the permits to start construction on the new building, also, on Line 2 there's a very excited young lady from the San Diego office."

"Oh, shit, I forgot about that."

Homeless Love

"Sabrina, you handle Line 2 and I'll handle Line 1. She'll bring you up to speed."

"Yes ma'am." She replied sweetly. "Oh, one more thing."

I sighed. "Yes?"

"Alex called, she'll be staying another week in Bermuda."

"Whatever, Sabrina. I'm too damn tired to fight another battle. I'll handle her when she returns."

"Yes ma'am."

g

After what seemed like several years of arguing with Orange County City Hall, I needed a drink, a movie, and a long nap in bed with a cold compress spread across my head. Everything was falling apart. The accounting wasn't adding up, the bills were not getting paid, and the Orange County permits were being delayed. The December opening was looking bleak. I needed to get the hell out of Dodge and take a month long vacation like Alex.

A light tap on the door brought me out of my slumber. Sabrina stuck her head in my office. "Good night, and have a wonderful weekend." She smiled.

"You too, Sabrina." I replied as I forced a smile on my face.

"Don't stay too late," she winked.

"I won't."

As I sat alone on yet another pitiful Friday night with nothing to do, I sighed at the memory of a couple of days ago. I had a friend that I could call on, someone who made these crazy, lonely nights bearable, but my pride got in the way.

The memory of Franklin's sad face seared my soul and the pain was too great for me to bear. I grabbed my purse and locked the office up for the weekend.

After running a few errands, with all intentions on staying in for the entire weekend, I arrived home a little before eight. The phone was ringing off the hook.

I found myself on the verge of tears when I answered it.

"Hello!"

"So you home, why you never return my calls?"

I dropped my shoulders. "Oh shit, Harold, things got a little crazy over here."

"Is everything alright? I tried to call your cell phone, but I kept getting a busy signal or a strange man's voice.

"My cell phone is disconnected, I'm going to arbitration regarding my phone bill."

"What happened?"

"Evidently, someone cloned my cell phone number and my bill got up to $2,500."

"Nina, I know damn well you can afford to pay that bill."

"Yes, I can. However I didn't run up the damn thing."

"I know you got my message, so is it alright if I come over?" He asked ignoring my issues, which pissed me off.

"I know damn well you don't want to spend a Friday night with me, so what's up?"

"Nothing's up."

"Like hell, what's up, Harold Jr.?"

I listened as he tried to come up with a good reason to use my house to commit adultery. "Just come clean Harold, what do you want?"

I heard him take a deep breath before he blurted out. "I want to use your place so me and a friend could spend some time together, that way if Maria calls, I can answer the phone."

"Oh, hell no. I don't want to get caught up in your madness, I got enough of my own. Besides, you shouldn't be treating Maria this way. You guys have only been married a hot minute."

"Why would you care how I treat Maria, you don't even like her, and she damn sure don't like you," Harold shouted into the phone.

"I never said I didn't care for your wife, so why are you getting so bent out of shape."

Homeless Love

"Whatever, Nina, like I said she sure as hell don't care for you."

"Whatever, Harold."

"It's not whatever, Nina, why can't you do me this one little favor?"

"Harold, I already told you, I don't want to get caught up in your drama."

"So the answer's no?"

I sighed. "Yes, the answer is no, besides, Maria can call you on your cell phone."

"She don't have this number and I left my other one on the dresser."

"You sneaky bastard, don't you see what creeping around got The Judge?"

"What did it get him?"

"Crazy-ass Rachel, for starters." I shouted.

"We use protection."

"Harold, that's not the point, what about the pain you'll be causing the mother of your unborn child?"

"She'll get over it. Mother did."

"Bye, Harold."

"Nina, I'm not far, can't I come over, just a little while." He begged. "I'll call her from there so she can check the caller ID, then I'll be out of your hair."

I slammed the phone down without answering him. I took a quick shower and was about to settle down with a good book and a bottle of wine, when the damn doorbell rang. I sat still, trying to ignore it, but he wouldn't go away. Rage almost blinded me when I swung the door open with full force; positioned for a battle. "I told you hell no." I screamed.

"Excuse me." The voice rang.

I flicked on the porch light. "I'm sorry I thought you were my brother. Can I help you?"

"I was wondering if you would be willing to help the homeless out?"

"With what?" I asked as I reached for my bat.

"Food, shelter, love." He smiled.

"Excuse me."

"Well, we are in desperate need of love mostly." He smiled.

My hand went to my mouth to stifle a scream. My eyes froze on a soaring dark handsome face standing in my threshold. His smile and his eyes told me he could be Franklin, but the well-pressed cream suit and white-rimmed shirt he was wearing said he must be someone else.

"It's me. Franklin." He said with a wide smile and a deeply imbedded dimple in his chin.

I was momentarily speechless with shock. I reached up, and passed my right hand over his bald head, which gave me chills. My hand moved from his head to his strong jaw line. His skin felt like warm silk.

"I never knew you were so tall," I whispered, as my heart raced in my chest. It felt as though I was seeing him for the very first time.

"May I come in?" He asked, as he wiped the beads of moisture that clung to his forehead.

I slowly stepped aside, never taking my eyes from his body. He was so handsome with a dazzling display of strength, when he strolled through my door, his gait spoke a language that I simply didn't understand.

"Why are you shaking your head, is something wrong?" He asked.

"No." I blinked once and only once, just in case he was a figment of my imagination.

He pointed toward me. "The door, you haven't closed it," he said softly serenading me with his bright smile and dazzling almond eyes.

"Oh, yes." I laughed, not realizing I was still standing with it open. I turned away for a brief moment as I laid my head on the closed door, trying to remain calm. I couldn't think of a prayer to say other than give me strength, Father God. "I'm sorry for staring."

"No need to apologize."

Homeless Love

Oh, be still my heart. I couldn't help but gaze at his black velvety skin; his beauty was strong and exquisite. The homeless man simply could not compete with the man that was standing in front of me now. I simply couldn't understand the transformation. "The other day at the café, I have to apologize for my behavior."

Kenny G ricocheted off the white walls, filling the room with the irresistible warmth of love. Now that the real Franklin was standing in front of me, I couldn't breathe. Even the fireplace seemed to glow more brilliantly. Then he placed one trembling finger to my lips.

"No need to apologize Ms. Lady, I understand. You can never be apart of my world, so." He opened his coat and spun around. "I have to come into yours."

Father help the day. I swallowed and turned away from him. "Would you like something to drink? I have wine, beer, and . . ." I said unable to say anything else.

He turned me around and took my chin into his powerful hand, "Nina, I'm an alcoholic." He said looking deep into my eyes. Thunder and lightening started between my thighs.

"Oh." I replied. As I watched the moonlight dance in his cold black eyes.

"Nina," he said again. "Did you hear me?"

I wanted to taste him so badly; I couldn't stand it any longer. I reached up and cupped his clean-shaven face in my hands as I brought his soft lips to mine. Franklin grabbed me around my waist and brought me into him so tightly I couldn't tell if it was his heart beating in my chest or my own. His kiss felt so good, so right I didn't want him to stop, but the damn doorbell forced Franklin to pull away from me.

"Are you going to answer that?" He motioned with his head.

"No." I whispered softly as I rose on my toes to taste his warm, soft lips once again. Then suddenly my heart leaped into my chest. "My brother." I said as I floated back to earth, shaking off a tense black silence that began to surround me. I looked down at the floor.

"I understand, I'll go into the another room." He said as he turned to walk away.

"Franklin, no, wait. I can do this." I lied and kissed him one more time. I turned to face the door. I knew that Harold was going to take the information right to the devil himself, so I braced myself as I placed two trembling hands on the cold doorknob. I took a deep cleansing breath and opened the door. Franklin stood behind me as I began to breathe again.

"You left Nina in my cab." The driver said.

"Oh, thanks, man." He took the sax from him and reached into his pocket. He gave the driver two dollars. "If I had more. . ."

"No problem sir, you enjoy your evening."

He placed the sax gently on the floor. "I will. Thanks," he said softly as he closed the door.

"You call your sax Nina?" I frowned.

"Yes, I used to call her Lynne."

"Lynne?"

"That was my mother's name, but after I met you, I knew she had to be a Nina, because she felt so right in my hands." He said, bringing me into his arms once again. "From the first day I saw you, your beauty was stamped on my soul."

"Franklin." I breathed.

"No, Nina, I mean it. Your will and pure determination to succeed is empowering. If only I had an ounce of what you've been blessed with, I could probably stay off the streets."

"But you can, Franklin, and I'll help you."

His hands slid from my body, and he turned away from me. "Nina, I need more help than you realize."

"I know, I can help you." He walked over to the fireplace. I followed him. "What's wrong?"

He turned to face me. "I'm wanted by the police."

I dropped to the sofa. "The police." I cringed.

As he looked deep into the fire, my childhood fears crept back into my soul. The Judge was right. When Franklin dropped to his knees in front of me. I wanted to run, but the tears in his eyes told me to stay. "Please, don't judge me when I tell you."

I bit my lip to hold back my own tears. "I can't make that promise, Franklin, but I have to know. Why are you wanted by the police?"

He took a deep breath, as streams of tears fell from his eyes. "I killed my family." He said softly.

"Excuse me." I said praying that I didn't hear him right.

He cleared his throat and spoke again. "I murdered my entire family," he said forcing my childhood fears to come between us once again.

Chapter Twenty-Five

Franklin

J looked up and saw terror spreading across Nina's face. I grabbed her wrist. "Nina, it's not what you think."

She rose to her feet; I could feel her pulse beating rapidly in my hands.

"Franklin." She mumbled softly and eased her wrist from my hands.

I stood and walked toward the plate glass window. I saw from the corner of my eye that Nina was slowly making her way toward the front door. "I was drunk, Nina." I shook my head. "I was drunk, and I crashed the car, killing our only child, my little baby girl." I said as my cries of regret filled the room. "My wife called me and asked if I could pick JoLee up from dance class. I said I would. She could tell that I had been drinking, she could always tell.

We got into an argument, and I jumped into the car and reached JoLee before she did."

"Oh, Franklin." Nina moaned as she touched my shoulders.

Biting back the familiar pain of a past that seemed to taunt me, I agonizingly continued. "I had been drinking with the guys to celebrate my promotion as senior homicide detective. I came home and continued to drink. I still can't remember till this day what happened, I don't know if I fell asleep behind the wheel or if I just ran off the bridge. I just can't remember, Nina. All I can see is our three-year-old daughter's bleeding skull in my hands." I jerked away when Nina touched my shoulders again.

"Franklin."

I held my trembling hands out in front of me as if something were laying in my palms.

"Franklin, you don't have to."

Her voice was so soothing to my soul. I didn't want to tell her about the tragedies, but I had to face the demons of my past.

"Yes, Nina, I do."

"My wife never came to the trial." I let my head drop out of shame as I gnashed my jaw teeth to hold in the tears. My knees refused to hold up my agony as I collapsed to the floor. "Oh, God, Nina."

"Franklin." Nina cried and hugged me, as I pressed my head to her stomach.

"My mother died the same day I was sentenced to eight years, eight lousy years in prison. That wasn't enough time. I killed my entire family; I should have gotten life or the chair."

"But you're doing life, Franklin, you've sentenced yourself to a life of hell." She groaned.

I pulled away and pointed to the carpet as if it were the courtroom floor. "My mother died, Nina, my best friend died in the courtroom, right there in front of me. She died of a broken heart." I inhaled as my past became a scalding memory in my soul. "That's why I left Chicago. I couldn't do four years of probation in the same city that I killed my entire family in."

Nina knelt down beside me and held me in her arms as I cried. I could feel her heart pounding.

Abruptly, I pushed out of her arms. "I'm worthless and I can't pretend that this time is going to be any different from the last three times I've tried to fight my demons and get off the streets, to get off the bottle. Look at these clothes, Nina." I shouted. "I had to pawn my father's watch and my Mother's pearl earrings just to be able to buy something to wear tonight." I stripped off the cream color jacket and threw it to the floor.

"Franklin, this is the first step."

"What in the hell am I going to do with a suit living on the streets?" I shouted as tears streamed down the side of my face.

"It's going to be alright, Franklin, we just have to pray," she said as she begun to whisper a prayer.

My throat balled into a knot so tight I couldn't speak. I tried to reject the 23rd Psalms she was chanting, but years of drinking to forget seemed to find their way from some dark place in my soul, and the words seemed to melt my hardened heart.

Holding her, smelling her, feeling her breast against my chest made me feel as though I was going to black out, from the ecstasy and the realism that I was actually holding Nina in my arms.

Suddenly her soft body overpowered me, I seized her face in my hands and kissed her soft salty lips. It made me shiver. And when Nina kissed me back, my dreams became a reality, I needed her to be mine. Curling her body into my arms, I imagined Nina's flesh touching as much of mine as possible. I sighed long and hard, almost collapsing in her arms. I continued to drink every drop that my Nina offered.

Nina

"This is not supposed to be happening." I whispered, trying to ease out of his arms, but once I felt his desire, I was unable to convince my body that what I was experiencing wasn't real. I tried to pull away, but my legs wouldn't budge. The signals were not connecting, at least not the right ones.

I became too weak to stand and I slipped out of Franklin's arms back to the floor. I stared into the blazing inferno; tormented by the confusing emotions I was experiencing. To love or not to love.

When Franklin sat in front of me, I tried to resist the urge to touch his chest, but his cologne filled my senses; with such urgency, I couldn't resist. I closed my eyes, and allowed my hands to slide down the front of his shirt.

He rested his head on my breast, and began to gasp slow romantic breaths, his soft moans abruptly woke me from my trance and I stopped caressing his chest and placed my hands on my lap. Simply not believing I was falling in love with a homeless man. I jumped to my feet and walked out onto the patio so the fresh air could clear my thoughts.

Then I heard The Judge's voice screaming. "Nina Marie Moore, I can't believe you're fucking a homeless man, when I have this perfectly hardworking, pocketful of money, white boy." I shook my head; I wanted what was in my heart. I wanted Franklin.

When he walked up behind me and wrapped his arms around my waist, my knees became butter.

"I understand I have nothing to offer you and you have everything you need."

"Franklin." I said softly as tears dropped from my eyes. "But I'm alone."

"Look at this house, girl, it's enormous, and a Jacuzzi on the deck so you can sit and look at all four corners of this earth. You're sitting on top of the world, Nina."

I turned to face him. "But I'm sitting alone," I sang as he wiped the tears from my eyes. "I'm sitting alone."

"I don"t even have a chair so I can come and sit with you Ms. Lady."

I took Franklin into my arms and cried. "My heart wants something that will cost more than I'm willing to pay."

"I know it's a price that you can't afford to pay right now, and I'm not asking you to do something you'll regret later. I have enjoyed your friendship, your company and your laughter. You've allowed me in your world and I won't stay if you don't want me to, I just wanted you to see me, the real me. So you wouldn't be ashamed to call me your friend."

"I'm so sorry, I didn't mean to hurt you." He silenced my apology by placing a finger to my lips.

C.F. Hawthorne

"You don't have to apologize, the two worlds should have never met, but I'm glad that I've had this chance with you."

"But I want you in my world."

His large hands took my face and held it gently. "Then ask me to stay in your world. Nina please ask me?"

I lowered my head as confusion took control of my senses. I looked back into his dark eyes and brought his lips to meet mine. "I can't Franklin." I cried. "I'm too scared. I can't ask that question right now."

He dropped his arms, and turned to walk away. The sound of his heels bouncing off the patio deck echoed in my heart, as he walked toward the front door. He turned back to look at me, I wished he would have kept going, but he didn't. There was something deeper than just tears in his eyes.

"Nina, my insides are screaming that I'll never get the chance to hold you again." He reached out his arms to me. "So may I please kiss you one last time? I understand that you're torn between two lovers. Your family and me." He rocked back and forth on his heels. "I'll never ask you to choose."

I walked into his arms and he held me, and for the first time it felt right. He kissed the top of my head and squeezed me tight. I could hear his heart beating so softly and sadly in his chest. When he kissed me, hot tears rolled down my cheeks. I didn't understand what love felt like, until now.

Ignoring The Judge's mocking voice inside my head, I took Franklin's hand as the last trace of resistance vanished. "I can't ask you to stay forever, Franklin, but can you stay just one night in my world?" I said as the creaking of all 13 steps ricocheted in my heart, causing my flesh to crawl.

Chapter Twenty-Six

Nina

When I pushed open my bedroom door, the sweet scent of raspberry engulfed me. I closed my eyes for a quick moment, as I began to float around my room. When I opened my eyes his beauty was magnified ten thousand times by the soft light from the hall. I felt tingling in the pit of my stomach that was too powerful to resist. I began to undo one button at a time, on his shirt. His firm ebony flesh released the butterfly in my world, making my stomach turn in response to his touch. I stood on the tips of my toes and took his chin into my mouth. He pulled me into his arms and held me there, taking in all that was going on around us. He pressed his body into mine as we were trying to become one.

Breathless, I took his hand and led him to the bed. Without looking from his gaze, I slid my hands into the night-stand. He breathed a sigh of relief when I handed him a handful of condoms. My Franklin gathered me into his arms and gently laid me on the bed.

His tongue was slow and thoughtful, sending shivers of desire racing through my body at full force. He removed my sweatshirt and I eased out of the pants. When he began to drag his tongue down my stomach, sending a new spiral of ecstasy through my bloodstream, I shivered. His kisses became urgent as he traveled around places that had never been explored before.

I melted and let go of any reservation I had as I reached for the heavens above. I shrieked, as his mouth excitedly discovered secrets that my body kept hidden from other lovers.

I could tell Franklin tried to keep control of his body as he discovered countless mysteries that made my soul quiver, but my cries sent him into full force.

"Franklin, please." I managed to whisper once he allowed me to catch my breath. "Please, Franklin." I moaned.

Understanding my soft whimper, he silently moved on top of me like a cougar stalking his prey. After finding the fortune he sought so deep inside me, he seized my passion and rocked me like a newborn child. We were in exquisite harmony with one another, until the involuntary tremors of my body destroyed the hard shell that he had built up around him. Thunderous sounds of ecstasy slipped past his lips.

I tried to open my eyes when Franklin cried out, but the pure force of ecstasy demanded they remain shut. Not wanting this moment in time to end, I obeyed his slow pulsating rhythms that told me time was near. I squeezed my eyes tighter as our bodies burst with exquisite pleasure. I was filled with an amazing sense of completeness when Franklin's warm breath slipped into my ears.

"I'd walk to the end of the earth to spend one more night with you." He whispered.

Franklin

When the sun allowed Monday morning to slip in. I realized that I'd held Nina the entire weekend. She felt so good in my arms, so right. Bones knew what he was talking about. I had to stop drinking, before I could make her mine. I shook my head realizing that I needed one more day with her, one more stolen moment in time.

"Can't you stay?" I pleaded, fearing that this was just a dream.

She looked at me with those big beautiful brown eyes, and kissed me on my forehead. "I wish I could, but I have to see the building inspector in Orange County today or I'll never get my permit," she said as she sat on my lap, half-naked.

"I understand." I mumbled. I don't know if it was the look in my eyes, but she slid off me and kissed me so gently on the lips.

"You're going to be fine. Just keep your mind on the Lord and your thoughts on me. Read some of those scriptures that we read, and by the way, she said as she slipped on her baby blue skirt. "You were fantastic yesterday."

Did this woman know how to make a man feel great or what? "Really?" I smiled.

"In church yesterday, when you played with the choir," I winked.

I drew her into my arms. "I knew that." I winked back and my lips brushed against hers. "You make me feel good all the time."

g

I stared at Nina as she drove away, thanking the Lord for giving a broke, alcoholic, convict one more chance, with a wonderful, beautiful woman like Nina. I had to agree with her father, there was no way I would have allowed my beautiful baby girl to get involved with someone like me, but the thought of never holding Nina again was more frightening than facing The Judge.

I strolled back into the house and sat in complete silence, trying to remember the many prayers Nina and I shared.

Around 12:45 I woke with a pounding in my chest. I was sober four days, three of which I had Nina to watch over me. Now that she's gone, the voice in my head told the ache in my stomach to began kicking the shit out of me until I gave it want it wanted. A drink, just one drink, one sip, so I could think, but she threw the booze away and what she didn't throw away, a large truck came by and picked up for some sort of wine auction.

The harder I tried to ignore the pain the more persistent it became. I rummaged through the kitchen for a small bottle of something, anything to take the edge off of what I was feeling. Just so I could think a little clearer. My trembling hands brushed across a small bottle of cooking sherry, I grabbed it from the back of the counter, and raced up the stairs.

I smiled, as the memory of my Nina's moans lingered in my ears, but once inside the bedroom, my spirit began to feel weak. I shook off the thought as the sherry called my name. I grabbed my sax and my cream jacket, along with a few of Nina's $20 dollar bills, then raced for the front door, shouting the 23rd Psalm.

Nina

At the end of the day, I finally made it to a place that I never craved before, home. The Orange County meeting took up my entire day, keeping me away from Franklin. But I was glad to be home to hold him one more time. Just so I would know this was not a dream, I dropped the keys several times as I rushed to open the door.

Excitedly, I ran into the dark house as the taut feeling of isolation slapped me in the face. I clicked on the kitchen light, and took in a deep breath staring at the appalling sight. My kitchen was in shambles. It looked as if a hurricane had hit it, destroying everything in its path.

"Franklin, baby." I yelled. "Are you still here?" Oh, God, please let him be here. I prayed. "Franklin." I said softly. I didn't want to jump to any conclusions, but I could feel my throat closing up. When I made my way to the living room, the solitude was heavy on my shoulders. No jazz filled the empty spaces of silence. No TV blaring, nothingness lingered in the air.

Tears slowly found their way down my cheeks. I knew it

was all a dream as I stood in the threshold of life. I walked deeper into the darkness to draw the blinds open.

Electricity jumped started my heart, Franklin was standing on the balcony with his naked back to me, my pulse pounded when the towel that was around his waist gently slid to the floor, and he softly began to play our song as he slowly turned around to face me.

"Father help the day," I said, his invitation was a passionate challenge that was too hard to resist, and I mean hard to resist! I hurried past the two candles, which sat on the patio table with a black tablecloth and my fine china.

He sat the sax down and took me into his arms and began filling me with a breathtaking pleasure that made my insides swell with excitement. Aching for the fulfillment of his lovemaking, and the protectiveness of his arms, I did what every woman knew she should never do. I cried. Completeness found its way to my soul.

I was speechless when Franklin let me fall out of his arms. What could I say, what needed to be said. I knew that I would walk to the ends of the earth to be with this man.

As we strolled up the short distance to my bedroom I turned to him, "You know a girl could get spoiled coming home to a naked man and a spaghetti dinner."

"That's what I intend to do." He smiled.

"Well, what about that kitchen. . ." I pointed before closing the bedroom door.

"Don't worry, I'll get that in the morning. It'll give me something to do, before my AA meeting."

"Oh, so you intend to stay." I smiled.

"Only if you'll have me."

"I'll have you, Franklin, if you'll have me."

Chapter Twenty-Seven

❧

Nina

Jdidn't want to return to Orange County on Friday morning but I had no choice, I had taken the rest of the week off to be with him, to bask in the loving he had to give me, to find myself and discover my meaning in this place I called life.

Those AA meetings are damn good. I discovered that I was a functioning alcoholic and that I could continue to fool myself as well as others for as long as it took.

As I sat in the Orange County meeting trying to focus on the matter at hand, I couldn't. I only had five days to get my shit together before Alex came home, but I didn't want to be apart from Franklin, when he wasn't making me laugh until my stomach ached, he was encasing me with a spiritual union like nothing I had ever experienced before. I didn't want him to leave, he couldn't leave.

My selfish needs were forcing me to set aside every decent thread of my proper upbringing to be with the man I loved, and I was willing to stand up to the devil himself to be with him. However, I still cowered at the thought of losing my family. It was a price too high for me to pay.

"Ms. Moore, are you ready to sign the final papers?"

I slowly looked up. "Yes."

On my way back to the main office in Riverside, I sang. *"Don't Worry, Be Happy."* Yes, everything was going to be all right. I was now the proud owner of three Legal Process Service businesses, another article was being published, and I found the man who was going to love me for the rest of my life. No one had to know he was homeless so how could anything go wrong? I had spoken all too soon as I turned down the street and saw four cop cars and a fire truck parked in front of my office building.

"Excuse me, what's going on?" I shouted as I exited my car.

Karen, one of my employees shouted. "Nina, over here."

"Karen, what happened?" I asked as tears began to build up in my eyes.

"The place was vandalized."

"Vandalized, when?" I whispered in total shock.

"When we got to work, the place was a mess."

"So why the fire truck?"

"Richard smelled gas so he called the Fire Department."

"Oh my God." I mumbled as I passed my hand through my hair. "Is everybody alright?" I asked.

"Richard sent everyone home."

I was numb with increasing rage and shock.

"Why didn't someone call me, you knew where I was."

"We couldn't get to the phone book, they wouldn't let us in, your answering machine at home picked up, but I didn't leave a message."

I gave Karen a brutal and unfriendly stare. "Where's Richard?" I asked through clenched teeth.

"Over there." She pointed toward the police officer.

When Richard spotted me, he waved me over, with an expression of fright pasted on his face. He put his arm around me.

"Richard, what happened to this place?"

"The police officer thinks it's a bunch of kids causing some trouble in the neighborhood." He mumbled releasing my neck.

"Kids!" I screamed.

Richard shook his head. "I think differently."

"And why is that, sir?" A tall red-faced officer asked.

Looking at me, then back at the red-faced cop, Richard

put his hand on his hips. "Kids would have destroyed everything, not just the computers and everything in the file cabinets. The entire office is destroyed, but the kitchen is in perfectly good order. Nothing's been touched. Why would kids miss the opportunity to break a few dishes?" He stopped, snapped his fingers, and turned away.

"Are you're trying to be a small time detective?" The officer said to Richard, who turned back to him with rage in his eyes.

Richard stepped in the man's face and put his hands on his hip. "I may act like a woman, but I'll kick your ass like a man."

I hurried and stepped between them. "Can we please go inside?" I asked, before Richard was arrested for threatening an officer.

"In a few minutes, ma'am." He held up his hands. "We have to wait until the investigator finishes in there."

"Okay," I answered, wrapping my jacket around me. "Can you hurry this up a bit, it's cold out here?"

He nodded, glared at Richard, and disappeared inside.
I took Richard's hand. "Let's go to the back. Did these kids leave anything behind?" I asked exhaustedly.

"Nope, not a thing." Richard answered, as we walked toward the back yard.

"How bad is it?"

He rocked a little. "It's pretty bad, Nina. I mean all the files are lost, the hard copy as well as the computer copy. Even if we worked with a staff around the clock, it's gonna take us at least a three months before we're up and running." Richard said as he made stick people in the dirt. "If it were kids, why didn't they take the Halloween candy Karen was hiding from her boys?"

I bit my bottom lip, willing the tears not to fall. "I don't know. Who would do something like this, Richard?" I closed my eyes. "I mean, why would anyone want to hurt me like this?"

"I don't know, but we're gonna get to the bottom of this, don't worry. And by the way, Sabrina quit yesterday."

"Yesterday, why wasn't I notified?"

"I didn't want your week of relaxation to be disturbed, of

which you still have to fill me in on." He winked and bumped my shoulders with his.

"There's nothing to tell, Richard." I blushed. "I think I'm in love."

"Oh, Nina-Girl. I'm so happy for you." He mumbled and looked away.

"What's wrong?"

"In the midst of all your happiness I had to be the one to let you down."

"You didn't let me down. Shit happens, then you move on."

He stopped and turned to me. "Oh, girl, what kinda shit is this man laying on you and does he have family?"

Chapter Twenty-Eight

✧

Franklin

J leapt out of the bathtub and ran to the window. I knew it was going to be trouble the moment I saw Alex slap money into the cab driver's hand. I stood frozen when the front door slammed so hard the windows rattled. I sat on the edge of the bed with a towel wrapped around my waist dripping wet and praying that I could just disappear. Boy, did I need a drink right now! I sat still, planning my escape as Alex's thunderous steps echoed through the house.

I stood to my feet and tried to run into the bathroom, but it was too late, her screams could be heard miles away.

"Who the hell are you?" She yelled, "Who let you in?"

I brought my hands over my chest, down to my side and back over my chest again. "I, I'm Franklin."

"Franklin, who?" She sneered, looking at me with her face all twisted up.

"Nina's friend." I managed to say between her flesh-burning gaze.

She put her hands on her scrawny hips and leaned back on one leg. "Nina ain't told me a damn thing about a friend named Franklin."

I smiled nervously and licked my lips. "We just met." Stupid thing to say once the words left my lips.

She zipped past me. "Is Nina here?" She shouted from the bathroom.

I seized the opportunity to grab something from the closet. "She's at work."

"And she left you here, alone?"

"She wasn't supposed to be gone the whole day." I answered as I slipped my legs into a pair of jeans. When I turned to face the bathroom, Alex was standing in the doorway gawking.

"Who did you say you were?" She squinted.

I slipped on a shirt and extended my hand. "I'm Franklin."

She looked at my hand and back at me. "Who?" She frowned.

"I'm a friend of Nina's, you can call her at work. She'll tell you all about me." My eyes lit up when the information finally hit her brain.

She brought her hands to her mouth. "Oh shit, you the homeless mofo she told me about."

Shame forced my head down. "Yes, I guess I am."

She walked around me smiling. "I was expecting to see a dirty, stinky, grungy man with open sores covering his body from not taking a bath."

I tried to pick my dignity off the floor. "Well, that's not me."

"I can see that." She raised both eyebrows. "Nina's letting you take a bath, right?" She said as she walked around me inspecting my goods.

I shook my head. Now I know why Nina was so afraid to tell her family about me. If they're anything like baby tigress Alex, I know the rest of the Moore clan would never accept me for who I am. Instead, they would always judge me for who I used to be.

"She's not letting you sleep here, right?"

I guess my silence told the whole story, because the bitch in her came out like wild woman.

She started waving her hands in the air. "Oh, you have to get the hell out of here. I don't give a damn where you go, but you're no longer welcome here. Now you can leave and never return or I'll call the police and you'll never see the light of day.

Our father is a judge, and he don't take no shit and he can't stand homeless folks like you." She pointed. "So get your shit and get O-U-T, out."

"I knew this was a bad idea from the start." I mumbled as I slipped on my shoes.

"You got that right, Mr. Homeless Man, now pack your shit and get the hell out of my sister's life, you can't stay here, you're not welcome here, bye-bye."

"But…"

"But, my ass." She added as she pushed me out the bedroom. "You have to leave. My father is gonna have a cow, when he finds out about you."

I grabbed my sax and my jacket, leaving the clothes Nina bought for me in the closet along with my self-respect.

"You ain't got shit to offer her and you ain't gonna steal all her shit from her including her self-respect."

As I began to walk down the stairs, I turned back to Alex who was right behind me, yapping in my ear. "Please tell Nina I said good-bye."

"There's no need to leave a message. She'll never get it. If you don't know anything about Nina, you should know this, it's all about the money with her, you're only a tax write-off."

"A what?" I turned.

"A tax write-off. Nina does this shit all the time. Helps folks out that's in a bind." She stopped talking and glared down at me. "Of course, she's never brought her charity cases home." Alex put her hands on her skinny hips. "You're the first and the last, now go." She waved.

I held up my hand to block off her offensive tone and continued down the stairs. "Okay, you've said enough, I got the message." I placed my hands on the cold doorknob. "Just tell her good-bye," I said as I slowly closed the front door. I tried to pick up the pace as I heard the door open.

"Franklin." She yelled.

With a calm temper, I stopped, turned to face the witch from hell.

"What?"

"My advice to you is never try and contact Nina again or I'll have our father on your ass so quick you won't have time to piss on a street corner. Have a great life." She said and slammed the door.

"Bitch!"

Nina

There was a cold, poignant feeling in the air once I walked through the garage door. I wasn't sure if it were some residue from my office being destroyed, or if I were really experiencing some unnatural entity that was taking over my life, but I wasn't enjoying the feeling.

"Oh, shit you scared me!" Alex screamed, when I threw my keys on the kitchen counter.

Then I knew it was an entity from hell that came to rob me of my joy. "What are you doing here? I thought you were supposed to be back next Wednesday."

"Walter had to fly to New York." Alex hugged me around my neck so tight I thought I was going to pass out. "We had to cut the trip short." She babbled.

I pried her hands from my neck and went to the kitchen sink to wash my hands. "How long have you been here?" I asked.

"A couple of hours." She slurred.

"Have you taken your things upstairs?

She grabbed me again. "No, I love you, Nina."

Once again I forced my way out of her arms. "I love you, too. Why you have to hug so tight?"

C.F. Hawthorne

"Cause I missed you, girl," She smiled, rubbing my arms.

I was a little leery at her warmness, but I returned her smile anyway. "Listen I didn't have a chance to move any of your stuff in here, I've been too busy."

"That's okay."

I glanced up the stairs. "I didn't give your landlord notice either."

"Hey, don't worry about it. I can get Harold and some of his friends to help move my things in here. Hey, any news on the party?"

"Well, some shit happened at the office today and we might have to push the party back a few weeks. I have to handle this before I can concentrate on Orange County."

"What happened at the office?"

"I'll tell you later, I'm exhausted and I just want to soak in a nice warm bath and take a nap." I slipped off my heels. "I have to be back at the office later tonight."

She sucked her teeth. "I would pour you a glass of wine, but we seem to be all out." Alex said, staring at me.

"I got rid of the alcohol."

"All of it?" She shouted.

I shook my head. "Yep, every bit of it."

"Even the ones you had imported from Italy?"

"Yes."

She waved her hands in the air. "Why?"

"I'm a functioning alcoholic, Alex."

"Bullshit, Nina, you had thousands of dollars worth of wine in that fucking closet and you threw it all away."

"Alex, it's only wine, it's being auctioned off, I'll get a fair price."

"That wine collection was your life."

"It was probably destroying my life. I was drinking two, maybe three bottles a day. I was depleting the collection anyway."

She shook her head. "I can't believe you."

"Listen, I've had a hard day, and all I want to do is go upstairs and rest, and once again if you going to be bitching about everything that I do, we might have to rethink you moving in here."

"Oh, so you have a problem with me moving in here, but you ain't got a problem with a low life, good for nothing, homeless man mooching off of your simple, black ass."

Her words stopped me dead in my tracks. I slowly turned around on my toes. "Where is he?" I asked through clenched teeth.

She raised her brow. "I sent him back to the pit of hell from where he came."

"What?"

"You heard me, I can't believe that you would sink so low, all these attorneys, doctors and even judges want to get in your pants." She gazed at me with a bold half smile. "And you give it up to a man that don't even own two pair of pants. How stupid are you?" She added, twisting the knife in a little farther. "How desperate are you?" She sneered.

"Franklin!" I shouted running up the stairs. "Franklin!" I screamed from room to room. I ran down the stairs into the game room and then outside onto the patio, where I lost control. Things started to fly across the patio in all different directions. My heart began to race as my soul began to slip from my body.

"How dare you." I screamed, madder than I've ever been in my life. I walked inside and went up to Alex. "How dare you? Don't you fucking back away from me." I shouted as I grabbed a handful of her braids.

"Nina?" She screamed and fell to the floor.

"How dare you come into my house and tell my man to leave. I've allowed you full run of my home, my cars and even my bank accounts." I slammed my baby sister's face against the refrigerator and I felt no remorse. "But you will not have full run of my life."

"Nina!" I heard her cry, but I couldn't stop.

I lifted her up by her hair and pushed her into a corner. I was only a few inches from her face. "I give you everything, I give this family everything, and what do I get in return, everyone on my ass about what's right. Well, I've had enough." I hit the pots that hung from a rack in the center of the kitchen so hard they went crashing to the floor. "I've had enough, Alex."

"Nina, please, it ain't that serious."

"Well, it's serious enough for me to kick your ass, now pick up your shit and get out." I screamed pointing toward the front door. "Go, Alex."

"Nina, please, you're not thinking straight!" She said, licking her split lip.

I could feel the blood slowly draining from my head leaving a slow pounding sensation behind. Then I saw myself crying at the foot of her grave. "Alex, you have to leave now or I'll have to plead insanity to the police. So please leave, now!" I said softly.

"I have to talk to you, you don't know what you're doing, and this man has done something to your mind, Nina this is. . . ."

I could no longer take any more of this simple bitch's pleading. I grabbed her by her skinny little arms and shoved her ass out the front door. She continued to scream and yell, pounding on the front door until I could no longer take it. I slowly opened the door, but only wide enough to throw her purse in her face. Her red and yellow suitcases followed shortly after that.

She stuck her bare feet in the threshold, blocking me from closing the door. I guess she thought the ass whipping was over. Bitch was wrong. I slammed her feet so hard in the door it bounced open, and I slammed it again.

"You're a sick bitch." She shouted. "I heard about lonely old women letting nice clean men into their lives to rob them blind, but this is fucking ridiculous." She screamed limping down the drive with her suit case dragging behind her.

The walls seemed to be closing in on me, as I strolled around the empty, cold house in lonely despair. I picked up the phone and called the one person who understood what I was going through.

"Hello."

"Richard, he's gone." I cried into the phone.

"Oh, sugar, I'm sorry, did he leave a note?"

"I don't know, I haven't checked the rest of the house."

"Maybe there's a note or something or maybe he just stepped out for a minute, you said he enjoyed walking around the neighborhood."

"No, Richard, Alex kicked him out, she made him leave."

"Alex? What the hell is she doing back here so early? I thought you had until next week sometime?"

"I don't know, I came home and found her here and Franklin gone."

"Oh, Nina, I'm sorry."

"God only knows what Alex's evil heart told him. This man could never speak to me again. What am I going to do without him, Richard?"

"You're going to get in your car and go and find your man, honey, don't let no mooching sister steal your good loving."

"That's what she called Franklin." I cried.

"What, a good lover?" He asked.

"A moocher Richard." I yelled. "She called him a moocher."

"Lord, I can't believe the skillet is calling the kettle black, that child don't work for the money you pay her as is, and she damn sure don't pay her way around your place. She has managed to convince you, that she should move in with you so you won't be so lonely, and she's never home."

"Richard."

"No, Nina, someone has to be the one to tell you that your baby sis, Lil sis, or whatever the hell you call her, is using the hell out of you."

"Richard."

"Nina, don't stop me, child, I'm on a roll. I have a great deal of pent up emotions where Alex is concerned."

"But, Richard, that's my sister."

"I don't give a flying pigs ass whose sister she is, that heifer has to go. The only reason she doesn't want Franklin around, because her stank ass will be out on the streets."

I was just about to step in and put out this fire, when his words hit me like a ton of bricks. For the first time Richard tantrums made sense, but I still needed some clarification. "Do you really think she's mooching off of me?" I asked.

"Oh honey. Please, everybody in the office knows that Alex has everything because of you. How many jobs has girlfriend got fired from before you hired her?"

"Seven." I mumbled.

"Seven freakin' jobs in one year. How in the hell do you get fired from a nursery? You pick up the plants, you put down the plants. You arrange the plants, you rearrange the plants. Oh, my God, you don't have to be a rocket scientist." Richard was screaming so loud he really was starting to sound like a woman.

"Richard." I screamed.

"Yes, girl."

"I have to go so you can calm down."

"No, what you have to do is get that homeless sister of yours out of your house and send her mooching ass back to The Judge, I bet he'll straighten her ass up real quick."

I lowered my head and slid to the floor sobbing, as the pain from my heart ricocheted through my body. I rocked back and forth, hugging myself across my aching stomach as I clenched the phone in my hand. I didn't understand what my body was going through as the pain began to glide down my back, around my legs, even my toes began to ache.

"Richard, I have to go." I mumbled. "I can't make it back to the office tonight."

"Nina, sugar, you okay? I'll come over there if you want me to?"

"No, I'm fine, goodnight." I mumbled.

"Good night, sugar."

Homeless Love

I placed the phone in the cradle as the room began to spin out of control. I crawled to the stairs, using the banister for support in order to steady my long ascent up those thirteen stairs. I swallowed a lump that was forming in my throat. "Franklin, baby, please come home," I cried into the darkness as I crept into the comfort of my bed, where I could still smell Franklin on the sheets.

"What do I see in him, Lord, that I couldn't see in others?" I prayed with my fingers locked so tightly together they began to ache. "Was it real love, dear God, compassion or companionship?" I whispered through clenched teeth. "Do I need him for all of the above? Tell me what to do? Father God, give me the answer."

The phone rang several times before I picked it up.

"Hello."

"Baby girl, I saw Franklin coming out of J and J Liquor Store." Richard sang into my ear.

I dropped the phone to the floor and threw off the covers. I ran down the stairs, frantically grabbing my keys from the counter top. I wiped the tears from my eyes and jumped behind the wheel of the Jeep, bound for downtown Riverside.

I searched every place I thought Franklin could be. I asked everyone that crossed my path; eventually I ended up in Fairmont Park. The one place Franklin demanded that I stay away from, especially at night. I swung the Jeep into the parking lot and jumped out.

"Franklin!" I screamed. "Franklin, baby, please it's me, Nina. Franklin!"

"Hey, shut up." I heard a voice shout.

"Have you seen Franklin?" I asked into the blackness of the trees.

"Who the hell is Franklin?"

"A friend."

"I can be your friend." A stranger insisted, walking out of the shadows of the night.

C.F. Hawthorne

I backed away. "No." I shrieked. "I don't want another friend, I want Franklin. Have you seen him? He plays the saxophone." I cried, as my mind became a muddy mess when the stranger grabbed my wrist and forced me into his arms.

"Come on, sugar, I need a friend just like Franklin needs a friend." He smirked, reeking of stale whiskey and dried urine.

Suddenly, it felt as if every homeless man was coming out of the darkness, like zombies, I took my key and jammed it into his face. As soon as he released his grip, I ran for dear life, by the time I reached the Jeep, I was in a cloud of tears. I raced out of the parking lot without turning back.

As my heartbeat returned to a normal pace and the mud cleared from my mind, I continued my search down the boulevard for my soul mate.

I spotted a couple walking hand and hand, they paused before crossing the street, and the woman reached up and gently kissed her lover on the lips. I froze as Franklin's passion surged through my veins. I drove home in tears.

Chapter Twenty-Nine

few days later I watched Alex as she walked toward the building, with big shades on. I felt sorry that I kicked the shit out of her, but only for a moment. Because I had something more waiting for her. When she walked through the front door, Karen greeted her with a smile.

"I'm still on vacation." I heard her sarcastically say as she stormed into my office without knocking. "Am I fired or what?" She screamed.

"I slowly turned around and stared at her. "No, you're not fired." I replied and turned my back to her once again.

"Then, what Nina," she screamed. "Karen has nested at my desk, placing her dime store shit all over the place. So where am I going to sit?"

I turned to face her again. "You have a new position."

"A new position?" She smiled and looked in Karen's direction.

"Yes, I decided to promote you."

"Me? A promotion?" she repeated as she squared her shoulders, let her head fall back for a few seconds, then smiled in Karen's direction once again. "Wow a promotion." She laughed sitting down in front of me. "About last night, I was only looking out for your welfare. I hope you understand."

I smiled and nodded. "And I'm looking out for my welfare as well. Your things are already packed and waiting for you in San Diego."

Everything came to a complete halt, as Karen's laughter raced through the double doors and landed in her lap.

"San Diego!" She shouted. "Nina, you know I can't live in San Diego," she begged.

"I didn't say you had to live in San Diego, dear, you just have to work there if you want to stay with the company."

"Nina, I can't do San Diego. I can't live that close to The Judge, I'll die."

"Oh, you'll live, Alex, because if you look deep in your soul, you'll see you're just like him and the two of you deserve each other." The intercom buzzed.

"Ms. Moore, the files are ready." Karen said trying to hold in her laughter.

"Thank you, Karen. Excuse me, I have to take care of this." I said without looking in her direction. She ran out of my office crying like a baby.

"What's all those tears for, child?" I heard Richard ask as he stopped her in the hall.

"I'm being banished to hell." She screamed all the way to her car.

Chapter Thirty

Nina

"Jt's way past 10 o'clock Nina, and I have to go home." Richard said as he put an arm around my shoulders. "Come on, let me walk you to your car and see you off."

"Go home, Richard, I'll be fine."

"Well, you don't look fine."

"Well, I am." I said as I broke down and started crying.

"Nina, Nina, Nina. This is not fine. Why don't you take a few days off? I can handle things here. The staff will be in early tomorrow, we're going to have this office back the way it used to be."

"But the files, Richard, my clients list. If I don't get things running soon, I can lose everything."

"If you don't get yourself together, you will lose your mind. Now go home. We can worry about the files later."

"I can't ask you to do that," I whispered wiping the tears away.

"Child, you're not asking me anything, I'm telling you, besides if I need you, I know where to find you." He smiled and kissed my forehead.

Breathing a sigh of relief, I shook my head and gathered my things. There was nothing to take home, almost everything was destroyed, so I secured my purse under my arm and left the cold, empty building.

Richard and I talked for a few minutes in the parking lot, and then we parted. I drove around and searched the streets again for Franklin. I didn't even see Bones who was always on one street corner or another. The bus station was empty, even the parking lot across from the station was free and clear of homeless people.

I drove by The Bar and The Music Box, praying that I might get a glimpse of him. But I had no luck. Reluctantly, I headed home.

As I shoved the key into the lock of the deserted house, I was still on the brink of tears. Having everything in the world isn't much if you don't have someone to share it with, I thought as the stillness surrounded me. I walked to the refrigerator and opened it, the half pitcher of red Kool-Aid forced the tears from my eyes.

Misery weighed heavily on my head as nothingness surrounded me. I missed Franklin: his laughter, his comical sense of humor, his conversation, and the sexual healing he gave me with his music. In my heart I've always been afraid of this kind of pain. The kind that you couldn't tell if it was your mind that was making your body hurt or your heart.

I slowly walked up the stirs, disrobing with each painful step. I fell onto bed and grabbed my heart as I pulled the blanket over my naked body and screamed in agony for Franklin, as painful spasms of lonely fear gripped my soul.

"We are one in the same Franklin." I cried. "You have love without a home, and I have a home without love. Together we're homeless love."

Chapter Thirty-One

✧

Three weeks later as I sat in my office, I wasn't in any better shape than I was the night Franklin left. If anything, I was angry with him. If he had any feelings for me, he should have come by or sent word by Bones or something, I mumbled as the buzzing intercom interrupted my thoughts.

I stared at the phone for a few minutes before answering it. "Yes."

"Alex is on line 1 for you." Karen said softly.

"Is it business or personal?" I asked hardheartedly. Even though Alex saved the Riverside office by making back up copies and storing them at home, I was still pissed at her.

"She didn't say."

"Well, find out, Karen, that's your job!" I snapped sarcastically before disconnecting her.

She buzzed again. "Nina, Alex said it's an emergency." I pushed line 1 and breathed heavily into the phone. "Is this call concerning my mother?" I asked through clenched teeth.

"Nina, it's not Mother, she's fine, but we really need to talk."

"We have nothing to talk about, Alex."

"Yes, we do, I was wrong I shouldn't have screwed in your life, I know that now, but you have a bigger problem."

"Yes, I know. I have the opening of Orange County and this damn party the WIB are having for me, which you forgot to cancel."

"I'm sorry, Nina, but it's not that."

"I know, Alex, you're always sorry. You know I don't have

time for this shit, I have a lot on my plate."

"After what I did and you sending me out here to work next to the devil, I've grown up and I'm sorry, really I am. But I have to talk to you, it's about Rachel."

"Alex, I told Mother that I was through passing information around, and I'm telling you. I don't want to hear anything unless you guys are sick. Is Rachel sick?"

"Nina, this girl is more than sick, she's demented. I think she's the one behind all your problems."

I stood to my feet. "What!"

"I saw her at Embarcadero Park last Thursday night."

"And?"

"And she was with Sabrina."

"So."

"Nina, think. Sabrina just moved here from Houston. How in the world did she ever meet up with Rachel?"

"Hell, I don't know."

"That's my point. She and Rachel have no reason to know each other. I read the police report and it did not mention anything about forced entry. I called the security company; no false alarms were ever reported. How does Mother and The Judge know everything that was going on in your life?"

I cleared my throat.

"No, it wasn't me, I never reported anything to these crazy ass folks down here. The Judge is evil, and he's dragging Harold and Mother into his lair. Sabrina is the culprit."

"Alex, you're bored." I huffed.

"Nina, listen to me. Didn't Richard say that Sabrina quit the day before the Riverside office was vandalized and everything was stolen?"

"Yes, but I still think it was kids."

"Why in the hell would a bunch of kids hit your place and not anyone else's?"

"I don't know, and I don't give a shit." I answered out of

breath.

"Everything that has happened to you, it has to be from the inside. I mean how else would someone get to your accounts and have all of them closed, including your cell phone, which has nothing to do with the company. Inside job, Nina."

"Alex, I've told you that I don't want to deal with this shit, and I don't think Rachel would go this far as to make me lose my company."

"She's not trying to make you lose your business."

"Then what?" I screamed.

"She's just evil and she's trying to make you lose your mind!"

"My mind. Why?"

"Nina, you're under a lot of stress trying to open two businesses, one right after another. The Judge is on your ass about the bloodline, Rachel's on your ass about kids, like she's your man or something."

"So?"

"So she's jealous and pissed off."

"For what, our childhood?"

"That too, but remember when she needed you to represent that crazy, crack smoking, husband of hers and you said no."

"It had nothing to do with him smoking crack, I didn't know he smoked cracked then. I just didn't practice law anymore."

"That's neither here nor there. Shit, girl, are you listening to me? Rachel doesn't care if you were practicing law or not, you turned a family member down. Her."

"Alex, that's crazy. I can't imagine she would do something like that."

"Lord have mercy, you have no common sense do you? If the Riverside office is cracking up and things going wrong, credit cards being cancelled, IRS on your back, thirty to sixty day freezes on bank accounts for no reason, come on, Nina, you were bound to nut up. What she didn't count on was the support of your staff."

"You got all this from one little meeting you saw? You never did like Sabrina."

"No, I didn't like the tramp, but I got all this from the notes I found at Rachel's place."

"You snooped around in her home?"

"Well, she was always coming over here with a briefcase to have private meeting with the devil. So I told her that I would baby-sit those little demons. Lord, those kids are bad as hell, especially that little yellow ass KayRon, that girl slapped the hell out of me the other night. I wanted to shake her little ass, but she so light, I knew I was going to leave a bruise. I already got the devil on my ass, I don't need Child Protective Services after me too."

"Alex, that's family, and we don't talk about family.

"Anyway." Alex went on. "I saw the briefcase."

I shook my head. "Where?"

"Well, it was sort of in the downstairs closet, on the top shelf under some blankets and old clothes."

"You actually went into that hell hole of a closet?"

"Yes, Harold said that would be the first place he would look."

"You told Harold?"

"Yes, anyway I got the briefcase down and saw all the papers, she has the letter that was sent to the bar association, stating that you weren't practicing law anymore and she had your address change, that's why you didn't know anything about your license being revoked. She was doing a number on you girl."

"That bitch." I screamed. "Does she know you saw the papers?"

"I think so, because that angel from hell asked me about those papers."

"Oh, my God, Alex."

"Girl, she was pissed. I thought she was going to shake the shit out of me. Thank goodness, she didn't find out about me snooping in her computer."

"Wait! Wait! You broke into her computer?"

"Yes, girl, I did, and found out that Rachel and Sabrina had a thang going on. Rachel frequents the Lesbian sites and that's where she found her soul mate Sabrina."

"She's gay?"

"Yes child. Oh and get this, Sabrina walked into the San Diego office looking for a job."

"A what? Didn't she think you were going to recognize her?"

"I almost didn't," she replied in a low voice, "she cut her hair and dyed it black. You remember how trampish she used to dress. Well, this girl had the nerve to dress like a preacher's wife from the country. I mean this chick had the dress past the knees and the high collar to the neck. I almost hired her."

"What stopped you?"

"She forgot to take off that hussy red nail polish."

"And you know hussy red when you see it." I laughed.

"You got that, big sis."

My heart stopped when Alex called me big sis. I took a deep breath. "Alex, I'm sorry for allowing Franklin to come between us, and I'm sorry for whipping your ass that night in the kitchen."

"It wasn't Franklin, Nina. It was me, I should have minded my business and let you handle yours. I mean, hell, you got three businesses and I'm living with Satan. If they put me out, I'll be homeless and I'm sure you'll take me in."

"Yes, I will," I mumbled. "but I'm still sorry for hurting you."

"Nina, I understand what happened to you in the kitchen that night, when you kicked the shit out of me."

"But my behavior was unacceptable, I should have never put my hands on my sister."

"Nina, I told you that I understood. If some ho' thinks she's gonna come between me and my soon to be husband she has a old fashion ass whipping coming her damn self. So I understand. Truly, I do."

My mind slipped away and it wasn't until I heard the word husband, that I began to pay attention.

"Excuse me, but did you say that you and Walter are getting married?"

"Yes, Nina," she screamed, "I'm getting married."

Homeless Love

"When?" I asked trying to sound happy for her.

"We haven't set a date. He wanted to be married before the baby's born, I wanted to wait until after." she said softly and slipped into a calm silence.

I sat motionless with the phone glued to my ear. I was speechless as the news bounced off my heart and echoed through my soul. I felt trapped by her words. I tried to fight another battle of tears, but I lost. My voice broke miserably and I cried, I don't know how long I cried before I regain my composure. Somehow, I managed to speak. "Alex, are you there?" I asked as I dried my eyes.

"Yes, I'm here." She said softly as her voice began to crack.

"Nina, I'm so sorry that you're so sad. It makes me sick that I caused your pain. If I could make it up to you, you know I would."

"I know, Alex." I mumbled as I sniffed.

"I was selfish and inconsiderate."

"That's okay. You've apologized enough, now all you should do is concentrate on giving The Judge a happy, healthy grandchild."

"He doesn't know and I'm not telling until I have to." She hissed into the phone.

"Okay." I said as I witnessed a little bitterness in her voice.

"Have you heard from Franklin?" She asked softly.

I was silently thinking of the many nights that I spent looking for him. I closed my eyes and swallowed the bitter taste of loneliness from missing him.

"No, I haven't heard a word." I said softly. "When I went into the bus station to get those sticky buns for the staff, I asked Lilly if she had seen Bones. She told me that Bones had died."

"Oh, Nina, I'm sorry to hear that," Alex said with genuine remorse in her voice.

"We had a memorial service for Bones. I took out a full page ad in the newspaper, hoping that Franklin would come or at least someone would know where to find him."

"Did he come?" She asked softly.

"Nope, I sat and waited until the entire church was

empty. I had no idea that so many homeless people knew Bones, but no one heard from Franklin."

"I have Harold checking every inch of this earth for him. He's checked at the jail, but we don't have much to go on since we only have his first name." Alex cleared her throat. "Maybe if you can give us more information, then we can check other places."

"I don't know if I want you to do that."

"Nina, please let me make it up to you. If I can find Franklin and tell him that I'm sorry for being such an ass, maybe he'll come back to you."

"It's not that I don't want your help, but we could be hurting him. The police back in Chicago want him just as much as I do. If they find out he's in California, he'll go back to prison."

"Prison? For what?"

"That's another ball game Alex, let that dog keep sleeping." I sat silently for a while not only craving Franklin but my baby sister as well. "Maybe you and the baby can come by on Friday and give me a hug."

That sounds like a date, but the baby wants spaghetti." She laughed.

"Spaghetti it is."

Chapter Thirty-Two

Nina

As I stood on my back balcony trying to enjoy the crisp Saturday morning air, I was saddened when the sun came up without Franklin holding me in his arms. I didn't want to believe that he would choose a life on the streets over a life with me. My heart was growing cold toward him. He's really a master at hiding. I've done all that I could to find him.

Alex's stretching and yawning brought me to my senses, and I wiped my eyes before turning toward her.

"You're up and dressed pretty early, Ms. Bride-to-be." I smiled forcefully, and rubbed her flat belly.

She rested her head on my shoulders as she slid her arms around my waist. I passed a hand over her natural black hair.

"Thank God, you finally took those blond braids out."

"I know, Walter likes the real me."

"So do I." I nodded and pushed her off me.

"You never told me what Mother said about you not inviting The Judge to the wedding or telling him about the baby."

"She's fine with it." Alex replied without a trace of concern in her voice.

"What?"

"Yep, she said to live my life and not The Judge's. She's changed, Nina."

"I didn't hear a change in her voice when I called the other day."

"You can see it, when she gets angry."

"Angry, Mother doesn't get angry."

"She has her mean days Nina, don't let her fool you."

"Mother has never been mean, now you're going too far with all this gossiping shit, Alex," I said as I sipped on the green tea.

"Well, she sure slapped the shit out of Maria the other day."

"Maria! For what?" I frowned.

"Because she and The Judge were behind closed doors planning Thanksgiving dinner for Mother."

"And she slapped Maria for that."

"Yep, walked right up to Maria and slapped the spit out of her mouth. I was speechless, I couldn't do anything."

"When I spoke to Mother she didn't mention anything to me about her and Maria fighting." What the hell was happening to this family, was everybody crazy?

"I'm heading back to San Diego." Alex smiled.

"So soon?" I asked.

"I told Mother that I'll be back early Saturday morning. You have to come and see her Nina, she looking bad, real frail."

"You're right, I'll sneak down tomorrow. Does The Judge still play golf on Sunday after church?"

"Yeah, and since I'm there he plays more often, so I'm sure he'll be gone by the time you arrive."

"Good, when I call Mother today I'll let her know that I'll be there tomorrow."

"You know The Judge is pissed at you because of all those family dinners you missed."

"Does he mention that I hung up on him?"

"All the time." Alex smiled.

"I had to get my head on straight. I lost my man; I almost lost my business and my mind. I couldn't deal with the family drama, if he don't understand that, then to hell with him." I said sipping my tea.

"Nina, I understand and I'm sorry that I made Franklin

leave. Truly I am."

I took Alex into my arms and hugged her tight. "Don't worry yourself, Lil sis. You made him leave, but you didn't make him stay away."

She buried her face in my chest and cried. "I'm still sorry."

I lifted Alex's head and looked into her tear-stained eyes. "Apology accepted, don't carry around the burden of guilt the way I did. If I never felt so guilty about hurting other's feelings, I would be holding Franklin in my arms and not you. So don't worry about it, I'll get over it. Now did Mother sound depressed?" I asked, walking back into the house with Alex at my side.

"You know it. If she gets from under The Judge she might feel better."

"Girl, you know she isn't going anywhere, that marriage is forever," I mumbled thinking that's the kind of marriage I would like to have. Forever.

"Well, I have a long drive ahead of me, so I'll see you tomorrow," Alex said before kissing me on the cheek.

"Okay." I nodded, waving good-bye.

I cleared away the breakfast dishes and put a load of clothes in the washer, after making a few phone calls. I returned to the patio and fell asleep in the mid-morning air.

My daydreams were of the wonderful, short-lived nights that I spent wrapped in Franklin arms. His sweet warm strokes and the gentle kisses he laid on my body made me shift in the chaise lounger, as the sun became my blanket, warming my body the way Franklin did.

Just as I was allowing myself to partake in the fantasy of Franklin making love to me, I was violently jerked from his arms by the loud ringing of my phone.

"Damn, damn, damn." I shouted and tried to ignore the rings as I searched my memory for Franklin's embrace once again. But the face of my mother forced me out of my fantasy.

"Hello," I said into the phone once I reached it.

"Nina, you have to get down here right away!"

I glanced at the clock, surprised that she'd made it home that quick.

"All hell is breaking loose," Alex shouted.

My heart was pounding in my chest. "Is Mother alright?"

"She's pretty upset."

"What's going on, Alex. Dammit! I don't have time for guessing games?"

"I don't really know, I just got here my damn self, right before Harold rushed into the house yelling and screaming at The Judge."

"At The Judge? What the hell is that all about?"

Alex's laughter filled my ears. "He even pushed him."

"Oh, my Lord, Alex." I shouted as I rushed up the stairs toward my bedroom.

"Harold is mad as hell, and you know if a black man turns red in the face, he's pissed off." Once again her voice was thick with laughter.

"Is he that angry?"

"Pissed off."

"At The Judge?" I asked again as I wedged the phone between my ear and shoulders while I slipped on my jeans.

"And Rachel." Alex said. "He's yelling something about they needed to mind their own business and leave other people's lives alone."

"Where are they now?"

"In the office, screaming and yelling at each other." I slipped on a shirt, dropped the phone and hit my head on the dresser when I bent down to grab it. "Dammit."

"Are you alright?" Alex laughed.

"Yeah, I'm fine. What are they saying now?"

"I can't make it out."

"Call the police?"

"Hell no!"

"Alex, call the police so they can break this shit up, it's

going to get out of hand."

"So."

"Alexandra!"

"The Judge's always said this family handles their own problems. You know we don't bring outside folks into the family business."

"Alexandra, this is serious."

"He needs to get his ass chewed out, for once."

"This damn family has more drama in it than the folks on the soap operas," I shouted as I slipped on my shoes with the phone still glued to my ear.

"Well, you know The Judge is drama his damn self," Alex added with a chuckle."

"Okay, listen."

"Oh shit!" She shouted, setting alarms off in my head.

"What, what, what?"

"Harold's screaming something about police and medical records."

"Alex, please call the cops." I begged.

"No."

"Alex, that's your father."

"And that's my brother, and I'm not calling the cops on my brother."

"Alex," I shouted as I heard doors slamming, people shouting.

"Harold!" Alex called out.

I pressed the phone so close to my ear it began to ache.

"I'm going to kill this man." I heard Harold shout and my heart stopped. He had never disrespected The Judge before.

"Oh, God, this is serious," I screamed and hung up the phone, called the police and jumped into the Jeep.

⚹

By the time I pulled into the front of my parents' house, the paramedics were driving away. I jumped out of the Jeep and ran into the house. Alex was sitting on the sofa next to Mother, holding her hand.

"Mother are you alright?" I cried, running to her side.

She patted my hand. "I'm fine, baby."

I looked at Alex.

"They think The Judge is having a heart attack."

"Why aren't you going with him?" I asked Mother.

She lowered her head. "He was asking for . . . ."

"He only wanted Rachel," Alex cut in. "I called Aunt Louise, which took me thirty minutes to tell her to come over and stay with Mother, so we can go to the hospital and kick the shit out of Rachel's ass."

"The Judge wanted Rachel to go the hospital with him and not his wife?" I snapped.

Alex shrugging her shoulders. "That's who he wanted and that's who went with him, hell, I don't care the two of them deserve each other."

"Alex."

"Sorry, Mother."

"Where's Harold?"

"I don't know, I called over to his house and that stupid wife said he was out of town and she didn't know when he would be back. That woman is such a liar." Alex shouted slamming her fist on her knees.

"She's not lying, Harold was out of town. He's been working on some big case that had him all confused." Mother said softly.

"Mother, Harold was not out of town."

"Your father went over to check on Maria just about every night; when you saw him today, he had just returned home."

"What happened today?" I asked.

"I don't know much." Alex said kissing Mother on her pale cheeks. "Harold stormed into the house with a manila folder and shoved it into The Judge's face, then he preceded to lose his mind and pushed The Judge into the office. Next thing we know, Rachel was shouting at The Judge.

I nodded in total confusion. I've been out of the family

C.F. Hawthorne

drama for so long the information was overwhelming.

"Harold told me to leave so he could talk to Mother, then the paramedics came rolling up to the front door, and The Judge ordered me to stay with Mother and for Rachel to go with him." She threw her hands into the air. "Like I said, I don't know much."

"Where's the folder?" I questioned Alex, who looked away.

"Girl, I don't know. Hell, I searched that office and I can't find anything."

I felt achy and exhausted. The Moore family drama was getting on my last damn nerve.

"Nina, I don't know what's going on, but you know Rachel's husband is smoking that shit real bad these days, and he did have a few court hearings. Maybe that's why Harold was shouting about police records and court docs."

"Alex, stop, The Judge will manipulate our lives, but he will not manipulate the system," I shuddered as Mother gave me a look that said otherwise.

"Girl, I don't know, I've seen some shady shit around here." Alex stated, kissing Mother on her cheek.

"Stop talking like that in front of Mother," I demanded.

"Oh, I don't mind, Nina, it's time for me to get my head out of the sand and start speaking up about things around me."

"That's my girl." Alex smiled and kissed her again.

"Alex, baby if you keep kissing me I'm going to get a rash."

"I love those little cheeks." Alex smiled.

"Lizzie! Lizzie! You alright baby?" A frightened voice shouted from the front foyer.

I threw up my hands. "In here, Aunt Louise." I yelled greeting my half deaf, elderly aunt with a kiss and a hug.

"Where's The Judge?" She asked as she rushed to her sister's side.

"They took him to the hospital," I shouted.

She sighed with exasperation. "No, thank you, baby, I

don't want no molasses pie."

Alex and I looked at each other. "No, They took The Judge to the hospital," I corrected.

"You feel shorter than a stick?" She asked looking at Mother. "What that girl talking about, Lizzie?" She asked in a state of confusion.

"He's gone, Aunt Louise," I shouted.

"Ole Lordly, The Judge done gone to the sky." she cried as she leaned on Mother with both hands clutching her heart.

"Let me handle this," Alex winked.

She stood and went to the right side of Aunt Louise's ear. "He's not dead, he's sick."

She stopped screaming and turned to Alex. "Go to the bathroom if you gotta shit."

I threw up both hands and walked over to the bar, reaching without thinking for the Scotch.

Mother reached over and stuck her finger into her sister's ear.

"Oh, shit, I turned the damn thing the wrong way." Aunt Louise grinned.

We had to explain everything to her again before leaving for the hospital. "I'll call you with any news," I said as I grabbed my keys off the barstool.

Once we were outside I turned to Alex, "So what do you think is going on?"

"Lord, Nina, I don't know, but Harold was some kinda mad. He was cussing and fussing like a crazy man. You and I both know when The Judge says jump Harold brings down a message from God."

"I know Alex, I just have to wonder what has Harold that upset?"

⅋

By the time, we made it to the hospital The Judge was already hooked up and being monitored. When Rachel looked up and saw me standing in the doorway, she backed deeper into the corner, but she had nowhere to run.

I eyed The Judge lying still, pretending to be asleep. I walked up to Rachel and slapped her so hard, spit flew across The Judge's face. I grabbed each side of her head and slammed it against the wall a few times."

"Oh, you gonna get an old fashioned Nina Moore ass whipping, now," Alex shouted with laughter in her voice.

As I held onto each side of Rachel's head I saw the fright in her eyes, it reminded me that I'd promised never to hit my sisters again.

Pointing my finger directly into Rachel's face, I bit my lip, "Don't you say a word to me, Rachel, you better get yourself a damn good attorney, I know what you've been doing to my company and you will pay for it."

I turned to walk away when I heard her whisper, "Bitch." As if my fist had a mind of it's own, I turned around and punched her so hard in her lip, The Judge sat up.

"Oh, shit," he shouted. "Nina, don't start fighting in here, people know us. Get out!" He shouted. "Get out!"

I glared at The Judge; his long, deep stare infuriated me. I saw Rachel trying to slither out of the room. I kept my gaze on The Judge.

"Girl, you need help." Alex shouted, and then another uproar broke out between Rachel and Alex.

I grabbed Alex and whispered in her ear. "The baby."

"You're just like us, Alex, so stop pretending that your not." Rachel managed to say when Alex released her throat.

"I'll never be like the two of you." Alex shouted pushing Rachel to the wall, again.

I grabbed Alex by the arm. "No, Alex, please don't. Lets go home, there's nothing here I need." I said glaring at The Judge one more time.

As we strolled past Rachel, she flinched. "Stay away from Mother." Alex pointed, jabbing her in the center of the forehead, "or I'll hurt you."

Chapter Thirty-Three

The Family

A few hours later when I walked back into the house, after regrouping from the hospital fiasco, I saw my mother staring into space, shaking her head as she hummed. See looked so frail, as if all the life was just sucked out of her.

"Mother," I said softly, as she continued to hum, holding a small brown, leather box in her lap.

Alex knelt down beside her. I took a seat at the bar.

"Mother," Alex said stroking her soft hand, "The Judge is going to be all right.

"I called Harold, he's on his way," Mother said softly without blinking.

Alex frowned. "Mother, Harold is not coming over here today, he's too mad."

"Yes, he is. I told him to bring Maria as well. I called the hospital; The Judge was released so he and Rachel will be home soon.

I stood in disbelief. "Mother, there was a small problem in the hospital earlier and I don't think the three of us should be in the same room. Not right now."

"Nina, sit down." Mother's order was so direct I dropped into a seat.

"Why do you want to put all of us in the same room under these conditions?" Alex asked.

"Because I'm tired of these conditions. I'm tired of sitting back letting The Judge rule this house." She lowered her head and tears began to stain the leather box. "I'm dying girls, I don't have bleeding ulcers, I have lung cancer and I'll not die with this man still ruling my family."

Life was immediately sucked out of me. I glanced sharply around, my eyes blazing with fear.

"Mother, no." Alex cried.

I was speechless, as I held the news close to my heart. I didn't want to cry, knowing that I would never stop, but Alex's tears began to flow like a hydrant. She laid her head on Mother's lap and wept.

"Why didn't you tell us?" I whispered, as pain choked my voice.

Her frail little face stared blankly at me as her lips trembled, "I wanted my babies to enjoy me for the time that I had left on this earth," she began to stroke Alex's head. "Hush now, child," she sang softly, "hush now."

"What am I gonna do without you, Mama?" Alexandra cried. "What will the baby do without you?"

"Alex, baby, you'll have Aunt Louise," Mother said smiling at her sister with tears in her eyes.

"Oh, no thank you, Lizzie, I don't want any cheese," Aunt Louise said rubbing her stomach, "it gives me gas."

Alex sat up. "Oh, Lord." Alex cried, standing to her feet. "Mama you can't leave us with her." She pointed. "She can't hear."

"Alex, don't worry yourself. You girls are going to be just fine. You're stronger than I ever was."

A flash of grief rippled across Alex face. "I don't want to be strong." She fell back into Mother's lap. I fought back my tears; because of Mother, we respected The Judge. What is going to happen to us now?

"Alex, you don't have a choice. It's time to grow up."

I sat still, almost numb. I never thought about life without my mother. I don't think I can understand life without her voice of reason. I may not always agree with her, but to understand life without her is almost unbearable.

"I hate my life, I hate this family," Alex shouted like a child.

"Alexandra, sit down and shut up," Mother shouted, pointing toward the stool next to her. "Rachel and The Judge will be home soon."

"Won't The Judge need his rest once he's released from the hospital?" I asked.

"It was gas, child, not a heart attack." Aunt Louise answered, "I ain't never heard nobody going to the hospital for gas pain. Ain't that a bunch of shit." She slapped her leg and laughed.

"You know how dramatic The Judge can be." Alex sniffed.

"Alexandra, I told you to be quiet."

"What has gotten into you?" Alex asked. "You've never raised your voice at me."

Mother gazed up at Alex. "Let's just say the devil has gotten into me."

"Mother, are you alright?" Harold shouted running to her side with Maria in hand.

"I'm fine, baby, sit and wait for Rachel."

"We're here, you don't have to wait on us," she answered with her lips curled to one side.

"Where's The Judge?" Mother asked.

"He went to lay down," Rachel said sitting next to Aunt Louise.

"Harold, go and get The Judge."

"Mother."

"Harold."

"Yes, ma'am," Harold said storming off like a child.

"Sit Maria, don't look so frightened," Mother smiled.

Maria slowly took a seat next to Rachel, looking as if she were going to deliver that child at any moment. I went and stood next to Mother. I was so close to jumping on Rachel my blood began to boil as she sat there, back straight, hands in lap and head held high. As if she hadn't done anything at all.

"What the hell do you want?" The Judge shouted, as he stormed into the room with a drink in his hand.

Harold walked past him, scratching his head. "I found him sitting in his office drinking, not resting."

"What is this all about? I'm a sick man, doesn't this family give a damn about the sick?" he yelled at the top of his voice.

"Alex, tell your sister what you did." Mother said, in an odd tone as she slowly opened the box.

Alex looked around the room in alarmed. She brought her finger to her chest. "Me?"

Mother pushed Alex toward me. "Go on."

She cleared her throat and looked down at her feet. "Nina, when you kicked me out I got drunk and called Rachel, and I told her everything."

"You what!" I said backing away from her.

Alex's eyes were filled with tears when she looked at me. "I told her everything."

The memory from that night still-haunted me. "Everything?" I mumbled softly, as the bile began to rise in my throat.

"Everything," she repeated, "I thought I was talking to Harold, but it was Rachel."

"And she told The Judge," Harold shouted.

I turned to Rachel, who shrugged her shoulders. "Well, he had to know, he's the head of this family," she said curling up one side of her thick lips, "He's our protector."

"You bitch!" I shouted and lunged at her.

The Judge stepped between us. "There'll be no fighting in my house, we'll love each other if it kills us," he shouted pushing me away.

I bumped into Mother who was holding a .22 caliber pistol.

"What the hell?" The Judge shouted, as I moved out of the way.

Her eyes were dull with pain, but she firmly pointed the barrel at The Judge's head. "I've sat back long enough and let you control this family, claiming this land as your own. I've watched you send innocent men to prison while you set guilty men free, just so you can one day call them for one of your wicked favors that would otherwise go undone."

"Mother no!" I cried, as her hands began to shake. My nerves were on edge at the thought of her spending any time behind bars.

"I've watched you stand in the way of each of your children's chance for love and happiness."

The Judge's eyes narrowed and his jaws tightened. "Lizzie, put that gun away," he said softly as he slowly walked up to her.

"No more, Judge Harold T. Moore III, no more!" She screamed so loud the room became still.

"Lizzie," he said with open arms, "come on, baby." He smiled.

She swallowed hard, trying not to cry. "I've waited long hours for you to return home."

"I always came home baby."

She shook her head. "But you never came to our bed alone, I always had to share my bed with other women."

The Judge appeared very confused. "Lizzie, what the hell are you talking about?"

"You never came home alone," she shouted, "you always brought the stench of another woman to soil our bed."

I couldn't believe what I was hearing and seeing. My mother had finally had enough of The Judge's shit.

"Mother," Rachel said softly.

She turned the gun on Rachel, then back on The Judge. Her soft gentle face became distorted with anger. "You asked me to raise your bastard child so as not to shame the family's name, but it was only your name you were protecting, not the family's."

I don't know about everyone else, but I was numb with increasing rage at my Mother's pain.

"Lizzie, you don't want to do this, I'm a judge and you're an old sick woman."

"I am old," she nodded. "I'm the old woman that has kept

your secrets," she screamed as a bullet whizzed past The Judge's head, making him spill his expensive cognac.

"Oh, holy day. Lizzie, I think that chemo done made you lose your mind," Aunt Louise yelled as she tried to get to the front door.

Harold ran toward Mother, but stopped when she turned the gun on him. Maria ran to Harold's side as the front door slammed.

"You can't shoot my husband." Maria screamed holding her stomach. "He has a child on the way."

Mother laughed and turned the gun back on The Judge. She cocked her head to one side. "No, my husband has a child on the way," she answered in a low, painful voice.

"Oh, shit!" Alex shouted.

Mother looked at Harold and started crying. "Harold baby, you can't have children." She shook her head.

"Oh, shit!" Alex repeated and threw both hands in the air.

"You had radiation treatment as a child. The doctor told me that you might not be able to have children. I never told anyone, especially The Judge. He was so proud to have a son to carry on the family name. I didn't want to disappoint him, and I didn't want him to stop loving you."

"What?" Harold shouted. "What, are you saying Mother?"

Maria backed away as silent tears began to spill from her eyes.

"The medical records that your father gave to you and Yolanda, are not fake, they're real. However, the names were switched by one of The Judge's friends," Mother said softly as her sweet tears continued to flow.

I was about to lose my mind from all the drama that was right in front of me. Harold stared at Maria, who kept her teary gaze fixed on The Judge.

"How? When? I mean." Harold turned his fiery stare on The Judge.

"Tell him, Judge," Mother shouted, making him jump,

C.F. Hawthorne

spilling more of his cognac.

He gulped down the rest of it. "Lizzie, we don't have to do this." The Judge laughed nervously. "We don't air our dirty laundry in public remember?"

"Look around you, Harold, its only family." Mother said waving the tiny gun in the air.

"You fucked my wife!" Harold shouted.

The Judge put both hands in front of him. "Son, it was for the good of the family."

"You sons-of-bitches were going to let me think that bastard was my child." Harold pointed to Maria's stomach.

"Somebody had to keep the bloodline going," The Judge shouted. "Rachel's breeding crack babies, and you can't breed at all. I have no hope of Alex even knowing who the father of her child would be, when she gets knocked up."

He turned his evil gaze on me. "And you." He said with so much disgust in his voice I wanted to punch him in the face. "My only hope for the future of this family wants to have babies for a homeless alcoholic that killed his first family. I just wasn't going to have it," The Judge screamed. "Not in my kingdom."

"This is getting good." Alex smiled and took a seat next to the bar.

"Alex." I snapped.

"What?"

"Be quiet."

"You slept with my wife." Harold cried grabbing his chest. I could almost feel the pain that Harold was displaying on his face. I tried not to cry, but I couldn't help it. I couldn't stop the pain from racing through my veins.

"Don't blame me, son." The Judge said softly. "You couldn't fulfill your duty as a man."

Harold lunged at The Judge, but Mother's words stopped him dead in his tracks.

"Tell him why Yolanda left him." Mother said, sending

everyone into a deep silent stillness. We all knew how much Harold loved the ground Yolanda walked on.

"Tell him, Harold." Mother shouted, as she sent another bullet into the wall.

He turned and gazed at all four of us. "What do you want me to say Lizzie." He asked as he slowly walked toward Mother. "She wouldn't sleep with you, Harold!" Mother shouted. "She wouldn't have your child. She loved your son too much to sleep with you. So you forced her out of the family and made it seem as if it were Harold's idea to divorce his wife."

"What are you talking about?" Harold cried.

"Your father and your brother-in-law planted crack cocaine on Yolanda's father, knowing that man was too sick and too old to stand trial and possibly go to prison."

"Shut up, Lizzie." The Judge shouted.

"I will speak the truth, I will not take your lies to my grave."

"Lizzie!"

"Yolanda loved you so much, son." Mother shook her head. "But she loved her old dying father more."

"In order for me to keep my father from going to prison," Yolanda said, as she appeared out of nowhere, standing in back of Harold, who stood shocked at the sound of her voice.

"Yo-Yo!" he whispered.

She took Harold's hand and kissed him on the cheek. "I had to agree to the divorce, and I could never tell you that you were the one who couldn't have babies, it wasn't me."

My Mother laughed and lowered her head. "It's amazing what we females do for love isn't it, Judge," she said smiling at The Judge's horrified face.

Harold's tears reminded me of Franklin's pain. He took Yolanda into his arms and held her so tight I could feel it.

Suddenly all hell broke loose. The Judge backed handed Mother so hard she fell to the floor. "Slut," he shouted.

I grabbed the gun that slid by Maria's feet and pointed it

at The Judge; my hands were shaking so violently I could've shot up the entire room.

Mother rose to her feet with the help of Alex, and stare in terror as Harold began to choke The Judge to death.

"Harold! Please let him go!" Mother pleaded as she sat, panting.

"Mother, he hit you!" Harold screamed. "He hit you!"

"There will be no fucking fighting in my house," The Judge shouted as he struggled out of Harold's grasp.

"It isn't the first time," she said softly and turned to The Judge. "But it's the last. If you want me to be quiet you better kill me like you killed Rachel's Mother."

Rachel's eyes widened as she stood straight as a board.

"I'll be damned." Alex barked. "And you said he couldn't have any criminal ties, he's the freakin' criminal!" She pointed toward The Judge. "No wonder you would always say what goes on in this family stays in this family. You were the one who had something to hide," she shouted.

"You said a homeless man killed my Mother!" Rachel shouted over Alex's babbling. "That's what you had us believing all our lives. That's why we feared homeless people all our lives. You fucking evil bastard." Rachel screamed.

"Rachel," The Judge said holding out his hand.

"Mother." Rachel cried, holding her chest. "Tell me, Mother, tell me the truth."

"Lizzie!" The Judge shouted, "You promised."

"I was young and in love, Harold." She turned to Rachel. "Your father killed your Mother and brought you home to me. All evidence pointed to a homeless man who witnessed the murder."

"No, Mother." Rachel cried, backing into the wall. "No." Mother limped over to Rachel and held her in her arms. "He said if I didn't take you, he would give you away. We didn't have any kids at the time and I felt so sorry for your sweet little face. I knew I had to protect you from this evil man," Mother kissed

Rachel's tear-soaked face. "He made me promise never to tell a soul or I would go to prison, for harboring a criminal. You were just a innocent baby and I loved you so much."

She shook her head and paused for a minute as tears fell from her eyes. "I never told a soul, Rachel. I was young and scared, and then I began to have babies. The Judge constantly reminded me that I would lose all of you if he were ever exposed."

She glared at The Judge. "Is that why you never cared what happened to my family? You never cared that I was the only one that didn't finish college. Because I was just some whore's baby that you had killed and not a real Moore." The room was still as Rachel's pain encircled her.

I turned to The Judge. "Where's Franklin?" I asked above the lies.

"Who?" The Judge grunted.

"Franklin?" I screamed gaining his attention with few rounds of the .22 into the ceiling.

"Nina Marie, I will not be intimidated in my home." The Judge shouted, as he stared at me with those cold evil eyes.

I must have blacked out for a few minutes, all of a sudden everyone was screaming and shouting trying to be heard. I stood in the center of the room with all the voices swirling around me like a whirlwind of lies. I stared down at the gun.

All that I knew and all that I thought I stood for was a lie. I could feel my life being drained from my soul. I opened my mouth to scream like a child that was in agonizing pain, but not a sound escaped my lips. Then I felt Alex whispering in my ear.

"I asked you a question. Where's Franklin?"

"You don't need a man like that, you need someone with some class, with a future: money, power, the freedom to move around this earth freely. Someone to come to your rescue when your business goes under. Not some brother can you spare a dime, mother fucking homeless man."

"You need those things, all I need is Franklin," I cried as

C.F. Hawthorne

a heaviness descended on my chest.

"You're not thinking straight. You've just opened your second business and the third one is around the corner. How will it look to have a homeless man on your arms? How will it look that the very people I ran out of San Diego are now living under my successful daughter's roof, the father of my future grandchildren. I can't have it, I tell you, I won't have it." he shouted as a tired sadness passed over his face.

My fingers curled into a fist. "This is my life." I said calmly. "And I need that brother can you spare a mother fucking dime kinda man."

His eyes became red and glowed like hot coals. "As long as I have breath in my body your life belongs to me." He screamed as he kicked over a table, knocking everything to the floor.

My mouth felt like paper, dry and dusty, and my heart raced uncontrollably in my chest. Torn between the love and respect that I spent all my life trying to gain from my father and the love I so desperately craved from Franklin. I didn't see the fairness in it all.

"Look at you, Nina; you are as pathetic as your Mother, believing in that love bullshit. Where has it gotten her?" He pointed. "And you'll end up the same way. Tired and broken from chasing something that doesn't exist. Power should be your first love," he shouted holding up his fist. "Power."

I could feel the last trace of obedience vanish, but I remained calm. "Let us be the judge of that, let us find out for ourselves. Now please, Judge, just tell me where's Franklin."

"Where is he?" Harold shouted. "Tell her for God's sake."

"You don't tell me what to do." He growled. "You're as pathetic as your mother and sisters combined. The only one that has any balls is Rachel." He reached down for her, but she scampered to a corner sobbing like a child.

Before all that was holy, we saw with our very eyes, Harold's fist slamming into The Judge's jaw, sending him crashing to the floor. Then he was bending over The Judge, fist raised for another punch.

"Baby, don't!" Mother cried. "You can't strike your father." She shook her head and buried her face in her hands. "Please don't hit your father."

"Stop protecting him, Mother," Harold shouted.

"I'm not protecting him, Harold, I'm protecting you. He's evil and he'll send you to prison," she cried.

The Judge stood to his feet. "You better listen to your mother, son, because you'll serve time in jail, I'll see to that."

The Judge turned to me and licked the blood that spilled from his lips. "As for you, you'll never see Franklin again, I've changed his name and buried him so far in prison, he'll never see the light of day. You'll not shame this family, Nina." He pointed, speaking as if he were out of breath.

I stared in disbelief as I walked up to The Judge with the gun at my side. "Most people with power wreaked havoc over others, but you wreaked havoc on your own family. How brainless is that." I said shaking my head. "Harold get Mother, Alex get her wrap." I ordered, as I turned away from him.

Harold pushed Maria toward The Judge. "Harold." She said softly. He turned and gawked at her. "I'm sorry," Maria, mouthed, "I'm sorry."

"What are you doing?" The Judge asked.

Still in my tranquil state, just the way The Judge taught me to win all my cases. Stay calm just before you strike with a sudden force that will crumble all mountains. I slowly turned back to face him, the tension was gone from my voice. I stood straight, shoulders squared. "If you're taking the one person that I love, then I'll take the one thing that you love."

His voice was heavy with sarcasm and fear. "And that is?" He smirked.

Power and relief filled my soul when I said. "Your control." The look on his face was priceless. I slowly began to walk toward the door.

"If you walk out that door, Nina Marie, you are dead to me."

I stopped in my tracks with my back still to The Judge. His words of judgment, disappointment, and condemnations wrapped around me and swallowed me whole. The sucking of his teeth brought me out of my thoughts.

"That's right, Nina, you'll not have a father."

I felt no pain when I turned around, held my head up and stared into the devil's cold, evil eyes. "I can't miss what I've never had, Judge. But you." I pointed. "On the other hand, will be miserable, because you've lost all that you've lived for."

"And that is?" He asked sarcastically.

"The respect of your family. I know that I'll never find Franklin and yes, my pain is deep, but it won't last forever." I smiled and sucked my teeth. "Your pain on the other hand, will."

"Pain doesn't bother me, and all isn't lost." He smirked and pulled Maria closer to him, as he rubbed his future growing inside of her.

I smiled. "The funny thing is, I've always looked up to you, admired your strength, now look at you, you're more worthless than these homeless people you've tried to run out of town."

"What the hell are you talking about?" The Judge said as he walked up to me with Maria following behind him. "I have a home, Nina, look around you this is not a cardboard box."

As I stared into his eyes, I felt nothing: no contempt, no shame, no sadness, nothing. I rocked back on my heels. "Yes, you have a beautiful home." I answered shaking my head. "But where is the love." I turned my attention to Maria who had no idea what she was in for. I extended my hand to her. "Now is the time to escape from hell."

She hesitated. Gawking at The Judge and then back at me. She placed her shaking hand in mine, I looked at The Judge one last time. "Where's the love?" I smiled as we turned and walked away.

"What the hell are you doing?" He shouted.

"Nina." Mother sang.

"Lizzie." The Judge screamed to the top of his lungs. "You're my wife Lizzie Moore and you promised the Lord that you would stand by my side, through good times and bad."

Mother stopped and turned to face The Judge. "It didn't say anything about standing by your side if you're a crazy shit." Mother said softly and closed the door behind her.

Chapter Thirty-Four

❦

December nineteenth. Five days after Mother passed, I stood in a backyard that I never used and accepted an award that I didn't want and gave a quick speech to folks that I didn't care for. I glanced up into the night sky and saw Harold leaning over the back balcony sipping on a tall glass of wine, lost in space. As I made my way up to him, accepting condolences, as well as congratulations, my heart still fluttered for the lost of Franklin and my Mother. However, I did what Nina always did, pretended that life was so wonderful.

"Are you okay, big brother?" I asked.

"Yeah sort of." He nodded. "You know that Mother would have been so proud of you. Especially after you named the Orange County office after her." He nodded as he tried to hold back his tears.

"Harold." I said softly, placing my hand on his back. "It's okay. She made everything okay for us before she died. She wanted this party to go on. She made everything alright for us."

He broke down. "The way she's always done." He cried.

"Everyone's okay." I smiled through my tears.

"I know, Nina, but it's not fair, I still feel as though our lives have been one fat ass lie."

I laid my head on his large bicep and slipped my arm through his. "You've mended those broken pieces, Harold. I mean you're not living in San Diego any more, your business is booming in Los Angeles, and when your divorce in Reno is final, you and Yolanda can get remarried, and maybe you guys can adopt a house full of kids." Harold nodded and smiled.

I looked over my shoulder. "We have a lot of things to be grateful for, Alex is happily married and her little stomach is finally poking out. Aunt Louise with her deaf ass will be 86 years old next in a few months. What more do we need?"

He swallowed hard and hugged me tight. "Now that everybody else is taken care of, what about you?"

I swayed in his arms. "I don't need anything."

"Nina, you're too good. Why in the world are you taking care of Maria and the baby?"

I took his glass and drank the rest of his wine. "Harold, what could I do? She had no place to go where The Judge could not intimidate her, especially after I had him served with those child support papers while he was on the bench."

"But, Nina, come on."

"That little baby is family. It's not Maria's fault that she was caught up in The Judge's evil lies. If I didn't learn anything from him I did learn the power of a family. And that baby girl is our little sister. Mother taught us to have a forgiving heart, remember you were no saint in the marriage, either." I said punching him on the arm.

"I know, Nina, but. . .."

"But nothing, Harold. Everything is working out. I don't understand why you're so gloomy?"

"This isn't right." Harold shouted through clenched teeth. "We all received what we wanted, except you."

I shrugged my shoulders. "Sometimes that's the way the dice rolls. I know that I'll never see Franklin again. If The Judge wanted to, he could get Franklin out or at least tell us where he is, but he chose not to, so I have to move on with my life."

"It's not that I didn't try, Lord knows I tried to find him, but The Judge held true to his word, he'll never see freedom, Nina."

He seemed so disappointed with himself. "Harold, I know you tried, so stop beating yourself up over this."

"He should pay for this! I mean, why can't we go to the police and tell them about Rachel's mother."

"We have no evidence and Mother has passed, so we don't even have a backup story."

Harold shook his head. "Nina, this is wrong."

"We've underestimated the extent of this man's power.

He's mean big brother. Just let the devil rest."

"He has to pay somehow, he destroyed our lives."

I hugged Harold because I understood his frustration. "He's paying." I said shaking my head. "He's lost his control."

Harold sighed, shook me off him and reached into his jacket pocket. "I have something to show you."

Reluctantly I took the papers from him. When I stepped into the light my heart fell to my feet. I was breathless as my eyes began to sting. "Oh, my God."

Harold shook his head, and smiled. "That's right Nina. Franklin's a very rich man. He invested money in the Internet. Nina, the man is homeless because he wants to be, not because he has to be."

I couldn't help myself as I burst out laughing. "Do you think he knows this?" I asked.

"I don't think so, it appeared that he made the investment right before his daughter died. The tragedy took precedence over the investment. The insurance money from his daughter's, Mother's and wife's death is still unclaimed."

"Harold I can't believe this."

"I want you to know. I took this information to The Judge, and begged him to set this man free, I told him that Franklin was a very wealthy man."

"What did he say?" I beamed.

Harold's eyes grew dim. "He shook his head."

Suddenly the papers became to heavy to hold, they

slipped from my fingers and fluttered to the floor."

"The bastard said this would be a lesson learned."

I swallowed the large lump that formed in my throat. "Lesson learned. What fucking lesson could I learn from this?" I laughed scornfully.

"Nina, he told me that Franklin has too much time for you to wait for him."

I spoke in a broken whisper as my head began to pound. "Time is all I have." I mumbled as I lowered my head and walked away.

§

A few hours later, I said good-bye to my last guest, and bent down to kiss Aunt Louise on her cheek. I reached over and rubbed Alex's belly. "Make sure you show Aunt Louise to her room Alex."

"You need to get some rest dear," Aunt Louise said loudly. "Your eyes look like you been crying all night."

"Rest is just what I need." I smiled

"This was a nice party." Aunt Louise commented. "I'm sorry that your mother wasn't here to see it. But she's proud of you." She shouted.

"I know, sugar." I smiled.

"Why didn't, Big Harold, show up?"

I looked over at Alex who was blowing her nose.

She winked. "We don't know, Aunt Louise." Alex said.

She turned and slapped Alex on her bare thigh. "Child, I don't smoke weed in public."

"Now look, we ain't going through this tonight." She reached over and turned up her hearing aid.

"I didn't say anything about you smoking weed."

"Oh." She smiled. "What you say?"

"I said we don't know why The Judge didn't show up."

"Good night, everybody." Harold and Yolanda yelled over

Aunt Louise's loud babbling as they walked up the stars heading for my guest bedroom.

Aunt Louise stood and began walking towards the front door. "Now look, I know damn well somebody knows something, hell, I'm deaf not dumb. Where the hell is that music coming form?"

"I don't hear any music, maybe your hearing aid is humming." Alex laughed.

"I hear music I tell you."

"Aunt Louise, don't open the door we have the alarm set." I shouted, but it was too late, she already had the doorknob in her grasp. The alarm started screaming, bells and sirens were blaring. I rushed to the wall panel and punched in the code.

"Lawdy be, child, you got some man playing a music instrument on your front porch." She shouted looking dumbfounded.

I slammed the panel shut. "Franklin." I whispered as I heard him softly playing our love song. I peeked around the corner and saw him standing there with one long stem red rose sticking out of the Saxophone. "Baby!" I shouted this time almost knocking Aunt Louise to the floor. He sat the sax on the ground and held me so tight I thought he was going to bring me into his soul. His kisses melted the tension that was consuming my entire body. My stomach trembled and my knees became weak. I stepped away from him in order to catch my breath.

"I never thought I would see you again," I cried. "Never again."

"We're soul mates, Nina, I need you to survive, I had a lot of time to think and sober up. I'm clean baby, and I remembered something while I was in prison."

"What?" I asked as I kissed him gently on his chin.

"I once asked a homeless man why would he get involved with a woman, when he had nothing to offer her." He kissed me once on my mouth "Want to know what he said?"

"Yes." I smiled.

Homeless Love

"He said he'll offer her all the love he has for the rest of his life, and that's all I have to offer you. All the love I have for the rest of my life."

Months of tears soared off the cliff of my eyes, as I held him in my arms, his voice was warm and comforting in my ears.

"Will you marry me, Nina Maria Moore, and be my life?"

I closed my eyes and shivered as that familiar tremor entered my soul. "Yes." I said softly. "I'll be your life if you'll be mine?"

His kiss felt like forever, when I opened my eyes, I saw The Judge standing alone in the sprinkler, staring at us.

I slowly turned away, pushing the gathered crowd back into the house. I closed the door softly and turned off the light.

"All was well in my home tonight." I whispered as Franklin and I walked up our not so lonely 13 stairs.